NAN: The Trifling Times of Nathan Jones

"Moses Miller skillfully pens a novel that will captivate readers from start to finish. Mr. Miller expertly documents what causes Nan to eventually live by the gun while attempting to survive on the run!!!"

 -- *Coast 2 Coast Readers Online Book Club*

"This book is a well written action-packed urban book that holds your attention to the end..Nathan Jones is a character readers will want to see depicted on the big screen for his brutal honesty, but watch out...he's dangerous."

 --*Heather Covington award winning author of Literary Divas*

"This is a beautifully written story with very vivid accounts of the events that unfold. I found myself cheering for Nan as he cleared each hurdle and for the man he became because of all he experienced."

 --*Sharel E. Gordon-Love, APOOO Book Club*

"Moses Miller is a genius whose unique style of writing masterfully tells a story that reads like a movie...you simply cannot read this book on the train or on a bus because you will miss your stop engrossed in this book. Congratulations Mr. Miller, this book puts you in a league of your own.

 --*Kasey Cameron, Essense Book Club*

"What more can I say other than this is one great piece of work. Moses Miller paints a picture that is so vivid and action packed that you feel as if you're a part of the scene. Follow Nan as he embarks on a trying journey into MANHOOD and the lessons that he learns along the way."

 --*Carla Berry, Mocha Moments Readers*

NAN:
The Trifling Times of Nathan Jones
Special Edition

As told to Moses Miller

Mind Candy, LLC
2007

Published by:

Mind Candy, LLC.
P.O. Box 2185
Garden City, NY 11531-2185
MindCandyMedia.com
info@MindCandyMedia.com

Copyright 2007 Moses Miller
ISBN 10: 0-9786929-0-X
ISBN 13: 978-0978692902

Written by Moses Miller for Mind Candy, LLC.
Edited by K. Porter for Mind Candy, LLC.
Cover design and graphics created by Marion Designs

Printed in the United States

This book is dedicated to my beautiful wife Robin and four major pieces of my heart: Imari, Eboni, Nyah and Josiah.

You each inspire me in your own unique way to achieve greatness. Words cannot capture the feelings and love only my heart can express. You've each made me realize that the opportunities are endless.

...Love can conquer everything. All of our dreams and goals can be accomplished through focus and effort.

Let's get it.

A Note From The Author

When I do book signings or have the opportunity to meet with book clubs around the country, I'm often asked, *"Why does the story say as told to Moses Miller?"* Well, when I wrote NAN, I actually realized that I was the voice for those that would otherwise go unheard. The invisible men and women that deal with the trials and tribulations associated with everyday life, but still remain unseen. My stories encapsulate the experiences of an entire generation. So, even without someone dictating a story to me, through knowledge and understanding I capture their pain, their suffering, their dreams and aspirations. I sincerely thank you for letting me take you on the journey. Keep Striving.

Moses Miller

the least known...last forgotten

Prologue

Blood Oath

Somewhere in a dense jungle in South America, a strategically planned mission had gone terribly wrong. The government had sent their elite units in first, but the enemy was better equipped than they anticipated and much better trained. A young Marine Lieutenant lay face down in the middle of wet jungle foliage, bleeding profusely from a gaping wound to his chest.

As he accepted his fate, and came to peace with the fact that he was about to meet his maker, a fellow Marine stumbled upon him. After hoisting him over his shoulder, he braved snake-infested swamps and dodged enemy fire, all the while risking his life for that of another human being he had never even met before.

From that day forward, the Lieutenant made a life long blood oath, to forever be indebted to the young marine that sacrificed his own well being, to save his life.

BETRAYAL: 1

THE ONLY LIGHT ILLUMINATING the front of the three-story brick apartment building on Albany Avenue, emanated from the half moon that was clearly visible in the darkened sky. A black van had been discretely parked outside of the building for the past hour, as the occupants patiently waited for the right time to make their exit. They were hardly in a rush. A thick cloud of smoke filled the van's interior, the by-product of the Sergeant's Newport addiction. He had quickly puffed his way through a pack and a half in the last hour alone, only putting down his cigarette to take a swig from his metal whiskey flask. Without much thought, he flicked his shrunken cigarette butt to the van's floor and stomped it out with the sole of his rundown leather loafer.

Being six-foot tall, the Sergeant had to bend down awkwardly as he paced back and forth inside the cargo van. Digangi and Dickson sat in the back leaning uncomfortably against the van's metal wall, resting their tired eyes. On the other side of the van, Rodriguez, the only female amongst the crew, rested her head up against the cold steel wheel well.

She clutched her black 9-millimeter in the palm of her right hand as she stared at the picture of her two sons, which adorned the heart shaped gold charm that she always wore around her neck. The youngest was only two, and his brother was four. She had left them with their father, who was in a deep sleep, when she quietly exited their apartment in Bensonhurst a couple of hours ago.

She tried to rest her eyes, but she couldn't get them off of her mind. Her husband, Jose wasn't exactly *Mr. Mom*. He was more like the absent-minded professor. She had purposely written down a list that intricately laid out everything he had to do for the boys in her absence, but she knew that he would still forget something.

"Rodriguez," the Sergeant yelled out in his gruff voice, just loud enough to startle her.

"Aye, Vie," Rodriguez responded, as she sat up and wiped her eyes.

"You should have gotten yourself some rest. I'm a need you completely focused when you go up there, Lisa," the Sergeant said. He was now kneeling down whispering, his face within two inches of hers. She squinted her watery eyes and held her breath as he spoke, putting up her best defense against the thick vapor he expelled from his mouth, which reeked of cigarettes and the undeniable stench of whiskey.

The Sergeant was what could best be described as a bubble invader. Whether it was a method of intimidation, or just the way he was comfortable communicating with others, he always conversed in very close quarters. He leaned his massive frame towards Rodriguez, and whispered quietly in her ear.

"Don't worry about a thing, Lisa. You'll be home hugging those two little sluggers before you know it."

"I know, it's just Jose. He—"

"Shh!!!" Sarge said, interrupting her mid-sentence. "Think about that shit later. You need to focus on what you can impact now...anything else will get you killed out there."

"You're right Sarge. I'm a get focused...I won't let you down," she responded, nodding her head in acknowledgment. She knew he was telling her the truth.

In an apartment a few stories above, Nan softly licked his girlfriend Leslie's belly button, before slowly working his way up her caramel complexioned body, only stopping once he reached her inviting breasts. She willingly opened her legs, moaning slightly as she felt his manhood enter inside of her. As he stroked, she moved her body in unison, letting him in deeper and deeper. He penetrated her wet insides, working the walls of her vagina in smooth motions.

"Oh, Nan...oh, baby you got some good stuff...oh, my god," she moaned passionately.

Her soft hands tightly gripped his back, pulling him into her as she panted in a soft whisper. Sensing her desire, he pushed himself deeper inside of her, feeling the warmth of her wet juices as his penis rubbed against her vagina walls. Her body shivered ever so slightly in his arms.

"I'm coming Nathan," she yelled out seductively. Nan got up on his knees as she moaned, arching his back as he began to stroke harder, but refraining from being overly aggressive with her. Still stroking, he held her legs over his shoulders as he began to climax as well.

The rhythmic rocking motion of the queen-sized bed slowly came to a halt, as Nan laid his sweaty body down on Leslie's exposed breasts.

"Are you all right? You don't have any pains right?" Nan asked in a concerned manner.

"You're so funny. You ask the same question every time we make love. You don't have to worry, the baby is all right Nathan," she said, as she stroked her hand through his short hair. "The baby can't feel anything that you be doing down there."

"Well, I don't know. I mean, you know I'm packing a little sumthin' sumthin'."

She mushed his head and said, "You are so silly."

Leslie was shapely and well proportioned. She was only two months into her pregnancy, 130 pounds and not even showing yet. As a matter of fact, only her close friends even knew that she was pregnant. Nan rested his chiseled frame back on top of her busty chest. She willingly obliged, letting him lay on her for a good five minutes before she had had enough.

"You gotta get up Boo," she said as she nudged his shoulder. "You're gonna be late for work…besides, you're smothering me and the baby."

Nan laughed to himself, kissing her on her forehead as he rolled over, preparing to get out of the bed.

"Oh, now I'm hurting the baby? How convenient," he said laughing out loud again.

He stared at the peeling paint on the bedroom wall, trying to will himself to get up and take a shower. Finally, he leaned over towards Leslie and kissed her softly on her neck, before whispering, "I love you," in her ear.

"I love you too, Nathan," she replied softly.

Sitting there, he looked Leslie directly in her light brown eyes. She always called him by his government name, and he didn't mind it. She was so beautiful to him...the second most beautiful girl he had ever laid his eyes on.

Leslie was a triage nurse at Beth Israel Medical Center. As fate would have it, she just happened to work a double shift the night that Nan had been wheeled into the emergency room on a gurney, bleeding profusely from gaping gunshot wounds to his chest and shoulder. Barely breathing, she held his bloody hand tightly as he fought for his life.

"Don't give up. You have to fight," she whispered over and over to him. Her voice sounded angelic. As he slipped in and out of consciousness, the touch of her hand clenching his own, gave him strength and lifted his spirits.

After Nan's successful surgery, she visited him several times while he was recovering. Nan was a lot more "street" than Leslie, but his enchanting personality and the fact that he was well versed on so many different subjects, made them connect immediately. They could easily talk for hours about anything, never growing bored of one another.

Everyday after Nan was released from the hospital, he sent roses to Leslie. Shy and reclusive, she purposely avoided his advances. But, within a few weeks they were dating...and three months later they were in love and living together. Leslie's friends teased her, because she was dating someone four years younger than her, but she didn't care. Nan was her soul mate, and she loved him with her complete heart.

Nan sat up in the bed, and rubbed the sleep out of his eyes with his right hand, before getting up and walking out into the hallway and entering the bathroom. He flicked the light switch on, and slowly closed the door behind him. The hinges made a creaking noise as it slammed shut. As he turned the knobs in the shower, hot water shot out of the metallic showerhead, spraying the green mildewed tile and the shower curtain with a light mist. He stepped into the shower, feeling immediately relaxed as the hot water beads slammed against his sweaty body.

It was approximately 1:45am. Nan had plenty of time to stop at the bodega and pick up a juice and something to snack on, before heading in to work. Less than a month ago, he had started working at a loading dock over on the other side of Brooklyn. The hours were awkward and the gig only paid $7 an hour, but Nan wasn't complaining.

This was actually the first time in his life that he held down a legal gig, and it was by far the most fulfilling job he had ever done. It wasn't much money, but at work he didn't have to look over his shoulder, or fear for his life. He was making an honest day's pay, for an honest day's work. Not the type of paper he was used to making, but he still felt as if he could definitely get used to this.

He rubbed soap all over his chest, making a nice soapy lather. The steady stream that shot out of the hot showerhead caused a thick steamy fog to form in the bathroom. Nan closed his eyelids, feeling fully invigorated in his relaxing surroundings.

"Let's go people, it's time to roll," Sarge yelled out in his deep baritone voice. Without much thought, Digangi and Dickson popped open the van's back door and the cold air from the wintry night immediately began to seep inside.

"You know the routine people, short and sweet. In and out. Plant the evidence, take out the perp...no witnesses"

Digangi, Dickson, and Rodriguez quickly exited through the rear of the van. They discreetly entered the small apartment house vestibule, and quietly headed up to the third floor via the steps. It was fairly quiet inside. They faintly heard the sounds of minor commotion as they made their way upstairs. Reaching the third floor landing, they pulled their guns out, slowly walking down the dimly lit narrow hallway.

Rodriguez gripped the barrel of her Mossberg shotgun, the stock handle concealed perfectly under her armpit. Her 9mm was holstered on her waist. There were three apartments on this floor, but they were looking specifically for 3B, which was located at the far end of the hall. Dickson holstered his glock, and pulled out a solid steel battering ram that he had hidden in an oversized black duffel bag he carried on his back.

As he grasped the ram tightly in his black hands, he looked over his shoulder at Rodriguez and Digangi.

"On three," he whispered, just loud enough for only them to hear. Sweat beads were visibly forming on both of their foreheads, as they anxiously stood behind Dickson with their guns drawn.

"One," Dickson mouthed, as Rodriguez used her free hand to bring the gold charm that hung from her neck, up to her lips in order to kiss it.

"Two." As the word left Dickson's mouth, Digangi the only white cop in the group, used the back of his shaky hand to wipe the sweat off of his brow. In order to muster up some saliva, he tried to swallow, but the inside of his mouth was bone dry from anxiety.

"Th...three," he whispered as he swung the battering ram swiftly, sending it forward with all his might. It smashed into the door, making a loud crashing noise upon impact. Wooden shards from the doorframe splintered into the air, as the metal door swung forward. Digangi and Rodriguez quickly entered into the one bedroom apartment, each of them heading in opposite directions as they surveyed the surroundings with their guns drawn. Dickson pulled out his piece, and stood guard by the front door, which he closed behind him.

The blissful sleep that Leslie had drifted into after the lovemaking session with Nan, was broken by the loud bang that reverberated throughout the apartment. Concerned, she yelled out his name. She waited a few seconds, but received no response. Hesitantly, she pulled the comforter and wrapped it around her body, concealing her nakedness as she got up off of the bed. Nan never left for work without kissing her goodbye. This concerned her greatly.

"Nathan," she yelled out again, as she opened the door and stepped out into the hallway. Nervous, her voice cracked as it echoed throughout the apartment. The hallway was pitch black, but hearing the sound of the shower running, she immediately felt relieved. She ran her hand along the plaster wall, searching for the light switch, just as a flashing yellow spark emanating from Rodriguez's shotgun, illuminated the hallway. A deafening blast rang out as the powerful shotgun's deadly shells whizzed through the air.

Leslie let out a faint scream, as the shells violently blasted through her back, sending chunks of her lungs and heart flying out of her chest plate. The comforter fell to the floor, as her naked body flailed forward crashing grotesquely into the dining room's glass table, which shattered into a thousand pieces under the weight of her lifeless body.

The sound of the shotgun had startled Nan, who was now standing outside of the shower, drying his body off with a towel. He quickly flipped the light switch off, scrambling to put his boxers on as he opened the closet door where the linen was stored. His heart was beating so fast, that he thought it would explode out of his chest.

He kneeled down on the bathroom's cold ceramic tile, and began scrounging through unopened toilet paper and maxi-pad boxes that were scattered about. He ran his hand around the back of the closet floor until he felt the cold steel of the 9mm semi-automatic he had stored there. He never told Leslie about the gun, and had purposely placed it way in the back so she wouldn't find it. Still fishing around, he finally came across the full clip that he stored separately.

Rodriguez noticed the light go out from a small crack under the bathroom door, and immediately started walking in its direction. She peered down the hall and noticed Digangi standing in the dining room, hovering over Leslie's body. Her body lay still, contorted from the fall and unsuspected blast. Digangi got down on one knee, checked for a pulse, confirming that she was dead. With a nod to Rodriguez, he completed a sweep of the kitchen area.

Rodriguez continued down the narrow hallway, stopping mid-stride before placing her back up against the wall just outside of the bathroom. She could hear Nan frantically fumbling about behind the door. She gripped her shotgun tightly in anticipation, and taunted, "Nan, just come out of the room, Poppi. We just want to talk to you." She waited for a reply, but received no response. Silence fell between her and the door, causing her anger to elevate sharply.

Her mock announcement alerted Digangi, who silently settled in on the other side of the doorframe. He positioned himself in preparation for an ambush. Grasping his glock in his hand, he looked at Rodriguez for direction. She pointed towards the door. Nodding her head, she held two fingers up, ordering their attack on the count of two. Digangi nodded intently, patiently waiting for the moment to pounce. Invigorated, Rodriguez begin her rant once again.

"Nan, we gotta talk baby. It don't gotta go down like this Poppi." This time she squealed a more condescending tone, overlapping her vile accent.

Nan kneeled on the bathroom floor, listening attentively to the voice on the other side of the door. He knew it very well. He also heard the other set of footsteps that crept across the hallway floor, before settling somewhere between the kitchen and the bathroom. He didn't know how many pigs were out there, but he knew that by the sound of things, Rodriguez brought a death squad with her. His mind drifted to Leslie. "What the hell had they done to her?" He heard her scream earlier, and the thought of anything happening to her made him sick to his stomach.

"The money's under the kitchen sink. Just take it all…don't fuckin' shoot!" Nan frantically yelled out in desperation. He was holed up in the bathroom with nowhere to go. The one window in the bathroom was too small for him to squeeze out of. Besides, it had protective steel bars on the outside of it, like the rest of the windows in the apartment.

Digangi looked over at Rodriguez, who whispered, "We gotta finish him."

Unknown to them, Nan was holding his breath, listening intently as he kneeled down right next to the door. Even though Rodriguez whispered, he was able to hear her chilling words clearly through the thin wood. Nervousness dissipated, as Nan began to realize that his fate had already been decided. The hot flow of adrenaline rushed through his body, as he squeezed the trigger on his 9mm multiple times sending four bullets ripping through the plaster wall and the right side of the bathroom door.

"Ah, shit! I'm hit. I'm hit," Rodriguez yelled, as two of Nan's bullets tore through her spine. Her body crumbled to the floor, as she continued to yell out in extreme anguish. "He's fuckin' shooting! That motherfucker's shooting through the door!"

Digangi kicked the bathroom door open, catching Nan by surprise as the impact sent him reeling backwards. In the confusion, Digangi emptied his clip into the dark bathroom. He was aiming high, not knowing that Nan had been kneeling down by the floor. One of the hot slugs grazed the top of Nan's temple as he fell backwards, but the rest of the bullets sailed wildly over his head. As Nan fell backwards, yellow sparks lit up the room.

In response, he squeezed the trigger of his glock twice. Bullets ripped through Digangi's upper chest and violently exploded out the back of his neck. Bloody mist splattered the wall behind him, as he dropped his gun, desperately using his hands in an attempt to stop the thick foamy blood that was streaming out of the gaping hole in his chest.

Nan felt his head with his free hand. The bullet had left a slight gash that barely broke skin, but cut deep enough to cause a small amount of blood to flow down his forehead. His heart was beating quickly, as he began to walk towards the door. Anxiety almost overcame him, as he struggled to make sense of the unknown. He didn't know how many police officers were in the apartment, or where they were positioned. But, he knew that he was a sitting duck inside the small bathroom.

He opened the door slowly and looked down at the hallway floor, glancing over his handiwork. Rodriguez was lying in a pool of blood barely moving, and Digangi was unconscious, expelling red foam from his nostrils as he breathed in and out shallowly.

"Leslie...Lez," he yelled out hysterically. There was no response. His emotions overcame him, causing his body to shake uncontrollably. "Leslie, I'm coming babe...I'm coming for you."

Nan peeked his head out into the hallway slightly, and glanced towards the apartment's front door. A minuscule ray of light shined into the apartment through a small crack in the door's frame, exposing a shadowy figure that was partially hidden in the darkness. Nan noticed him leaning against the wall in stealth mode. Slowly, he leaned back into the bathroom unnoticed, kneeling down by the doorway. He wrapped his gun hand around the wall and out into the hallway. As he unmercifully squeezed down on the trigger, the dead calm that had briefly overtaken the apartment, was broken by the sound of the four gunshots that echoed throughout the hallway.

"Ah, fuck! You motherfucker!" Dickson painfully yelled out, as one of the hot slugs slammed into his lower abdomen.

Groaning, he opened the door and lurched out into the apartment house hallway crawling on his hands and knees at a turtle's pace. With the door ajar, bright light from the hallway seeped inside of the apartment. Nan peeked out of the bathroom, to the left and then slowly glanced down the hallway to his right, before tensely walking out towards the kitchen.

Leslie's body lay in the middle of the dining room floor, surrounded by a puddle of thick red blood and shattered glass shards. Nan dropped to his knees when he saw her. Her lifeless eyes were still wide open, as they blankly stared upwards toward the ceiling.

Nan's voice cracked as he painfully whispered, "Come on Lez, let's go...I'm a make it better. Please just let me make it better, Lez. *I need you.* Don't leave me." He didn't know what to say or do. Inside he felt completely shallow, and outside his body grew numb.

"Why God? Why didn't you take me? Why, didn't you take me?" He asked emotionally, as he shivered uncontrollably. He was unable to concentrate. His mind was completely flooded with thoughts of her...thoughts of their child inside of her.

The sound of police car sirens nosily blared outside, breaking the peaceful silence on the streets. The loud disturbance forced Nan to regain his focus. He leaned over and kissed Leslie softly on her forehead, before closing her eyelids shut.

"I love you, Lez...I love you. You didn't deserve this. I'm a get all those motherfuckers back for this shit. I promise you...I promise you."

Nan heard the tires of another squad car come to a screeching halt in front of the building. He slowly stood up off the floor, and covered Leslie's naked body with the comforter, before frantically running into the bedroom. He scooped a black hoodie and blue jeans off of the night table, and quickly put them on. His forehead broke out in a cold sweat as he sat on the bed, and slid his feet into his Timbaland boots, lacing them up tightly. He tucked the black 9mm into the back of his pants, securing it in his waistband, before throwing on his black leather goose.

Nan ran back into the apartment's hallway, and glanced down at Rodriguez.

"I...I can't feel my arms and legs," Rodriguez said in a painful whisper.

"Good, then you won't need this then bitch," Nan responded coldly, as he grabbed her shotgun off of the floor, and tucked it beneath his black leather bomber.

He heard shuffling in the apartment house hallway. Instantly, he moved to the doorway and peered out slowly. Diagonally across the hallway he noticed his neighbor Ms. Cooper's door slightly opened. Through the crack, he saw her staring into the hallway. Her young grandson, D.J. stood behind her, nosily looking over her shoulder as they both stared in horror at the chaos around them.

As Nan walked out into the hallway, his eyes met Ms. Cooper's. The eeriness compelled her to speak.

"Nathan...Nathan, what's going on? Please, tell me what's happening?" She shuddered in amazement, cupping her mouth, as she stood paralyzed. D.J., who was also gripped by terror, gazed at Nan wide eyed as he noticed the 9mm clutched tightly in his hand.

A feeling of tenseness immediately overtook the hallway, as Ms. Cooper slowly started to close her door ever so cautiously. She was doing her best to avoid any unnecessary attention. Nan struggled to get his thoughts together. His mind raced frantically, and soon afterward a makeshift plan washed over him. His movements were guided almost subconsciously, as he pushed Ms. Cooper and D.J. into their apartment and slammed the door behind them.

"Omigosh, Nathan. Please, baby. Whatchu doing to us? Please…what's going on? Where's Leslie? Please tell me you didn't hurt that girl," she started to cry out loudly. She was distraught. Nan didn't want to hurt them, but he needed her to be silent. There was mayhem all around him…he just needed time to think.

"They killed her, Ms. Cooper. They killed her," he repeated as he unconsciously shook his gun at them. He paced back and forth in the living room, waving the glock as he tried to regain his composure. His actions immediately hushed Ms. Cooper's questions while she mentally prayed for her well being.

Nan glanced over at D.J., who stood just inches away from him. Nan saw himself in D.J. The innocence was there. He tried to gather his thoughts, but the blaring sirens and lights outside hindered his ability to focus. Ms. Cooper decided to take a chance. She decided that she would approach Nan and attempt to rationalize with him.

She couldn't believe that the kind young man who lived directly across the hall was standing in her apartment drenched in sweat, brandishing a gun. Wasn't he the same gentleman that helped her with her groceries every now and then? Didn't Leslie joyfully tell her about the baby that they anticipated? Nothing made sense, but her heart beckoned her to coach him out of his insanity.

"Nathan. Whatever is going on, God can provide an answer. God can take care of it baby. I promise I won't let nothing happen to you. Please just tell me what you need," she pleaded.

Nan just shook his head. "I ain't trying to hurt you Ms. Cooper," he said apologetically.

"I know baby. What do you need from me? Is it money...anything?" She reached out and gripped his hand. Her frail fingers shook, as she held onto him, still in mental prayer. Nan's eyes quickly scanned the room, noticing a window, just in the master bedroom. To his luck, no protective bars were present.

"I need to get outta here. I need to go...from there," he said, pointing in the direction of the bedroom window. Ms. Cooper was bewildered by his suggestion, but keeping her promise to help him out, she escorted Nan through the bedroom as quickly as her old legs allowed.

Ms. Cooper rested her hand on his back as a coddling tactic. It was subconscious, but needed nonetheless. Her touch soothed him for the moment, as he opened the window and inspected the alley below. Before he slid through the window's frame, Ms. Cooper embraced him angelically, another subconscious action that her heart compelled her to perform. In her mind, she recited another mental prayer. This time she prayed for Nan's well being, just as he propped himself on top of her twin sized bed, and slowly worked his body backwards until he was holding onto the window ledge by the tips of his fingers.

Nan's legs dangled freely in the air beneath him. Flashing lights blared frequently, but surprisingly, there was no police presence. Apparently, no one had the foresight to stakeout the alley. After a half a minute or so passed, he let go of the ledge, landing securely on his feet after making the twenty-foot drop. His body jerked from impact, as the shotgun slammed against his thigh, bruising him slightly.

Concealed in the darkness of the alleyway, he leaned his back up against the wall as he plotted out his next move. Cold wind blew in his face, filling his nostrils with the disgusting stench of stale urine. The police cruisers were less than forty feet away from him to his left, and there was a fence that led to a lot down the far end of the alley, which was off to his right. He was just about to start walking towards the fence, when a light that he saw in his peripheral vision startled him.

To his left, a figure had entered the alleyway and sparked a lighter in order to light his cigarette. Puzzled, Nan stayed still, patiently studying the individual's movements closely before deciding his next move. Even in the coldness of the night, sweat slowly trickled down his chest.

The man's back was facing towards Nan, but he undoubtedly knew who it was. Nan's instincts told him to start heading towards the fence. He had time…he could disappear unnoticed. But, he gave into his heart and conflicting emotions.

Slowly and stealthily he walked towards the street, using the dark shadows of the alley as concealment. Perspiration slicked his face, as he lessoned the distance between himself and the street. He was so angry, so engulfed and overtaken by hate, that he didn't notice the discarded Pepsi can lying directly in his path. When he was within ten feet of the street, his foot kicked the can. It wasn't a hard kick, but it was enough of a disturbance to get the Sergeant's attention.

Startled, he dropped his cigarette, turning to look into the darkened alley. He immediately saw Nan as he crept through the shadows. The Sergeant recognized his face as he looked into his cold bloodshot eyes, and immediately went for his gun. Nan hesitated to raise his shotgun, only reacting after a bullet sailed past him closely.

He refocused his attention, reacting to his opponent's attack by squeezing down on the shotgun's trigger. The shotgun blast rang out loudly, lifting the Sergeant clearly off of his feet. He yelled out in a painful shriek as he landed on his back, and his head slammed onto the hard concrete in a pool of blood.

As Nan prepared to retreat, a young white uniformed policeman ran around the corner with his gun drawn. "Freeze motherfucker!" He yelled.

Nan thought about trying to turn the gun on the cop, but it would have been to his own detriment. The police officer had the drop on him. He had caught him by surprise. Nan threw the shotgun down in front of him, and raised his hands over his head.

"Get down on your fuckin' knees motherfucker!"

Reluctantly, Nan followed the officer's orders. He had no choice.

THE DIARY OF ~~DESPAIR~~:

Winter of 1985 - Spring of 1987

Before you judge me for what I became,
I only ask that you take the time,
to fully understand what I was forced to become...

Nathan "Nan" Jones

Void

⅁he painful events that took place on Sunday, December 24th 1985 would forever be etched into the minds and hearts of those that lived through them. Braving the cold bitter wintry weather, many families had ventured out onto the streets to do some last minute shopping. Christmas and the spirit of giving was in the air, and not even Mother Nature could stop the would be Saint Nicks from making the necessary preparations for tomorrow's festivities.

But, the spirit of giving wasn't on everyone's mind that night. A homeless career criminal named, Jerome Reddy had wandered into a liquor store in the Bedstuy section of Brooklyn. His mind was racing wildly from the hot shot of PCP he had injected into his veins only minutes earlier. The bright interior lights caused him to uncomfortably squint his wild bloodshot eyes. He glared out through a narrow blur, barely comprehending what was going on in his surroundings.

John Hayes was a middle aged black man that owned *Hayes Liquors* on Fulton Street. A very devout family man, he considerately gave his full time employees the day off, and found himself working the counter at ten o'clock that evening. His wife Marie and his fourteen year-old son, Joseph had arrived about a half an hour earlier. Marie was tidying up the shelves, while Joseph sat in the back room watching a repeat of *Chips* on a 13-inch black and white television.

Joseph was still giddy in anticipation of the gifts he was going to receive the next morning. He had been begging for a *Nintendo* for the past three months, and he was confident that his father had come through for him. Plus, he overheard his mother asking one of their neighbors where she could buy the silver name belt he wanted so badly. It was definitely going to be a Christmas to remember.

Completely consumed with thoughts of the gifts he was going to receive and the festivities that were going to take place the next day, he drifted off to sleep. Not even the loud crashes and explosions from a car chase scene on the television were able to awake him from his deep sleep. The hustle and bustle of the past few days had caught up with him, and he now lay unconscious on the small sofa, snoring lightly.

Out front, Marie tidied up the small store space, mopping the muddy footprints and collecting the scattered trash that patrons had brought in with them. She glanced at the disheveled looking man almost immediately as he stumbled into the store, noticing his wild menacing eyes. Instinctively sensing danger, Marie picked up her mop and quickly headed towards a door that led behind the counter.

Glancing up at a round mirror strategically placed near the ceiling in a corner behind the counter, Marie observed the man slowly walking towards her. She fumbled with her key ring, struggling to open the door. Just as she turned the lock and stepped into the doorway, the butt of a handgun slammed into the back of her skull, sending her staggering forward before hitting the wall with a loud thud.

John was kneeling down, transferring cash from the register into a small reinforced steel safe, when he heard the disturbance. He jumped to his feet quickly, and carefully scanned the room. He checked the mirrors that he had placed at strategic locations around the store just a month earlier, immediately noticing that the door that allowed entry to the back of the store was ajar…and Marie was nowhere to be found.

Fear shot through his body at a feverish pace, clouding his thoughts as he contemplated what to do next. Should he call the police? Should he check on Marie? A thought immediately came to mind, as his eyes settled on a black revolver that he kept hidden under the register.

As he reached to grab the revolver, he felt the aura that accompanies another human being in your presence. He looked up just as the coldhearted killer squeezed down on the trigger, heartlessly sending a bullet exploding through his skull.

John was thrown on his back, flailing his arms as he struggled vainly to hold onto the remaining life force that existed in his body. The killer coldly stepped over his body and satisfyingly rifled through the loose cash in the safe, stuffing about one thousand dollars worth of crumpled bills into his ragged pant's pockets.

As Jerome padded his pockets, he was startled by a noise that he heard behind him. Sweating, and still charged off of the PCP, he turned around and pulled his trigger twice. The bullets ripped through Marie's petite frame as she stumbled into the room. The blast from the .45 caliber slugs exploding in her chest, killing her instantly.

Jerome looked at Marie's lifeless body through glazed unfeeling eyes, as he quickly stumbled towards the front of store, and exited out onto the cold street. Joseph was awoken by the sound of bullets reverberating through the small store. Paralyzed with fear, he lay on the sofa, unable to muster the courage needed to move his limbs. After what seemed like an eternity, he heard the chime of the steel bells that hung from the front door. Upon hearing the loud shriek of car tires outside, he got up from the sofa and hesitantly walked out into the hallway.

One of the workers at the deli next door, had dialed 911 when he heard the sound of the bullets echoing in the liquor store. Three police units that happened to be in the area responded quickly, arriving within minutes of receiving the call. Jerome Reddy's car was just pulling away from the curb as the police arrived. Two squad cars followed in hot pursuit, while the officers from the remaining squad car stayed behind to secure the crime scene.

Cautiously, they entered the liquor store, immediately taken aback by the gruesome scene that greeted them. Bloody footprints led towards the front door, originating from the cash register area that was behind a reinforced plastic divider. As the officers made their way to the back of the store, their hearts dropped to the pit of their stomachs.

A pool of blood drenched the carpeted floor. John's lifeless body was lying halfway into the room in a sea of blood by the cash register. Glancing down towards their feet, they fixed their eyes on Marie's bloody frame. Young Joseph lay next to her, hugging her tightly, as he shook uncontrollably, tears streaming down his face. His pants were drenched, soiled with his own urine and dark red blood that leaked from his mother's wounds. He mumbled deliriously under his breath, noticeably in a state of shock.

Outside on the busy streets of Brooklyn, Jerome Reddy sped down Atlantic Avenue, weaving in and out of traffic as two squad cars followed behind him in hot pursuit. Sweat dripped from his forehead, as he navigated his way towards downtown, through halfway opened eyes. He had more than enough money in his pocket to get high for a week.

As he neared Nostrand Avenue, traffic began to congest, due to a red light and several pedestrians that had just descended the staircase from the nearby railroad. He changed lanes, pulling along the right shoulder to avoid the cars, all the while maintaining the same frenetic pace. A crazed smile came over his face as he saw the police lights grow faint behind him. They were unable to fit in the small space that he was able to squeeze his compact Chevy Vega through. Looking at the rearview mirror, he smiled realizing that he had successfully ditched the pigs.

Jerome glanced back at the road, regaining focus through his blurry eyes, just as he plowed through a sea of unsuspecting pedestrians crossing the street. With his foot glued to the floor, his car was now traveling in excess of ninety miles per hour. Some bodies flew violently through the air on impact, before they landed on the hard gray pavement seconds later. Others were mowed down quickly, as they slid beneath the Vega's steel bumper, crushed under its tires.

Unscathed and still elated, Jerome continued racing down the street, disappearing into the darkness. Back at the scene of the accident, a plethora of dismembered bodies lay in the street, as bystanders scrambled to help those that had fallen victim to this senseless act. The police that had been following Jerome, stopped their pursuit and immediately offered emergency aid to those that were still clinging to life. Twelve people in total were injured. Three individuals lie on the ground lifeless.

As emergency workers arrived on the scene, rushing as fast as humanely possible to provide aid, a thirteen year-old boy stood in the middle of the street, looking on emotionless. Clutching a shopping bag in one hand, young Nathan Jones stared down at the mangled flesh of his mother and father. A night of last minute shopping as a family had resulted in their vicious deaths. His blood felt cold in his veins.

He told the emergency workers that he had seen the bright headlights of the car peering down on him, but couldn't move out of shear terror. In the midst of the madness, his mother sacrificed her own life, by pushing him out of the car's path and into a safe haven. Her blood stained his blue snorkel. In less than a New York minute, he had become an orphan. He never felt so alone in his life.

Lemonhead and Bazooka Joe

Saint Mary's Refuge was an orphanage in the Crown Heights section of Brooklyn. It had been around since the depression, functioning as a haven for orphaned and abandoned teens. Due to the fact that they took in any child between the ages of thirteen and eighteen, the orphanage became more of a group home than anything else in the early eighties, as the influx of minorities and foster children increased. But, the self sacrificing staff of devout Catholics did their best to run *Saint Mary's* in the image of the perfect man that was strapped to the ten foot cross that hung from the ceiling in the main lobby.

Joseph Hayes sat on a bench in the middle of the empty courtyard, glaring up at the sky during his scheduled recess break. On a typical summer day, this area would be filled with teens and supervising staff members. Today, even though the sun's rays deceivingly peeked through the clouds, the temperature outside was still bitter. This was Joseph's routine daily. He had become extremely introverted since his parent's brutal murder that occurred only three months ago.

Coming from a middle class family, Joseph was having a hard time adjusting to *Saint Mary's* environment. He didn't like eating every meal of the day in a mess hall, or the fact that he had to take showers with fifteen other boys each day. He was a recluse before being brought to the home, and as of late he had become even worse.

The in house psychiatrist had attempted to get Joseph to open up on several occasions unsuccessfully. He wouldn't speak a word. Therefore, the staff didn't let him attend school with the other students just yet. Realizing that he had witnessed such a traumatic event firsthand, they approached the situation gingerly.

After some thought, they decided to keep him out of school the remainder of the year, getting him up to speed with a tutor. He would attend *Boys & Girls* high school next year, or when the time was right. But for right now, they gave him time for his deep wounds to heal.

As the wind blew a chilly breeze through the air, Joseph slouched his lanky five-nine frame on the cold metal bench. His small afro was nappy and matted down, looking as if it had gone uncared for for several months. His chocolate complexioned hands were ashy white from the cold. He slowly rubbed them together creating some friction, in order to warm them slightly.

Drifting off in a trance like state, he stared straight ahead, unaware of anything taking place around him. Constantly, he replayed the last day that he saw his parents alive over and over in his head. He blamed himself for their deaths, feeling that he could have saved their lives if he didn't hide in the room like a gutless coward. Still daydreaming, he didn't even notice the man that approached him with a young black teen trailing closely behind.

"Joseph," the tall sharply dressed black man said lightly in his deep baritone voice. A second or two passed before he came out of his trance, and slowly glanced up at the man acknowledging his presence. He stared coldly at him through unfeeling eyes, before the man spoke again.

"Joseph, my name is Officer Mark Carson," he said, pausing to extend his hand outward.

After waiting a few seconds, and realizing that Joseph wasn't going to shake his hand, he pointed towards the skinny thirteen year-old black kid standing by his side.

"This little guy over here, I call him lemon head, because he went crazy when I bought him a couple packs of *Lemonheads* the other day."

Joseph's eyes dropped downward towards the ground, revealing his disinterest. The cold wind rustled brutally through the courtyard causing Carson and the young kid with him to tuck their hands inside of their jacket pockets.

"I don't really like them either…too sour, ya know?" Carson said, continuing to talk as if he was having a two-way conversation. "You look more like a bubblegum man yourself. That's why I bought you a bag of *Bazooka Joes*."

Carson pulled a crumpled brown paper bag full of *Bazooka Joes* out of his trench coat pocket, and placed it on the bench next to Joseph. He glanced over at it quickly, and then stared back towards the ground.

Unfazed, Carson smiled slightly and said, "They don't stay sweet long…even taste a little rubbery after awhile, but I bought you a bunch of them anyway."

Joseph continued looking downward, barely paying attention as the scrawny kid stepped from the side of Carson and sat down on the bench next to him.

Turning his body to face towards Joseph he said, "Yo, I know how you feel. I deal with the same stuff everyday," he paused mid-sentence, swallowing deeply before continuing. "The same person that killed your parents killed mine too."

Slowly, Joseph lifted his head up and looked the boy directly in the eyes. For the first time in months, his face revealed a glint of interest.

Extending his hand outward, the boy said, "What's up Joe? My name is Nathan…Nathan Jones."

With that, Joseph grabbed Nathan's hand and warmly gave him a pound.

Carson

Officer Mark Carson was a beat cop that had been on the force for almost ten years. His father had been a detective at the 17th, and he proudly followed in his footsteps after finishing a couple of years at a junior college and a short stint in the Marines. At thirty-seven, he had recently gone through a bitter divorce. The hustle and bustle that came along with his job hadn't actually helped his relationship, so he never really got the chance to have the family he desperately wanted.

Mark had been the first officer on the scene, after the car chase he was involved in on Christmas Eve, reached a violent climax. He felt like his heart had been ripped out of his chest, when he saw Nathan standing alone in the intersection of Atlantic and Nostrand, clutching his mother's bloodied hand. The mangled bodies of his father and a few other pedestrians were also disgustingly littered across the street. He had never seen a look of pain and emptiness like the one he saw on the teenager's face that day.

When he heard that another child had suffered a similar fate, his heart compelled him to reach out to some friends he had in the Department of Social Services. After several calls and arm-twisting being done behind the scenes, he was able to get *Saint Mary's* to accept both of the youths. It made him feel some degree of accomplishment, figuring that if they didn't have their family, they would at least have one another.

Nathan had been receptive to him almost immediately, when he first visited him at the home. He didn't know if it was due to the fact that he remembered him from that fateful night, but they clicked like they were old friends. From that day on, he decided that he would always be a part of both boy's lives. No matter what it took, he would be that father figure that they both had lost. He would be the mentor that he knew they both desperately needed.

The staff at *Saint Mary's* had urged Carson to give Joe a little time before he introduced himself to him. They were extremely concerned about the way that Joe had reacted to the death of his parents, slipping into a reclusive state. Understanding their concerns, Carson kept his distance while the psychiatrists worked closely with Joe, until he got the go ahead for their meeting a week ago.

Carson didn't have a feel for Joe yet. Just like Nathan, he could only imagine the gut wrenching pain that he was going through on the inside. Joe was definitely the colder of the two, but he figured that his cold heart would soften up over time. In any case, he would be there for him no matter how long it took.

Carson headed over to Albee Square Mall and picked up a couple of pounds of *Bazooka Joes* and *Lemonheads* from the store inside. Recognizing him as Five-O, the owner of the candy shop gave him the candy for free. That was the usual routine. Instead of protection money, local business owners generally just gave him things for free in hopes of him keeping an eye out for them. It was against departmental rules, but he considered it one of the perks of the job.

After grabbing a bite to eat and finishing up his tour, Carson headed home to Park Slope. He lived in a luxurious brownstone, decorated with expensive European furniture and plush wall to wall carpeting, that looked like it was way beyond his means. But, somehow he managed to pull it off. He never half stepped when it came to staying fresh with the flyest things life could offer.

Carson popped the top off of a Heineken, and settled down on his leather couch imported from Italy. He grabbed a fat Cuban out of his blazer pocket, lit it up and slowly pulled from it. As the smoke entered his lungs, he immediately felt at ease. Tomorrow, he planned on heading over to check on the boys and drop off their candy. He couldn't wait to see the excitement on their faces.

Blood Brothers

After the revealing day in the courtyard, Joe and Nathan became inseparable. Bonded by the same tragic event, they began to trust one another as the months slowly passed, confiding in each other often. Joe slowly began to come out of his shell, expressing himself more freely with his counselors as well. They finally agreed to him attending classes with the other kids his age, at the beginning of the new school year in September.

But, when September arrived, school was tough on him. The teachers didn't really understand his shy and reserved manner. So, instead of spending the time needed to develop him academically and socially, they stuck him in the overcrowded classes with other students identified as needing "special ed". These were the kids he used to spitefully make fun of when he was younger, and now he was sitting amongst them.

Nathan on the other hand, was very popular with his classmates. He handled the trauma associated with his parent's death fairly well, so he didn't miss much school the year before. He was physically smaller than most of the other ninth graders, but he had an undeniable gift of gab and an infectious personality.

He flattered the young females with his sly comments, and impressed his male peers with his colorful stories. It was nothing to see a group of students surrounding Nathan in the hallway between classes, as he told one of his stories in his animated fashion.

This was his method of defense, to keep the vultures at bay. The thugs that would normally prey on a kid his size left him alone, enchanted by his style. He had mastered the art of storytelling so much, that even though his tales seemed exaggerated, they all contained some believable elements that made you want to think that it was really the truth.

Nathan and Joe barely got to see one another during school, but they always got together at the end of the day for the walk home. They used this time to get up to speed with the events that took place during the day. Surprisingly, Joe was the more talkative when the two of them were alone. He looked forward to the long walks home with his best friend.

"Yo, I was looking around the lunchroom and I kept seeing Latoya with the short Anita Baker cut staring at me. I think she likes me B," Nathan said with a huge smile on his face.

Joe frowned his face up in disbelief and said, "Yeah, right. You wish, B."

"Nah, for real. I'm serious."

"Yeah, whatever. She's a year older than you."

"Yeah, I know. But watch, you gonna see her rockin' my name belt by the end of the week."

Joe held up his right hand and made the "ok" sign. They crossed an intersection after traffic slowed up, and continued walking towards *Saint Mary's*.

"Yo, why they always able to trick *B.A. Baracus* into getting on a plane?" Joe asked, changing the subject before pausing to look at Nathan. "I mean, every episode they gotta get on a plane to go somewhere, and he always lettin' *Hannibal* or *Murdock* trick him into drinking or taking some sleeping pills or something?"

Nathan kicked a rock across the sidewalk, as he laughed under his breath. "Maybe he's just stupid. What big black dude do you know that be walking around talking about, *I pity da' fool?*"

Joe punched him lightly on the shoulder, as they both laughed out loud. The *A-Team* was their show. They watched it each and every Tuesday religiously.

Even though it was autumn, they were receiving the benefits of a prolonged Indian summer. The sun shined brightly through the clouds, and even though they needed light jackets, it was beautiful outside. They stopped at a corner store packed with other students for a *quarter-water*. That was what they called the sugary drinks that came in small little plastic containers with foil lids. *Saint Mary's* was right around the corner. They stood outside the store talking before they headed back to the home.

"Was your mother nice, Nate?" Joe asked, as he took a sip from the blue liquid that resembled antifreeze in his container and munched on some cheese doodles.

Nathan looked down at the ground momentarily, as he thought to himself. Then he smiled and said, "Yeah, she was so cool. Real cool. I miss her cooking."

"Yeah, my mom used to make the best fried chicken and macaroni n' cheese," Joe said excitedly, as he thought about the Sunday dinners he used to have after church.

"Your mother couldn't cook no macaroni, man. My mother could cook much better than your moms," Nathan said facetiously in response.

Joe slapped him playfully on the face and spitefully said, "Screw you, punk. Your moms couldn't even cook!"

They slap boxed playfully for a few minutes, throwing their hands through the air, but failing to connect with one another.

As they started walking again, Nathan took his drink out of his pocket, and pulled back on the foil top to open it. As he carelessly tugged on the foil, a jagged piece cut the tip of his index finger.

"Damn," Nathan yelled out, as he waived his finger in the air. A small amount of blood trickled down his hand slowly.

"You alright?" Joe asked concerned.

"Yeah, I'm ok," Nathan said, still shaking his hand to relieve the pain.

Joe timidly bit down on his lip before he said, "Yo, Nate…you know you're my best friend, right?"

"Yeah, you're my best friend too man," Nathan responded.

"You wanna be blood brothers?" Joe asked in a sheepish manner.

Inquisitively, Nathan asked, "What's that?"

Joe held the edge of his drink container to his finger, and slid the jagged foil across the tip of his thumb, causing a small cut. As the blood slowly began to flow out, he held his finger towards Nathan. Nathan held his finger up as well, and they touched them together, before giving each other a pound.

"Now you're my brother...my blood brother. Nothing will ever come between us. We're family now," Joe said.

Nathan gave him a pound before saying, "Brothers forever."

From behind them, a female's voice could faintly be heard over the sound of passing traffic yelling, "Nathan!" When they turned around, they saw short-haired Latoya that they had just been talking about, walking up with two of her friends. A look of shock came over Nathan's face, as Joe sarcastically whispered, "Give her your name belt. Go on I dare you, give her your name belt." Nathan quieted his chatter, by nudging him with his elbow.

He had been telling another one of his tall tales earlier when he said that Latoya was looking at him. Contrarily, she had caught him staring at her a few times that day, causing him to shyly look away. Now she was standing in front of him, and his stomach was fluttering with butterflies. He glanced over at Joe who was wiping his hands on his pants, trying to get the orange cheese doodle dust off of his fingers.

"Hi, Nathan," Latoya said. They stood in front of each other like two nervous kids, but she mustered up the courage to look him directly in the eyes.

He shyly looked downward before saying, "What's up?"

Latoya was a brown skinned cutie in the tenth grade, with the fly haircut like Anita Baker. She giggled lightly and then said, "These are my friends Shawn and Michelle." Her tight smile exposed a perfect set of teeth.

Nathan looked at the girls quickly, and then pointed to his side and said, "This is Joseph. He's, he's my brother."

"Hi, Joseph," Latoya said in her soft voice. "You go to *Boys & Girls* too?"

"Uh-hmm," Joe mumbled, as he stood there uncomfortably.

"Oh, I never seen you before, but nice to meet you," Latoya said, before asking Nathan, "Can I speak to you in private for a second?"

Nathan walked off with her, leaving Joe and the two other girls about twenty feet behind. His knees felt weak beneath him as he walked, not knowing what to expect. Latoya was gripping her books in front of her by her chest. Finally, as they stopped mid-stride to talk, she peeked over them, and stared directly at Nathan with her deep brown eyes.

"There's a boy at school that I think I like," Latoya said in a soft whisper.

"Yeah?" Nathan asked.

"Yeah," Latoya responded with a slight grin.

"Do I know him?" Nathan responded uncomfortably, with an uneasy smile pasted on his face. Not really knowing what to say.

"Uh-hmm?"

"What's his name?"

"Guess."

Nathan wanted to say his own name so bad, but he didn't want to be embarrassed if it wasn't him. He didn't even know what to do if it was him. He looked down at the sidewalk, as his mind raced, thinking of a name to say. Finally he said, "Mike?"

"No. Iiilll", she said, as she frowned up her face in disgust.

"How about Malcolm? I seen you talking to him outside of your math class between periods," he said.

She laughed out loud, before saying, "No way. I was just asking him about the homework."

"I don't know who then," Nathan said, with a dumbfounded look on his face.

Latoya confidently looked him in the eyes again and said, "Well, his name begins with an "N", but you don't have to guess anymore, I'll let you think about that. Besides, I have another question for you."

"What's that?"

"You know Nathan Cooper?" She asked.

"Yeah, I know him."

"Well, I can't stand him. And, everybody calls him Nate."

"And?"

"Well. I don't want to call you Nate too, cause then I'm gonna think of him, and I can't stand him, so I don't want to call you that," she rambled, before catching her breath.

"So, what do you want to call me?" Nathan asked, with a smile on his face.

"Nan."

"Nan? That's not cool. That sounds like a girl's name. Everybody would laugh at me."

Latoya paused briefly before she said, "Not if they know that you're my Nan."

Momentarily flustered by her bluntness, Nan blushed and looked down awkwardly. For once, he found himself tongue tied. Latoya broke the awkward silence by walking back towards her friends, leaving Nathan behind still blushing. Once she reached her friends she smiled and said, "I'll see you tomorrow, Nan."

"Ok," Nathan responded.

Joe teased him about his new sobriquet all the way home. From that day on, he became known to everyone he came across as "Nan", and the two youths bonded by a similar tragedy, became known to everyone as brothers.

When they got back to their rooms at *Saint Mary's*, there was a paper bag waiting on each of their beds. At least once a week for the past few months, Carson left a bag of *Lemonheads* for Nathan, and a bag of *Bazooka Joes* for Joe. It had become the regular routine since they all met in the courtyard earlier that year.

He Man versus Man -At- Arms

*N*an didn't get the same degree of admiration at *Saint Mary's* that he got at school. The staff had changed considerably in the months that he had been at the orphanage. This was due to several cutbacks, and also the influx of dysfunctional misfits that seemed to be flooding through the front doors more frequently as of late. Crack cocaine was prevalent on the ghetto streets, and this had a profound impact on family units in the urban areas throughout the city.

For the first time in its seventy-year existence, *Saint Mary's* had to start closing its doors to teens due to overcrowding and its decrease in staff due to cutbacks in state funding. Unfortunately, the environment was becoming overrun by the petty thugs and lowlifes that they had already taken in. So, when they closed their doors to new entrants, it didn't really do anything to help this developing problem.

Nan and Joe had come from middle class families. Even though they lost their families brutally, they hadn't lived the hardened lives and witnessed the drug abuse that some of their peers had. These were kids that were raised and abandoned by drug fiends. The epitome of a hard knock life. Undoubtedly, they had a harder, rougher edge to them. Slowly, this new breed of teens formed various clicks, and fights became a frequent occurrence at the home.

The Five-Percenters were a radical offshoot of the Nation of Islam, taught to believe that the black man was God, and that all white people were the devil. They weren't the biggest click in *Saint Mary's*, but clearly, they were the most respected. The boys that were down with them had adopted the surnames "Sha" or "Ra," and everything revolved around the day's mathematics with the god bodies. Besides them, there were a few other clicks, but none that were as organized and feared.

Nan and Joe stuck to themselves most of the time when they returned home from school, spending most of their evenings in the room that they shared. Even though they were both in high school, and girls and other adolescent thoughts were steadily racing through their minds, they were still young at heart.

On the down low, Joe still liked to collect action figures, his pride and joy being his small *Master's of the Universe* collection, that his parents had bought him a few years back. Deep down, both of them were still desperately trying to hold on to a piece of their past. The time in their lives when they were unfamiliar with fear, and before they understood the pain that accompanies the death of loved ones. A time of innocence.

"I think that if it was *He-Man versus Man -At- Arms* in a head up for real, *He-Man* would get beat down," Nan said, as he sat on the bottom bunk of his bed and studied the *Man -At- Arms* doll he held in his hands.

"Nah, *He-Man* would get him. Plus, *Battle Cat* would help him out if he needed him," Joe responded defensively.

"Yeah, he would need help cuz *Men -At- Arms* would kick his ass," Nan said, as he picked up the *Sword of Power* and put it in *He-Man's* hand.

Just then, the door to their room swung open and Shaborn walked in with a couple of his cronies flanking both shoulders. Shaborn was a stocky sixteen year-old that had showed up recently at *Saint Mary's* door after his mother was convicted of armed robbery. He wore a tight green Letigre shirt that gripped his frame, highlighting his slightly developed physique and plump biceps. He had on matching suede Ballys.

Shaborn had quickly become popular amongst the other Five-Percenters at *Saint Mary's*. He was treated sort of like the leader of sorts, probably because he was the most fluent with the god body lingo. Plus, he had a little rep that he carried with him, from getting into street fights when he lived in Bedstuy.

When Joe and Nan saw him, they immediately stopped playing and looked up defensively.

"What's today's mathematics god?" Shaborn asked Joe in his gruff voice. He purposely called out Joe instead of Nan, because he was the bigger of the two.

Joe looked at him dumbfounded, before responding, "I don't know what you're talking about?"

"Yeah, you niggas sitting up here living large playing with toys and shit, benefiting from the devilish ways of the eighty five percent," Shaborn said, pausing to point his index finger around the room.

Joe and Nan were in *Saint Mary's* before the tremendous influx of kids. Teens that came around the same time as them had their own rooms, and in their case they had been sharing one for the past six months. As for the newcomers, they had to share bunk beds in an area that used to function as a gymnasium. This caused a degree of jealousy.

"Seriously, I don't know what you're talking about," Joe said, as he shrugged his shoulders and looked towards Nan.

"Non-cipher, nigga…non-cipher. God cipher divine, you know what the hell I'm talking about. Don't look at him," Shaborn said in a harsh tone, pausing to point at the *Castle Grayskull* that they were playing with. "This nigga got toys and games and shit. Spoiled ass nigga."

Joe looked confused, and was noticeably uneasy. Realizing this, Nan stood up in his defense and walked over to Shaborn. He was just as scared as Joe, but he mustered up the courage to look him in his eyes and say, "Yo Sha, why don't you just leave him alone? He's not bothering you."

Shaborn pointed his skinny index finger in Nan's face and venomously yelled, "Why don't you mind your fucking business, nigga?"

Nan didn't want any beef with Shaborn and his crew, but instinctively he pushed his hand out of his face with authority. And just as he did, one of Shaborn's boys clocked him across the temple. Nan forcefully fell to the floor on impact, but quickly gathered himself. Without hesitation, he scrambled back to his feet courageously, throwing a couple of glancing blows at Shaborn. Nan put up a valiant effort, but he was quickly overwhelmed by his assaulters. Driven by rage, he tried to get on his feet again, but decided that it was better to curl up in a defensive position as Shaborn and one of the other boys used the heels of their sneakers to stomp him out.

He was getting walloped, but the rest of the crew made certain that Joe received the brunt of their fury. Amidst the turmoil, he had froze up in fear, too scared to even get up to help Nan. As he sat motionless, one of the boys kicked him forcefully in the temple, sending him reeling backwards. Before he could recover, his *Castle Grayskull* came slamming down on him, bloodying his head and knocking him momentarily unconscious as it broke on impact.

As Nan lay curled up in the fetal position, Shaborn reached over him and grabbed a patch on the rear waistband of his pants that his belt went through. Tugging on it forcefully, he ripped the Lee patch off of his pants and said, "Lee inspection, nigga!"

After the boys walked out of the room, Nan helped his friend get up off of the floor. The thick blood on Joe's forehead made the cut look a lot worst than it actually was.

Other boys nosily came to their room after they were sure the coast was clear, quietly voicing their concern for Joe and Nan's well being. They looked over their shoulders as they spoke, not wanting to invoke the wrath of Shaborn and his crew. Nan angrily dismissed them though. He had no respect for punks, and he knew that none of the other kids were really concerned about their well-being, or else they would have helped them earlier.

As Joe wiped the blood off of his forehead with the sleeve of his shirt, he looked over at Nan. Nan was biting down on his busted lip, the acrid taste of blood filing his mouth.

"I'm sorry, Nan. I'm real sorry," Joe said apologetically, as his voice quivered.

Nan looked directly at his shaken friend and said, "It's alright, Joe. How's your head doing?"

"It's just a cut, I'm a be alright."

Sitting on the edge of his bed, Nan looked around the room and surveyed the damage that had resulted from the altercation. The toys they had been playing with were mostly broken up and scattered about.

Still looking downward, he noticed the *He-Man* doll lying on the floor, its arms and legs had been broken off during the ruckus. Smiling slightly, he reached down and picked it up, before grabbing another doll as well.

"Look Joe," he said, holding the damaged *He-Man* doll in his right hand and the unscathed *Man -At- Arms* in his left.

"See, *Man -At- Arms* took his beating like a man, but look at *He-Man* all broken up."

Joe smiled back and said, "Yeah, *He-Man's* soft."

"Yep, I told you *He-Man's* a pussy."

As they threw the broken toys away, they both laughed to hold back their tears, nervously smiling to mask their fears. But deep down, they knew things would never be the same again. Their childhood had come to a screeching halt. Even as they joked with one another, they were fearful, both realizing that it wouldn't be the last time they would have a run in with Shaborn and his crew.

A teenage love

℘veryday since their conversation outside of the corner store, Nan walked Latoya home from school. They never officially said that they were "boyfriend and girlfriend," but they each kind of assumed it. Holding hands, and laughing at each other's corny jokes kind of makes it official. That's when you know you have a teenage love affair going on.

Nan was real close to his mother before her death, so being able to talk candidly with another female filled a certain void. And plus, Latoya was a good girl from a decent family. She was very smart and had been raised with morals. She wasn't one of those girls that stood pigeon-toed, trying to look cute, lying about having Indian in their family. She had her own style.

He often wondered what someone so beautiful and smart would see in him. But, as she once told him, "You're my diamond in the rough...my rose that blossomed out of a crack in the concrete." He would never tell Joe that she said that, because he would have jokes for days. But, it always made him feel good when he thought about her saying it.

Nan was in deep thought. He was thinking ahead, wondering what would happen between them when school was out. That wouldn't be for several months, but he wondered if they would still be together, or if they would grow apart? As they walked, she read the expression on his face, and knew that he had a thought on his mind.

"What are you thinking about Nan?" Latoya asked inquisitively, her smile exposing the deep dimples in her cheeks.

"Nothin," he responded.

"Are you still having problems with Shaborn and his crew?"

"Yeah, but I ain't thinking about them niggas."

"Then what's a matter?"

"Nothin."

"You know, it's a shame that we hate ourselves so much, instead of just getting along with one another, you know? Have you ever read any books by Dr. Henrick Clarke?"

"No, why? Who's he?" Nan asked inquisitively. He loved reading and studying history.

"He's a scholar. I learned a lot about our history and why we are how we are as a people by reading his books. My grandfather got me into him."

"Word? Ask your grandfather to let me borrow one of his books. I'll read it."

"Ok."

"Have you ever heard of Ricky Walters?" Nan asked.

"No, what did he write?"

"A few interesting stories. One called *A Teenage Love* and another one called, *Lodi-da-di*," Nan said sarcastically as he laughed out loud. Latoya laughed back, punching him playfully on the shoulder.

"I'll get my grandfather to lend you a book, and you get him a copy of Slick Rick's album, ok?"

They both laughed out loud again. They could have these type of conversations all day long. Both of them could be very serious and introspective, but they both were silly and had good sense of humors that complimented one another. As they walked along, Nan's smile quickly faded, as he looked at Latoya, his mind was still flooded with depressing thoughts.

"Life is strange, you know? Not that I didn't love my father, but my mother was like a piece of my heart. When I lost her, I…I didn't think I could go on." Nan said, as his eyes dropped downward.

"But, you did go on, because your parents raised a strong young man."

Nan smiled and looked into her eyes, "It's hard sometimes, you know? When I think about them. I dream about that night."

Latoya looked downwards, and grabbed Nan's hand tightly. Her eyes begin to fill with tears. "I need to tell you something…something real personal."

"What's wrong?" Nan asked in a concerned manner.

"Were your parents close?"

"Yeah, they were always holding hands and kissing and stuff. Why do you ask?"

"My stepfather beats on my moms," she said as her voice cracked and her lip quivered uncontrollably. "That bastard busted her lip and gave her a black eye last week. I…I told her to leave him, but she loves him too much. I can't stand to see her like that."

Nan's face looked slightly confused, as he tried to think of the appropriate words to say. The right words to comfort her in her time of need.

"He only started after he lost his job at the Port Authority and started drinking a lot. He comes home drunk all the time now," she said as a warm tear rolled down her cheek. She looked in Nan's eyes and tried her best to muster up a slight grin.

"I can't believe that I have you tongue-tied. You always have something to say. But, I can read your mind just by looking in your eyes…I love you so much, Nan."

Nan cracked a huge smile and said, "You love me?"

She giggled lightly before responding, "You know I love you."

"How do you know you love me?" Nan asked sheepishly.

"Because even when I try *not* to think about you, you stay on my mind," she replied in a soft tone.

Nan blushed, before he pulled her closer to him and kissed her on the lips. He slid his tongue into her mouth and began tonguing her, just as some younger kids walking behind them said, "Ooohhhhh!!!!"

They both giggled and continued walking along. Latoya held his hand tightly. She always felt safe when she was in his presence, because he was so conscious of their surroundings. He would never let her walk on the side of the sidewalk closest to the street. It was little things he did that she truly adored.

As they neared her brownstone, she looked at Nan and asked, "Why were you surprised when I said that I love you?"

He smiled and said, "Because I didn't know that you felt the same as me. And, because I never wanna lose you."

"You never will, Nan. I'm a be yours forever"

She gave him a soft peck on his lips, and he caressed her cheek lightly with his hand. They were both young and still virgins. Just touching each other's skin turned them on. As he ran his fingers across her cheek, he noticed that her face was a little swollen. Barely noticeable, but he picked up on it because he always played with her face. She explained to him that it always happened to her during the spring because it was allergy season.

As she walked towards her building, she sarcastically asked, "Now you gonna break up with me cuz my cheeks is a little swollen?"

Nan giggled and responded, "Even with puffy cheeks, you're the best looking girl in school."

She blushed shyly and walked into her building, as he strolled off towards *Saint Mary's* feeling like he was on cloud nine. There was so much more that she wanted to tell him, but she didn't know how.

Wu Kung-Fu

Joe was giddy with excitement as he walked home from school. It was his sixteenth birthday, and he was walking home all alone, which had been the routine since Nan met Latoya. Deep down, he really missed the deep conversations they used to have on their way home. But, he couldn't blame Nan. If he had a girl as fine as Latoya, he would have kicked him to the curb too.

Lately, he had been trying to come to grips with the loss of his parents. The police hadn't found their murderer yet, but he had a recurring dream each night, in which he stood face to face with the cold-blooded killer. In his dream, he walked out of the back room and confronted the heartless bastard before he gunned down his parents. He stabbed him violently in his stomach with a switchblade, and ripped it upwards towards his heart as he begged for his life and gasped for air.

The dream was so vivid and real. Even though he was in control, he felt scared. Even though he tightly gripped the knife in his hand, he felt as if the blade was ripping through his own flesh.

Just as the killer fell to the ground and succumbed to death, Joe would wake up in a cold sweat. This had been happening to him around two o'clock in the morning every day for the past two weeks. But, the look in the killer's eyes is what confused him the most. As he delivered the deathblow, the faceless man looked back at him blankly and almost innocently.

Joe would hold a flashlight under his covers and skim through his photo album until his eyes got heavy in order to go back to sleep. He thought about discussing the dreams with his psychiatrist, but he knew they wouldn't understand. Plus, in his mind, they already thought that he was nuts anyway.

As he walked down the street, a familiar looking vehicle pulled up next to him. Carson rolled the passenger's side window down slowly and excitedly said, "Zook, come here my man."

Zook was the nickname he had for Joe. It was short for *Bazooka Joe*. Joe smiled excitedly as he walked over to the car.

"Hey, Carson," Joe responded.

"Get in partner," Carson responded, as he unlocked the passenger's door. Joe hopped in the car, and after he sat down and securely buckled his seat belt, Carson slowly pulled away from the curb.

"Where's Nan?" Carson asked inquisitively, as they drove down Myrtle Avenue.

"He's walking Latoya home."

"Ahh, that pretty young thing got him whupped, huh?"

Joe laughed out loud before he responded in an exaggerated tone, "Nan's in loooove."

"Yeah, I remember those days. First kiss, first love...have you thinking crazy thoughts and everything," Carson said, as he popped a cassette into his car's tape deck.

On cue, Force MD's *Tender Love* began to pump through the speakers. He smiled and looked at Joe.

"See, that there is some good music. This ain't like that Hip-Hop be-bop stuff yawl be listnin' to. Run-DMC...Fat Boys...that crap will be played out in five years."

Joe nodded in agreement, as the soft music played.

Carson turned the radio off after a few seconds, before saying, "That there is knocking boots music. You play that for your girl. Not when you in the car with another dude," they both laughed out loud, then Carson tapped him on the shoulder and asked, "You got you a girl yet, Zook?"

"Nah, not yet."

"Don't worry, it'll happen. It will get to a point when you'll have to beat the chicks off of you."

Joe smiled and shyly said, "I can't wait for that."

"Ha, ha. It will happen soon. Trust me," Carson said, as he paused to light a cigarette. "So, what do you want for your birthday? I know you didn't think I forgot. Did you get the *Yankee's* cap I left on your bed last week? That wasn't for your birthday or nuthin'. I just seen it, and thought that you would like it."

"Yeah, I got it," Joe responded, sounding dejected.

"But?" Carson asked, sensing the lack of excitement in his voice. Joe just shrugged his shoulders, and didn't respond.

Carson looked at him closely and asked, "Why ain't you wearing it? You didn't like it?"

"I…I liked it," Joe responded lightly, his voice drifting off.

"So, where's it at?" Carson asked, growing agitated.

Joe bit down on his lip uneasily before saying, "Sha…Shaborn took it."

"What?" Carson asked, sounding bewildered. He pulled the car over to the curb and angrily glared at Joe. His insides were burning with fury.

"Zook, you let some motherfuckin' hood take the hat I bought you?"

Joe was noticeably shaken. This was the first time he had seen Carson so angry, or even use such foul language with him.

"I didn't want to, but—" Joe managed to spit out, before Carson rudely interrupted him.

"Fuck that! You don't let no motherfucker punk you," Carson said as he sped off towards *Saint Mary's*.

He was fueled by his emotions, and couldn't wait to confront the boy that had stolen Joe's hat. Joe and Nan were like sons to him. He knew the pain that they had suffered through in the past year, and would be damned if he let anyone hurt them again.

As he drove down the street that led to the orphanage, he saw Nan walking on the sidewalk. He could tell his distinctive bop from a mile away.

Slowing the car down to a crawl, Carson pulled over to the curb right next to Nan, who cracked a smile when he saw him. He was sporting some dark blue jeans that matched his blue *Yankee's* cap.

"Hey, Carson," Nan said, enthusiastically walking over to the car bopping. He grabbed the back door handle, and hopped into the backseat.

Carson turned around and made eye contact, barely looking enthused as he asked, "Who's Shaborn?"

"Some Five Percenter," Nan responded calmly.

"*And?*" Carson asked, pausing before saying. "I see you wearing the hat I bought you, and Zook told me that he stole his."

Nan reached over the backseat of the car and tapped Joe's shoulder. Before he could fix his lips to say anything, Joe said, "I didn't tell you anything cuz I just noticed that it was missing last night. I thought I lost it until I saw him wearing it earlier today."

"So, what yawl gonna do?" Carson asked as he turned in his seat, facing Joe now. "This Shaborn. What is he, some little hard rock hoodlum or something?"

"He's a god that used to roll with some cats named the Supreme Team, before he moved out to Bedstuy. Got people following him around the home like he's Jesus Christ or sumthin," Nan said as he rolled his eyes in disgust.

"So in other words, yawl niggas is scared of him?"

"I ain't scared of shit," Nan said in a matter of fact tone.

Carson looked him in the eyes coldly and said, "You better watch your mouth, Nan."

"My bad," Nan said apologetically.

"So, if yawl ain't afraid of him, why's he punk'n you?"

"Cause we ain't talkin' bout *what's the science god,* and all that other nonsense. Plus, he got a little crew and shit…I mean stuff," Nan said.

"A crew ain't shit," Carson said, catching the disapproving eyes of Nan.

"I can say whatever I want. I'm a grown ass man, and I take care of myself. When you get a little older, you can do the same, but until then, respect your elders."

Nan cracked a sarcastic grin and said, "Sorry father."

"Listen smart ass. Do you want me to pay Shaborn a visit? Do you need me to handle this?" Carson asked.

"Nah," Nan responded.

"Zook?" Carson asked, looking directly at Joe who quickly shook his head from side to side.

"Well, if you two are going to try to handle this beef on your own, I guess it's my job to at least show you how to fight," Carson said, as he pulled his car away from the curb and drove off down the street.

For twenty-five minutes he weaved in and out of traffic in silence, as his two young passengers wondered where they were headed. After crossing the Manhattan Bridge and heading to midtown, he found a parking space in front of a fire hydrant on 42nd street. He put his police parking permit in his window before hopping out of the car and commanding Nan and Joe to, "Come on."

For the next two hours they watched, *The Chessboxer's Last Stand*. At first, they laughed at the dubbed voiceovers noticing that the words didn't match the lip movements, but before long they sat in silence completely amazed by the fight scenes and martial arts techniques displayed.

The whole ride home from the movies, they talked about Li Yin Mi and the fights with the bushido masters. Carson had accomplished exactly what he hoped for. After picking up some *Chicken Littles'* from KFC, he dropped the boys off at *Saint Mary's,* and promised to pick them up first thing the next morning. They excitedly rushed inside to their room and practiced their techniques until they both fell asleep late that night. All night long, they dreamed about Kung-Fu fighting. Both vowing to someday master Wu Kung-Fu.

Master Thaddeus

*E*arly the next morning, Carson picked the boys up as promised and drove them over to a two story building in the Flatbush section of Brooklyn. This is an area traditionally known for its West Indian influence, which explained the Jamaican bakery that occupied the building's ground floor. Carson pressed a brass bell positioned right next to a black steel door on the side of the building. After being buzzed in, he walked the boys up a musty staircase that led to a spacious loft.

As Nan and Joe walked into the loft, the first thing they noticed was how bare the interior was. No furniture sat atop the unpolished wooden floor. Only thin blue pads were scattered about, similar to those that they used in gym class occasionally. The dingy white walls that adorned the room were also relatively bare, with the exception of a yellow, black and green flag that hung from a wall at the far end of the loft. There were approximately ten windows scattered about, but the dark colored blinds that hung, only allowed minimal light to enter into the room.

The sunlight that managed to filter in exposed a thick smoky haze that filled the room. Nan recognized the scent that accompanied the cloud of smoke. It was the smell of the reefer that he saw some of the older boys smoking after school sometimes.

After staring into the open space for minutes that seemed like an eternity, a figure appeared out of the distant shadows. He was extremely dark skinned, stood about six feet tall, with a chiseled medium sized build. The middle-aged man had dreadlocks and a deep menacing scar that ran through one of his eyelids, and half way down his cheek. Stone faced, he stared at them through his one good eye for a few seconds before speaking.

"So, these are the two brethren that you told me about, huh?" His deep voice and West Indian accent echoing throughout the huge room.

"Yeah, some kids at school are using them as punching bags. I need you to teach them how to defend themselves," Carson said.

The man pulled a chew stick from above his ear and put it in his mouth, biting it a few times before he said, "Defense starts with a deep rooted inner sense. Thus, in order to defend—"

"You must first comprehend," Carson said, smiling as he completed his sentence for him. "You never change man, you never change. Boys, this is Master Thaddeus Strong, the best self defense instructor in the world."

Carson's description of Thaddeus may have been a little exaggerated, but his skills were undeniable. He had learned from the best, and thoroughly studied many ancient cultures. This allowed him to become fluent in five different languages, and deadly in twice as many fighting styles. His technique was a combination of so many different elements. His style was to never become subdued by any one style.

Still stone faced he responded, "To instruct is to provide instruction. To direct is to instill direction. But, to perfect—"

"Is to achieve perfection," Carson said, completing Thaddeus's sentence again. "Man, I thought that the weed would have burnt your brain cells out by now. But, you're more profound than ever."

"The way of the Rastafari is not so unlike that of the Samurai. Gratitude, obligation and bravery. Understanding life, by constantly preparing for death...*seen?*"

Carson left the boys in Thaddeus's loft, where they spent the rest of the day learning about the importance of discipline and self control, which were two of the basic principles that he felt all warriors should understand. He shared from his vast knowledge base, quoting *The Art of War, Machiavelli,* and various scriptures from the bible, which the boys absorbed like a sponge. Nan was noticeably the most focused, as he listened intently, taking in the knowledge.

The next day, Nan and Joe returned to the dojo bright and early in the morning. After being buzzed in, they were surprised to find Master Thaddeus patiently waiting for them at the top of the staircase. He had a white tight fitting t-shirt on, with the words, "Semper Fi" written on the front of it in bold red letters. The scent of weed was gone, and even though it was seven thirty in the morning, he looked bright and alert as if he had been up for hours.

"So you want to learn how to defend yourselves? To free yourselves from the shame that accompanies a humiliating defeat?" Thaddeus asked, while standing at the top of the steps with his muscular arms folded in front of him. The boys both nodded their heads in agreement.

"We shall start with the basics, and continue to aggressively grow from there. The regiment will be very demanding, but when we're done, the same blows that your enemies delivered to you only weeks ago, will seem as if they were thrown at a snail's pace. As they say, no pain, why train? You'll learn how to develop an unstoppable offense, and an insurmountable defense. Your enemies will bow down and worship, or rise up and perish."

"So, we're gonna learn to fight like they do in the kung-fu movies?" Joe asked, sounding real giddy like.

"A proper defense assures that your limited offense is delivered with purpose. Every blow counts. Recognize your opponents flaws and pounce," Thaddeus said, his accent echoing as he paused mid thought and stared closely at Joe.

"A strength overused, quickly becomes a weakness that's abused. Your parents were brutally murdered, and you are both fueled by a deeply embedded anger. Put that aside, until the time is right. As the bible says, vengeance is mine. So, rejoice in the hope, endure under tribulation, and persevere in prayer...*seen?*"

Nan looked up at Thaddeus, his facial expression revealing the fact that he was in deep thought. He paused, shrugging his shoulders before saying, "So a warrior must rid himself of his inner demons, before he can outwardly extinguish his enemies?"

Thaddeus cracked a slight grin, exposing his top row of yellow teeth. This was the first time the boys had seen him smile. He waived his hand, directing them to come into the dojo. As they walked past him he said, "Now you're getting it. I couldn't have said it better myself. Let's capitalize off of this moment, and be zealous in our pursuit of honor. I have so much to teach you both."

AL: **2**

NAN SLOWLY KNELT DOWN on the hard pavement, with his hands raised above his head. The rugged concrete felt uncomfortable and sharp against his kneecaps. The young officer walked towards him cautiously, pointing his revolver at the middle of his back. His hand shook anxiously as he venomously spewed, "Lay down on your fuckin' stomach."

A frigid winter breeze blew through the alley as Nan laid down on the cold concrete. Following instructions, he placed the left side of his face on the pavement, pressing it against abrasive pebbles and shattered glass that littered the alleyway. As he closed his eyes, he felt a sense of inner peace that he only experienced during his meditation sessions. He no longer heard the blaring police sirens, or the other noises that usually accompany the night. At that very moment, he stopped thinking about Leslie.

Concentrating deeply, Nan could hear his own heartbeat. He controlled its rhythm, willing it to slow to a snail's pace. Focusing even deeper, he could faintly hear the police officer's footsteps as he walked towards him. Even with his eyes closed, he envisioned his enemy's movements. Inexperienced and scared, he moved forward hesitantly. Nan could smell his fear.

In the blink of an eye, Nan rolled over to his left side and delivered a vicious sidekick *(Cechuatui)* to the top of the young officer's shin. A grotesque cracking sound echoed throughout the alleyway, as the bone cracked, separating the cartilage in his knee. As his leg buckled, his revolver fired wildly in the air. A bullet hit the ground ricocheting a foot from Nan's head, just as he had anticipated.

The officer reeled backwards, trying to regain his balance, as excruciating pain shot through his body. Before he could steady his pistol, Nan hopped to his feet and delivered a straight striking fist *(Zhiquan)* under his throat. He purposely held back the power he delivered in his blow, not wanting to completely crack his windpipe. The officer dropped his gun, and grasped his neck with his gloved hands while he gasped for air. Pain and fear were etched across his face.

The disturbance made by the officer's gun firing, caused the other policemen that had just arrived on the scene to quickly filter into the alleyway. Nan's muscles tightened as he did a forward dive roll, and in one motion grabbed his shotgun off the ground and sent two shells blasting in their direction. The officers returned fire, sending bullets whizzing closely past his head. He could smell the gunfire. His body felt numb as he saw the sparks emit from their burners, illuminating the darkened alleyway.

Nan pressed down on his trigger again, as he trained his gun on a white officer that was attempting to hide up against the wall. The shotgun jammed, just as a bullet went through the puffy shoulder of his leather goose, burning his skin on impact. Feathers flew in the air as he turned and frantically ran towards the other end of the alley, tossing the shottie as he gained speed. Adrenaline quickened his instincts.

The sound of gunfire exploded loudly, lighting the alleyway up like the fourth of July. Nan reached the chain-linked fence at the end of the alley, and quickly scaled it, safely landing in an adjacent lot. Unconsciously he sprinted through the tall weeds, trash and debris that littered the vacant lot. The police trailed about twenty-five yards behind him, still firing shots in the air. Undaunted, he continued to run like a cheetah…with thoughts of an assassin.

Before he knew it, he found himself on Kingston Avenue. It was the wee hours of the morning, and barely no one was out on the block as Nan continued to run full speed down the sidewalk, weaving left and right to avoid bullets. He ignored the distractions around him, focusing solely on the task at hand.

As he reached the corner of Dean Street, he saw an elderly man sitting inside an idling car at the intersection. Nan yanked open the old station wagon's door and forcefully pulled the startled man out of the car. He placed him on the ground lightly, purposely not wanting to hurt him.

Behind him, silhouetted by the light from the street lamps, the cops closed in. As they got within twenty feet of the vehicle, Nan threw it in drive and sped off down the street. The rear glass shattered from a volley of bullets, as the officers emptied their gun clips. He slammed down harder on the gas pedal, causing the tires to shriek loudly as he drove off blindly. He was ducking down in his seat in order to avoid the gunfire, as glass exploded over him.

Sweat slicked his forehead, as his body shuddered in the seat, reacting from the adrenaline rush he was experiencing. Butterflies fluttered throughout his empty stomach. His hands felt clammy as they gripped the steering wheel.

Aggressively he navigated a few corners at high speed, the old car's bald tires barely gripping the road as he continued to press down hard on the gas. A cool breeze blew against his face, the result of air flowing in from the windows shattered by the gunfire. After a few minutes passed, he was on Flatbush Avenue heading downtown. Surprisingly, there were no sirens blaring or lights flashing behind him. He had successfully ditched the police.

His mind raced briefly as he contemplated pulling over and switching the car with one that didn't appear so battle damaged. But, he decided to take his chances for the time being with the gun-riddled Plymouth. The police knew what he was driving, but he didn't have time to hot wire a new ride now. He had to regain focus. His next move had to be well thought out. He couldn't afford to make any mistakes.

After hopping on the BQE and traveling at the speed of traffic for a few minutes, he exited in the rough area of Brooklyn known as Red Hook. Shortly after getting off of the highway, he pulled over to ditch the car. He took a skullcap out of his pocket, and pulled it down over his eyebrows, as he exited the car and walked down the street at a brisk pace.

While he was fleeing the police, he thought about an around the way chick named Kimba. She was a chick that he messed around with for a bit, before he met

Leslie. It was nothing serious though. But, with three kids, no man and no job, she was always up at night. He knew he could chill at her crib until he figured things out. And plus, Kimba wouldn't ask any questions. When he stopped at a corner store and called her, she was wide awake just as he expected, listening to a cassette of the *Red Alert* show that she had taped the other night.

He put his head down as he walked through the courtyard between two of the tenements in Red Hook, and headed to the door of her building. A handful of hoods were standing outside, drinking forties as they waited for some business to come through. They looked him up and down suspiciously, before a young shorty no older than fifteen recognized Nan after ice grilling him for a few seconds.

"What up, Nan," he said, as he took a swig from the forty in the brown bag he gripped in his ashy hand. Nan nodded his head in response, as he stepped inside the vestibule and headed up the stairwell that was filled with the disgusting stench of urine.

Kimba waited in eager anticipation for Nan to arrive, scouring through a pile of dirty clothes until she came across a pink see-through negligee. Her curvy five-foot frame looked sexy in the skintight piece that fit her to perfection. It gripped her snugly in all the right places, highlighting her perky breasts and exposing her thick round ass. Looking at her body, you would never believe that she had spit out the three rug rats that were sound asleep in the bedroom that they shared down the hall. She had bounced back beautifully from the pregnancies, looking even better than she did at sixteen when she first got knocked up.

A beautiful longhaired redbone, she was a prime target for the hustlers in the neighborhood who were always out on the corner scrambling when she walked home from school. It didn't help that her moms worked two jobs and was gone most of the time, forced to provide for her only child after her deadbeat husband abandoned them when Kimba was only seven.

But through all of the adversity that she faced, Kimba still managed to be a good student with a good head on her shoulders. She would always ignore the advances that the local dealers would make at her, knowing that they were up to no good. That was until the right nigga with the right game pulled up in the right car…and then things changed.

That nigga was Yang, a Chinese Jamaican from Flatbush. He ran with the Poison Clan, and had mad loot and expensive whips that he changed like his underwear. He was Kimba's first, and he turned her out in the fashion that so many hustlers do their hoes. He wined and dined her til he got the drawers, wore the vagina out until it was more flexible than silly putty and then he kicked her to the curb for the next piece of tail.

With dealers, chicks come and go just like their bankroll. And when Yang got locked, Kimba was left with the reality of raising a seed on her own, as well as trying to convince herself that the fantasy of eventually returning to school one day would come true. She never returned to school after the eleventh grade, but she continued naively falling for the "niggas of the minute" from around the way. All of them promising her the world, then running up in her and moving on.

Inside, Kimba was like a giddy teenager as she waited for Nan at her apartment's front door. Like all the other niggas she messed with in the past, she thought that Nan was going to be her man. But, he had stopped coming around months back, right before another one of her men came home from lock down. Still giddy, she smiled to herself confidently and said, "I knew this nigga would be back around." In her mind, there was no pussy better than hers.

The steel apartment door was cracked halfway open and Nan could see Kimba's hazel eyes looking on from within the darkness. He had forgotten what apartment was hers, until he remembered to look for the door with three small bullet hole impressions in it. Murder and mayhem was commonplace in Red Hook. Kimba's kids spent many a night seeking refuge in the cast iron tub in the bathroom to avoid gunfire.

He pushed the door open slowly, and gave her a quick peck on the cheek as she wrapped her hands around him in a tight hug.

"Hey, baby!" She yelled out enthusiastically.

"What's up, Kimmie," he replied, sounding drained and noticeably less excited than her.

Feeling the coldness, her eyes dropped downward as she asked, "What's wrong Nan? Is everything alright, baby?"

"Yeah, I'm just tired as hell, that's all," Nan said, as he walked into the apartment and headed towards the living room.

Children's clothes and toys were scattered all over the floor, and dinner plates with old food pasted to them were left out on the coffee table. The place looked exactly the same way it looked the last time he was here. Kimba embarrassingly moved some of the mess off of the sofa, and as Nan took a seat she said, "You always drop by right before I'm about to clean."

He had heard the same line every time he stopped by in the past, and regardless of the time he strolled through, the apartment was always a complete mess. He never looked down on her though. He knew that she was overwhelmed. Being twenty-three and trying to raise a six, three and two year-old was not an easy task. She wanted a savior, and he knew that he could never be that man. So, he never made her any promises that he didn't plan on keeping.

As he rested the back of his head on the sofa, Kimba stared at him with a look of concern on her face.

"What's wrong?" Nan asked as he read her facial expression.

"What happened to your arm?" She asked, pointing towards his shoulder. Nan glanced down at his left shoulder and noticed a hole with bloody goose feathers protruding out of it. Functioning off of pure adrenaline, he had forgotten that he had been hit. He unzipped his goose down expecting to see a gaping hole in his arm, feeling relieved when he only uncovered a flesh wound. He glanced over at Kimba who was quietly looking on glassy eyed.

"Some niggas tried to rob me over in Fort Greene," he said in the sincerest tone, before proceeding to tell a story in the same animated fashion he had been doing since he was a youth. Kimba looked on, listening intently before she walked into the kitchen. Seconds later, she came back with a plastic bowl filled with warm water and a dampened rag. She patted the one-inch gash on his arm until she was satisfied that all of the dried blood was removed, and then she cleaned the small wound on his head. Afterward, she went back in the kitchen, returning seconds later with a tall sugary glass of cherry Kool-Aid.

Nan gulped down the liquid, quenching his parched throat. He was dehydrated, and the sugar only increased his thirst. Realizing that he was still thirsty, Kimba brought a pitcher of ice water into the living room and placed it on the coffee table. Nan finished it off in less than a minute, and put his feet up on the table. Kimba sat next to him and put her thick legs across his thighs, while smiling seductively at him.

"You gotta be careful out there. I told you before that you need a good woman to take care of you, then you wouldn't have to be out on the street all the time," she said, a slight glint was noticeable in her eye as she blushed.

"You're right," Nan said softly as his thoughts drifted and he thought about Leslie. Only hours ago, he had been thinking about spending the rest of his life with her. He was finally going to get the opportunity to be the father that his own pops never really got to be before his own life was cut short prematurely.

A deep feeling of depression and sadness came over him. Emotionally overwhelmed, he closed his eyes and drifted off to sleep. Kimba nudged him with her foot a couple of times, trying to wake him out of his deep sleep, but he remained in his comatose state. Just looking at him made her vagina wet, and she was feeling horny as hell. Realizing that she wasn't going to get her some, she sucked her teeth in disgust before drifting off to sleep herself.

Nan snored lightly as his mind became filled with thoughts of the past. He dreamed that he was a little boy walking down the street with his father and his mother. It felt so lifelike, so real, as the street lights illuminated a crowded Atlantic Avenue. His parents appeared to be so happy. His father was walking in front, and he followed behind with his mother holding hands tightly as they strolled across the street feeling carefree. It was so blissful outside…everything seemed so serene.

It happened so fast. The headlights looked so bright as they peered down on them. There was no time to move, barely enough time to think. Seeing no other option at hand, Nan forcefully pushed his mother out of the way. As she fell to the ground, safely out of harm's way, the car mowed him down, pinning his frame under the bumper before his body slipped beneath the tires. He lay on the ground, blood seeping out of every orifice as his mother looked down on him in a state of shock. Her deep brown eyes welled up with tears as she stared into his lifeless pupils, feeling helpless.

Lying there, Nan's eyes closed slowly just as he began to drift off into eternal sleep. He felt an unbelievable state of bliss as his life force began to leave him. He had saved his mother. He smiled slightly as he stared deeply into her beautiful face. Just as he prepared to finally meet his maker, he awoke from his deep sleep in a cold sweat. He looked around the room full of anger when he realized that it was only a dream.

Kimba was in her bedroom now, sitting on the edge of her unmade full sized bed with her ear pressed to the phone. It had rang minutes earlier, waking her out of her sleep. She hurriedly ran to her room and answered it, not wanting to awake the kids. The last thing she wanted was to be bothered with them this early in the morning. She recognized the voice on the other end of the line immediately.

"Yo, Kimba. What up?" It was Melquan.

"What's up Quan, you know what time it is, nigga?" She responded annoyed.

"Yo, Dee told me that he saw that *niggaNan* at your building a couple of hours ago. Is that motherfucker still there?"

"Why? You keeping tabs on me now and shit?"

"Are you by a fuckin' TV?"

"Yeah, why?"

"Is that nigga by you now?"

"Nah, he's sleeping on the sofa in the living room. Why?"

"Put it on channel two."

"Why, nigga?"

"Just put the shit on channel two!"

Kimba pulled the small power knob outwards and turned it slightly to the right, purposely keeping the volume level low as she turned to channel two. The early morning news was on. She adjusted the metal hanger that she used as a makeshift antenna, clearing the static on the screen until she was able to see the image of a black male reporter that was standing in front of an apartment building. The words, "News Flash" appeared on the bottom of the screen. Pointing his hand towards an area of Albany Avenue, sectioned off with police tape, the reporter said:

"This is John Jeffries on the scene of a violent gunfight that took place only hours ago on Albany Avenue. Police units are still combing over the area trying to piece together the events that took place upstairs in a apartment and spilled over into the alleyway off to our left. The events are sketchy, but what we do know is that the police were here to serve an arrest warrant on Nathan Jones. But, this is where things get fuzzy."

The reporter paused as the camera panned over to his right, focusing on three stretchers being carried out of the front of the building by paramedics.

"As you see folks, things escalated quickly. Apparently, Jones ambushed the officers, killing one and severely injuring several others. Also slain in the murderer's vicious rampage was an elderly grandmother and her grandson that we're being told lived in an apartment across the hall from a woman identified as his girlfriend who was reportedly slain by the crazed gunman as well. Their names are being withheld while police notify the next of kin, but we're being told that a brief hostage situation took place before the killer took their lives and absconded from the scene. As more details come in, we'll be sure to fill you in. What we do know is that Jones is on the run, and he's armed and very dangerous. Here's his picture folks. If you see him, call the number on the bottom of the screen 1-800-C-R-I-M-T-I-P. Jones is suspected of the gangland murders of several lower level drug dealers as well, including James Griffith, Tyrone Deans and Lamont "Power" Givens—"

The phone fell onto the floor as Kimba's hand trembled, and her jaw dropped downward in disbelief. Lamont "Power" Givens was Melquan's younger brother and also the father of Kimba's three-year old son, Darnell. She stared at Nan's picture on the screen in a state of shock, as Melquan yelled her name on the other end of the line. "Kimba! Kimba," could faintly be heard through the receiver that lay on the floor. Finally, after a minute or two, Kimba picked the phone up from between her legs by pulling it by the cord. Melquan was still yelling her name when she put the phone to her ear.

"What?" She said, her voice sounding weak.

"You seen that shit? That nigga killed my motherfuckin' brother."

"Yeah, I...I seen it."

"Keep that nigga there. We on our way over there now."

"I can't have no drama over here Quan. My kids is in the house sleep and—"

He interrupted her rudely and said, "I know your motherfuckin' kids is over there...my fuckin' nephew is one of them motherfuckers. You think I'm a let something happen to him?"

"No," she said in a deflated tone. Melquan came by with money every week for Darnell, and picked him up on weekends. He had nothing but love for his nephew.

"Just keep that nigga there. I'm a be through in a minute. I'm a scoop Black, and then we coming through," Melquan said before hanging up the pay phone.

Kimba hung her phone up on the receiver that was on top of the night table next to her bed. Her knees felt weak beneath her. Power had been her heart. He was her on again off again boyfriend when he was out of jail. Sure he was a crack dealing hustler, but he had a huge heart and he genuinely cared for her. But, the cold unforgiving streets had been cruel to him. And recently, she witnessed him getting brutally gunned down, apparently over a drug deal gone bad. Or, so she thought.

She didn't even believe it when it happened. Power wasn't large or nothing. He didn't have any enemies that she knew of. But, he had slipped up that night and some money hungry nigga had taken advantage of the opportunity. Reliving that fateful night in her mind made her feel hollow inside, and cold chills overwhelmed her body. She had often wondered who the bastard was that snuffed out her man...and now she knew.

She turned off the TV just as John Jeffries was beginning to talk about the city-wide manhunt that was underway. She walked out of her room slowly, taking time to be deliberately cautious. Her legs still feeling weak, and her mind was still flooded with thoughts of Power. As she walked into the hallway almost incoherently, she didn't even notice Nan standing outside of her room until she nearly bumped into him. Her facial expression revealed confusion and fear, as she glanced upwards towards his forehead, purposely not making any eye contact.

"What's going on?" Nan asked, noticing her awkward demeanor. "You look like you just seen a ghost."

Kimba looked him in the eyes quickly, before glancing downward towards the floor. Taking a deep breath, she tried her best to regain her composure. Her hazel eyes still looking glassy, and the skin on her face looked flushed.

"I...I just don't feel well. I think I'm getting my period," she said as she rubbed her stomach.

"Oh, poor baby," Nan said jokingly, as he pinched her softly on her pudgy cheek.

"Fuck you, Nan," she said, as she pushed his hand away from her face and looked into his eyes. She mustered up a smile, but inside her blood was boiling with fury. She wanted to see him dead. If she could do it herself, she would.

"I know you must be hungry, right?" She asked.

"Starving, for real...I feel hungrier than a hostage."

She forced herself to laugh before saying, "Have a seat back in the living room and I'll make you some breakfast."

Nan looked at her and said, "You sure? You don't feel well, right?"

"Nah, I'm ok. Go have a seat. I'll take care of you."

Nan walked back into the living room, and Kimba followed behind him. She stopped briefly to peek in on her kids. After making sure that they were still sound asleep, she headed into the kitchen and turned on the stove. The clock on the stove said four twenty four. She bit down on her lip as a sense of uneasiness and a slight chill came over her. When she spoke to Melquan, he said that he was just about to pick up Black, who lived only a few blocks away. She knew that him and his boys would be arriving any minute. Shit was about to hit the fan.

THE DIARY OF ~~DESPAIR~~:

Spring - Winter 1987

Step dad

     After school, Nan and Latoya spent the rest of the day at Prospect Park. They both had a half-day, because of the testing that normally goes on at the end of the school year in high schools, right before the summer months. The weather was so beautiful and inviting outside. The warm sun rays peered down on them through the huge oak trees that lined the stone path as they strolled along hand in hand.

     Nan held both of their notebooks under his arm, as he bopped slightly with a slight grin on his face. He had just admired how sexy Latoya's legs looked as she walked beside him. She had a knee length denim skirt on, and a pair of red and white low cut Nikes with no socks on. She looked so fine to him. In turn, she complimented Nan on how sexy he looked since he started working out.

     He had been doing a few hundred push-ups and crunches a day, ever since he started training with Master Thaddeus. In less than two months, his skinny frame seemed to be developing cuts and bulking up noticeably. It was just as Thaddeus had told him, "When a body is in unison with nature, it shall grow like the flowers that blossom in the spring." Therefore, he didn't lift weights, nor did he encourage any of his students to do so. Nan heeded his advice.

     Latoya rested her head on Nan's shoulder as they sat on a bench. She loved being in his presence, and dreaded when they had to part ways after school. Lately, she had been purposely going home late. Her mother was a nurse, and because of the demands of her job, she was frequently forced to work nights at the hospital. Therefore, Latoya found herself home alone with her stepfather more often than not during the past couple of weeks.

     After a few hours of talking and not so innocent flirtation, Nan walked her home. They hugged briefly in front of her house, and Nan kissed her lightly on the cheek before she reluctantly walked inside. As she strolled off, Nan felt as if he missed her already. He waited until she turned the key in the lock and opened the door, before he walked off towards *Saint Mary's*.

Inside the house, Latoya's step dad James was sitting at the kitchen table drinking some warm rum and smoking a cigarette that was burned down close to the menthol filter. Ashes were scattered on the floor in front of him, but he ignored them. He had become an overweight slob ever since he lost his job, letting his facial hair become overgrown as he sat around drinking and smoking most of the day.

With no job, he was bereft of any degree of confidence, and was purposely being reclusive not wanting to be bothered by anyone. Emotionally weakened, he allowed himself to slip into a funk. So, when Latoya walked in the house hours after school had ended, he barely acknowledged her presence. He glanced up briefly, before slipping back into his zombie like state.

As a young girl, she had been so close to her real dad. He was always attentive to her, and played an active role in her life before his untimely death seven years ago. It was stomach cancer that ate at him, deteriorating his inner core at such a young age. This condition would eventually take his life a week before his thirty-eighth birthday. Latoya was daddy's little girl, and she missed him dearly.

When her mother met James about five years ago, she had hoped that he would fill a void that was missing in Latoya's life. James seemed up for the task, saying all the right things and treating Latoya as if she was his own child. But, this quickly changed only weeks after the wedding, when James began to show his true colors. That's when his addiction to liquor became evident, but it was only as of late that his abusive tendencies started to really come out.

Latoya ignored James completely, and headed up to her room. The humidity and hot sun beaming down on her all day had made her feel clammy and uncomfortable. After dropping her books on her bed, she immediately grabbed a towel and some fresh satin underwear and pajamas, before heading into the bathroom that was in an adjoining room attached to her bedroom.

She closed the door behind her securely, before stepping into the tub and turning the hot water knob in the shower stall all the way to the right. A hot misty fog quickly filled the room as she stepped under the hot spray. She adjusted the knobs, until the water temperature felt soothing against her skin. As she rubbed a soapy lather over her tender flesh, her body loosened up as visions of Nan filled her head.

Her thoughts were sexual as she ran her hands across her soft breasts. How badly she wished his hands could replace her own at that very moment. Even though they hadn't been intimate up to this point, she wanted him to be her first. She dreamed about him making love to her every night when she went to sleep, always feeling ashamed when she ran her fingers between her thighs. She would stroke herself lightly until she climaxed while fantasizing about something she never had. She didn't want to pretend any more. She desperately longed for the real thing.

After a couple of minutes passed, she stepped out of the shower and grabbed her towel off of the sink to dry off. She immediately felt a cold breeze against her skin. As she wrapped the towel around her body, she noticed that the door to the bathroom was ajar. Looking deeply through the fog, she noticed James standing on the other side of the door. His beady eyes were staring at her through the crack. Through unfocused eyes, she thought that she saw one of his hands wrapped around a glass of liquor, and the other one in his pants.

Instinctively, she looked downward to make sure the cloth towel was still covering her nakedness. After confirming that her body was covered completely she said, "James, do you mind. I'm getting dressed. What do you want?" Her voice quivered as she spoke, partially due to anger, but mostly out of fear.

James continued to look at her through the fog, for a drawn out minute. His eyes were bloodshot red, and he had a crazed look on his face. Finally he said, "You look a lot like your mother, you know that?"

She didn't respond, so he took a swig from the brown fluid in his glass and said, "A lot more beautiful though."

Latoya walked over to the door and slammed it shut before locking it securely. A warm tear streamed down her face as she leaned her back up against the door, before she slowly slid down to the floor. She hated his guts.

"How long had he been looking at her?" She wondered to herself.

This wasn't the first time that she felt his eyes on her, but it was the first time that he had stepped into her bedroom. She didn't know how to tell her mother about this. And she didn't want to burden Nan with her problems, when he had so many of his own.

After sitting on the floor for at least a half an hour, she opened the bathroom door and cautiously walked into her bedroom. James was gone. She locked the bedroom door and turned on her air conditioner full blast. It was only seven thirty in the evening, and the sun was still out. She laid down on her bed and quickly drifted off to sleep. Her thoughts were consumed with visions of Nan, as they had been every night since they first met. He was her heart.

Confrontation

Joe and Nan had adopted a steady regiment that included a change in their eating habits and five intense workout sessions with Master Thaddeus a week. The summer had just begun, and Nan was especially happy that he would be able to commit more time to training. Joe jokingly called Nan, *"Luke Skywalker"* and Thaddeus *"Yoda."* It was very clear that Nan carefully studied his teacher's moves and strived to master the art form with the zeal of a Jedi Knight.

Thaddeus had done so much to develop the boys both spiritually and emotionally, believing that inner strength promotes outward invincibility. Joe had definitely made significant strides, escaping out of his shell more frequently, and even surprising Thaddeus with his quick wit and humor. Nan on the other hand, was a different story. Thaddeus felt that he kept his emotions concealed, and only revealed what he wanted others to see.

Ultimately, he wondered if Nan had actually adjusted to his parent's deaths as he led others to believe, or if he harbored a deeply embedded pain that ate away at him daily. Sometimes during their training sessions, Nan would put forth an aggressive attack that could only be fueled by anger. Uncontrolled, he was ineffective. But, Thaddeus knew that if his young student was able to harness his anger, he would become quite a dangerous warrior.

In any case, Carson and Thaddeus looked at the boys as a project, and under the circumstances they were both happy with the progress they had made. Carson was very proud of his "sons." And for Thaddeus, he recognized Nan as a unique specimen that soaked up everything that he could absorb. There was only one other student that he remembered training in his past, that had picked up just as quickly. There was only one other that perfected techniques and executed moves so effectively that it seemed like second nature.

On the thin blue mats in the middle of the dojo, Thaddeus taught Nan and Joe the history of bushido and introduced them to the timeless blades. Carefully, he explained the strokes that lead to a balanced attack and the foundation for a crushing counter attack. With speed and precision, he swung the blade in front of him making it cut through the air so swiftly that it was almost naked to the human eye.

"More chi," he yelled out, as the boy's eyes followed him closely, their facial expressions revealing their amazement.

After his demonstration, Thaddeus allowed the boys to practice with the blades for a little while. Then after working out on the combo dummy and a sparring session, Thaddeus sat the boys down in the back room of his dojo. This area functioned as a shrine to his late master. He lit several candles positioned around the room, which discharged a therapeutic aroma, before sitting down and crossing his legs in front of him Indian style. Feeling blissful, he closed his eyes and fell into a deep meditative trance, before he spoke to the boys.

"The intricate strokes that highlight the character of a man, is often painted over imperfect canvas," Thaddeus said, as he stood up and grabbed a plastic pitcher from the table. The boys looked on, still trying to figure out what his last statement meant, as he poured liquid into three glasses.

As he sat back down, he took a sip from his glass before telling the boys, "Go now get yourself some sorrel."

The boys each grabbed a glass and hesitantly sipped from the dark liquid. The strong taste of ginger and cinnamon quickly burnt their throats and rushed to their heads. Thaddeus laughed as he looked at their facial expressions and said, "Sorrel for the soul. It's a mixture of Golden Seal, Echinacea, peel of de orange, ginger, and *supum* secret...*seen*?"

The boys smiled and continued sipping from their cups. The more they drank, the looser they felt. It was the secret Jamaican rum ingredient that was starting to make them feel a little nice.

After they finished off their first cup, Thaddeus filled their glasses up again. The ginger no longer burnt their throats, as they gulped the liquid down.

"Ya, feel a likkle nice, huh?" Thaddeus asked.

"*Seen*," Joe responded, as he tapped Nan and they both started laughing. "This is some good tea, *Sho-nuff*."

Even Thaddeus had to laugh when he heard Joe refer to him by the name of the evil Kung-Fu instructor from *The Last Dragon*. Joe was feeling the effects of the sorrel, and it made him act sillier than normal. Nan finished off his glass and looked over at Thaddeus and asked, "How did you learn the arts?"

Thaddeus nodded his head, acknowledging that he heard the question. Before he responded, he seemed to think deeply, as if he had a lot on his mind.

"I was trained to be a killing machine by the government that occupy a place me call home, *seen?* Marines, Special forces and a ghost for the CIA, I've done it all…probably lick a shot on every continent, *seen?*" He paused and took another sip from his glass, his eyes remaining focused as he continued talking in his deep accent. "Listen yout…don't ever tell no one ya soon come back, when you don't know if ye really come back soon, *seen?*"

Nan and Joe nodded their head, even though they didn't know what he was talking about. The sorrel obviously had Thaddeus feeling nice too, and he was beginning to babble.

"My master (Sifu) was a nobleman named Chi Hung Li. Father was Chinese, mother was Japanese, but he studied both cultures and their way of life manifested itself through his actions. A student is bound to a teacher, to give his life in place of his masters if the situation calls for it. A true Samurai is bound to any man who has put his life on the line, to preserve the life force that exists within the Samurai. Therefore, I am bound to two men for eternity. One of which died exactly ten years ago today. Even in death, I serve him with life. The other my life, I'd give to save him from death, *seen?*"

Nan and Joe continued to look at Thaddeus closely, listening to the slurred words he mumbled out. His eyes wildly looked around the room, until they settled on Nan. Looking directly in his eyes he said, "Your mouth deceives your heart. I live with the pain of a promise that I made to my master prior to his murder, you too must face your demons."

Nan frowned up his face and angrily said, "I don't have no demons!" He was infuriated as the blood began to boil and his thoughts became consumed with visions of his mother.

"Nan, what happened the night your parents die? *What ya say bout dat, brethren?*" Thaddeus asked in his deep accent.

Nan shot Thaddeus a piercing glare as he stood up from the floor. Angrily, he kicked over the table in the middle of the floor, spilling the small amount of sorrel that was left in the pitcher. The glasses he and Joe had used also sailed to the ground shattering on impact.

As he turned and walked away he said, "I'm outta here man."

Concerned, Joe started to get up and follow behind him, but Thaddeus grabbed him by the arm and said, "Let him be, Zook. When you're running from the past, the last thing ya want deal with is someone chasing you, *seen?*"

Joe reluctantly sat back down. He still wanted to follow his friend, but when he heard the door at the bottom of the steps slam, he sat back down. Thaddeus started cleaning up the mess on the floor with a rag, while Joe assisted by picking up the pitcher and broken pieces of glass. He was visibly saddened. He knew the pain Nan must have been feeling inside, and he wanted to be there for him. But, deep down he knew that Master Thaddeus was right.

Outside, Nan walked up to a corner store. He didn't have a quarter, but he had his paper clip that he always carried around for use in times of need. He placed one end of the clip into the receiver, and the other in the metal key slot of the phone. The phone made a sound similar to the tone you get when you deposit change into it. When he got a dial tone seconds later, he keyed in Latoya's number. After a couple of rings, a male answered the phone in a gruff tone and said, "What?"

Caught off guard, Nan hesitated before responding. Latoya's stepfather never let him speak to her, so he was tempted to hang up. But, because he really needed to hear her voice at that very moment he asked, "Yes, uh can I speak to Latoya please?"

"Who the hell are you?" Her stepfather said rudely.

"I'm Nathan, I—"

The phone went dead on the other end. His heart sank to the bottom of his stomach, and his throat became dry.

"Motherfucker," he mumbled to himself. Pissed off, he started to call back, but he decided to start his trek home instead. He walked towards *Saint Mary's* with a head full of emotions and thoughts that were pulling him in all directions.

He barely took in his surroundings as he traversed the concrete jungle. His feet were on autopilot. Before he knew it, he was opening the front door of the home and heading towards his room. His rush of adrenaline was finally coming down, and he couldn't wait to see his bed.

Father Donlan, the most senior member of the staff, greeted Nan as he walked in. Nan acknowledged him, and continued heading towards the steps looking downward. He didn't even notice Shaborn and his crew coming down the stairs straight towards him.

"Faggot!" Shaborn yelled in his face as he walked past. Nan ignored him and continued towards his room as the rest of the crew followed suit, hurling verbal insults at him as well. Reaching his room, he sat on the edge of his bed and stretched out his legs. Joe wasn't home yet, which made him feel relieved in a sense. He didn't feel like talking about the events that had taken place earlier.

As he leaned back on the mattress and prepared to close his eyes, he glanced at the small dresser that was up against his wall. He had mistakenly left his *Yankees* cap on top of it when he went to train in the morning, and it was gone now. He hopped up from the bed and rushed out of his room swiftly. Without a shadow of a doubt, he knew who had taken his hat.

Shaborn stood in the courtyard talking to some of the other Five Percenters in his god body lingo, when Nan approached him. It was after eight o'clock, and the sun was starting to set. Curfew time was in a half an hour. Nan was fuming, and his anger only helped to amuse Shaborn. He smiled and turned the brim of the *Yankees* cap on his head so that it faced towards his back. Grinning even more sarcastically, he looked at Nan and nonchalantly said, "What's the science god?"

Without hesitation, Nan swiftly swung his right hand through the air, and bitch smacked him on the side of his face. Shaborn was caught completely off guard. He rubbed his face embarrassingly, before he bit down on his lip and nodded his head. Venomously he said, "I'm a whup your ass nigga!"

By now, the other boys that had been scattered about conversing in the courtyard noticed the ruckus and began to move in for a closer look. Shaborn's boys began to strategically form a circle around Nan and Shaborn. The two boys that settled in behind Nan were just waiting for the fight to start so they could snuff him out.

Shaborn looked at Nan confidently, as he got into a fighting stance and balled up his fists. He was bigger than Nan and had been in several scuffles in the past, so he wasn't the least bit intimidated by his small foe. Rhythmically he moved his head from side to side and rolled his fists in a circular motion in front of him.

Nan looked on, concentrating deeply. He was timing his movements and predicting his enemy's plan of attack, as Master Thaddeus had taught him. Shaborn continued moving from side to side, cracking a sinister smile as he said, "I like your hat, G. The shit fits me better than your fuckin' faggot roommates." His boys that were now completely circling him and Nan, laughed out loud at his humor.

Nan kept his fists in front of him by his crotch. His feet were planted firmly, but there was no indication that he was prepared to fight. Shaborn became even more confident when he, observed what he perceived as Nan's lack of preparation.

"I'm a whup ya ass like your momma, nigga," Shaborn said with a smug grin on his face. "Oh, I forgot…you ain't got no mother."

Nan's blood was boiling inside of him. He struggled not to let his anger consume him. When Shaborn got within two feet of Nan, he threw a short feint with his left, followed by a powerful overhand roundhouse with his right. Both punches were telegraphed, and Nan swiftly adjusted the positioning of his feet, as he leaned to his left in a crouching motion, avoiding the attack while he delivered a vicious pushing palm strike *(Tuizhang)* to Shaborn's lower abdomen in the same motion.

The impact caused Shaborn to keel over in agony, as he grimaced. Nan shifted his body weight and the positioning of his feet, before delivering a left foot sweep *(Mopan Saotui)* and a swinging fist punch *(Baiquan)* with his right hand that viciously landed against Shaborn's temple. His body crumpled to the floor in slow motion, as the crowd that was gathered around looked on in disbelief. Nan moved quickly with unmatched precision, jumping midair in order to perform a roundhouse kick *(Biantui)* that connected to the chest of one of the god bodies standing behind him.

The other boy that had settled in behind him only minutes earlier, attempted to snuff him with a punch to his head. He only threw the blow halfheartedly out of fear, because he really wanted to run. Surprisingly, the blow hit Nan solidly, catching him on the left side of his forehead and dazing him slightly. Seeing the blow land, gave the young god some confidence. He planted his feet, and threw a right cross with evil intentions behind it. Unfortunately for him, Nan was better prepared for this attack.

Timing the punch perfectly, Nan shifted his body weight, as he focused his mind solely on his attacker. Defensively, he caught the punch mid air, twisted his attacker's arm slightly, and viciously yanked him forward. A grotesque cracking sound could be heard as the cartilage in his joint tore and his arm came out of the socket in his shoulder. The teenage boy let out a scream of anguish as he collapsed to the ground. Shaborn was languishing in excruciating pain beside him, like a wounded dog licking his wounds. He was on one knee struggling to stand up, his jeans dirtied from the ground in the courtyard. Emotionless, Nan methodically walked over to Shaborn and delivered a powerful sidekick to his chin. As Shaborn fell backwards, a bloody mist sprayed in the air.

Nan menacingly stood over him and snatched the baseball hat off of his head. As he lay defenseless on his back, Nan grabbed him by the collar of his shirt and rapidly unleashed a barrage of punches in his face. Just as Shaborn slipped into a state of unconsciousness, Father Donlan and two other staff members knocked Nan to the ground and restrained him forcefully.

Even with all three men holding him, he continued to struggle wildly. His temper and anger were fueling his uncontrollable emotions. As he finally settled down, he marveled at how easily he had delivered a vicious beat down to his enemies. It was just as Master Thaddeus had told him. Their attacks seemed to be delivered in slow motion.

When they sparred in class, he always beat Joe. And he thought that he faired pretty well against Master Thaddeus, until he would stop toying with him, and began doing all types of well-executed moves that he never trained them on. But even still, Nan couldn't believe what he had just done. Several of the moves he performed hadn't even been taught to him yet. He had just observed Thaddeus performing them.

As he thought about Master Thaddeus, his own unwarranted outburst from earlier came to mind. He deeply resented their argument. Thaddeus didn't deserve to get treated like that. He had earned Nan's respect. As soon as he got the opportunity, he would offer him a sincere apology.

One on one

The sun had only been up a half an hour when Carson's phone began ringing off the hook, prematurely waking him out of his deep sleep. It was Father Donlan on the other end. His voice sounded agitated. His words slurred from exhaustion as he explained the disturbing events that transpired the night before. Carson was in a state of shock as he listened on. Thaddeus had given him the 411 about what went down at the dojo. He took it lightly, figuring that it was an isolated incident, but now he was a little concerned.

He called in to the station house and advised the duty cop that he would be using one of his days, before showering and heading over to *Saint Mary's*. When he arrived, they still had Nan isolated from the rest of the kids. He had calmed down considerably from the night before. But, with Shaborn and one of his cronies in the hospital recovering from various injuries, Father Donlan was in a bit of a quandary. He liked Nan immensely, but he didn't think he could let him remain in the home. They had a strict policy on violence that Nan had definitely violated.

Carson pleaded with Father Donlan, and after some arm twisting he agreed to let Nan stay if Carson could assure that there would be no more violent outbreaks. Carson gave him the assurances that he needed, and they mutually agreed that it might be a good idea for Nan to at least spend the day away from *Saint Mary's*. He probably needed some time to get his head together, anyway.

Walking to the car, they barely said a word to one another. Nan looked as if he hadn't slept a lick. Beneath the brim of his baseball cap, his bloodshot red eyes could barely be seen.

Carson looked at him and said, "What's up?"

Nan nodded his head slightly with little enthusiasm. He had a headache, a side effect of a hangover brought on by the sorrel laced with Jamaican rum. As Carson pulled the car from the curb, he broke the uncomfortable silence by calmly asking, "What the hell were you thinking? You almost killed him, Nan."

Nan shrugged his shoulders and said, "He took my hat, so I got it back." His words were cold and without feeling. Carson observed his demeanor. His defiance and stubbornness reminded him so much of himself, that it was almost sickening. But even still, he admired the fact that he didn't let himself get punk'd. At least he had the heart to stand up for himself.

"A hat ain't worth nobody's life Nan," Carson said, still maintaining the same calm tone.

Angrily, Nan said, "You bugged out when Joe got his hat vic'd. I thought you would be happy that I got mine back."

Carson had come down a little hard on the boys, but he didn't expect such a violent reaction from Nan months later. Driving along, he thought about it for a little while, but then he dismissed Nan's outburst as more of an excuse than anything else.

"So, why'd you bug out on Thaddeus then? He told me all about what happened yesterday."

"Cuz he tried to tell me about myself, and he don't know me. He don't know what I been through, to be telling me about demons. He don't know about my demons."

Carson looked over at him and shook his head as he said, "That's where you're wrong. He knows more about demons than you think. He's experienced more pain than you could ever imagine."

Carson pulled his car over to the curb in front of his brownstone in Park Slope. Nan had never been to his crib before, and was surprised to see how dope it was. He was even more amazed when they walked inside and he saw the cherry wood furniture and the thick white carpet.

"You gonna have to lose the shoes my man," Carson said to Nan as they walked into the living room. Nan obliged, taking off his Nikes and letting his feet sink into the plush rug.

"You hungry," Carson asked as he walked into the eat-in kitchen that was right next to the living room.

"Starving," Nan replied.

"I figured that," Carson said in return, as he grabbed a black nonstick pan and put it on top of one of the burners on his gas stove. He dropped some butter in the pan as it warmed up, before pulling some onions and peppers out of the refrigerator and dicing them up quickly. Like a master chef, he threw some eggs in a bowl and mixed all of the ingredients together. Within minutes they were enjoying some cheesy omelets.

Nan inhaled his eggs quickly, and then he ate a couple of slices of toast before gulping down a large cup of OJ. Carson finished his breakfast shortly afterward, before sitting in silence as he read through an article in the *Daily News* on John Gotti.

Nan saw what he was reading and said, "John Gotti is a ruthless man."

Carson closed the paper as he said, "Nah, that dude just kills people over money. That's not ruthless, that's just business."

"Yeah, but that still seems kind a foul," Nan responded.

"Nan, money makes the world go round. Show me a man that says that *money don't make the man*, and I'll show you *a man that don't make no damn money*," Carson said as he paused to look around his house. "Look around you. How do you like my crib?"

"It's dope," Nan responded emphatically.

"How about my ride?"

"That's dope too."

"Exactly. It says a lot about me. It shows that I handle my business. So, when you see someone kill a cat over money, it's usually just business."

Nan remained in deep thought for a couple of seconds before asking, "Would you kill somebody over money?"

Carson's facial expression seemed to reflect that he was pondering the question, before a smile came across his face.

"Why do you ask? Did you steal some of my shit?" He asked sarcastically, as they both laughed.

"Come in the living room," Carson said, as he stood up from the table and walked out of the room. After they sat down on the black leather sofa, Carson got up and pulled a Nintendo Master System from out of the entertainment center, and unraveled two white controllers.

"How's your *Double Dribble* game?" Carson asked with a slight smirk on his face.

"You know how to play *Double Dribble*?" Nan asked in amazement.

"Man, this is my shit. I'll whup your ass!" Carson said emphatically, as he blew into the open end of the grey cartridge before placing it into the deck.

"Well let's get it on then!"

From the start, Carson showed his dominance by raining three after three on Nan. Nan was a worthy opponent, but he couldn't stop Carson's patented flying threepointer from his sweet spot on the corner of the arch. Nan bragged every time the slow motion dunk played, as he drove to the basket. But, he was still getting his butt handed to him royally.

Carson looked over at his young challenger, eyeing him as he glared at the 50-inch projection television screen. He chuckled lightly to himself, while marveling at Nan's persistence. Every time he lost, he would ask Carson to run it back. After whipping him out five games in a row, Carson looked over to him and said, "Damn, don't you ever give up?"

"Run it back one more time," Nan said pleadingly.

"Nah, I don't feel like bringing it to you anymore. You're wack. Play the computer a few times and get your game up before you play me again. I'm a go get some sleep."

"One more time, come on."

Carson shook his head, letting Nan know that he had no plans on playing the game again right now. Then he said, "Listen, you know what I told you about your hat? About not letting nobody take nothing from you and everything?"

Nan nodded and said, "Yes."

"Well, there was more to that statement. I thought I would be able to explain it to you before you ran off and went upside somebody's head."

"What's the rest then?"

"You ever heard someone say that he snuck up on them like a thief in the night?"

"Uh hmm."

"Well they was talking about Jesus, but all real niggas move in silence, Nan. They handle their business one on one. Understand what I'm saying? What you did was sloppy."

"How you figure? What would you have done?"

"Don't get me wrong. I would a whupped his ass. But, I would a found a way to do it bringing the least possible attention to the whole situation. Mano a Mano...man to man, *knowwhati'msaying?* One on one. That's how real men handle their problems. I had to bail you out this time, and deal with your problem. I didn't mind, cause you're like a son to me. But, the shit was embarrassing for me to have to plead with Father Donlan to keep you at *Saint Mary's*. When shit hits the fan, you have to learn to deal with it one on one. Whatever the consequences. Whatever the repercussions."

Nan spent the rest of the day at Carson's, until he drove him back to *Saint Mary's* that evening. Even though Nan tried to bait Carson, he couldn't get him to play *Double Dribble* again that day. Instead, he just chilled and watched Video Music Box, as he thought about what Carson had told him. He was like a father to Nan. Even more so than his real father was when he was alive. He admired Carson, and cherished their relationship deeply.

When Nan returned back to the home, the other teens that were still out and about greeted him with admiration. As he walked to his room, he heard the whispers.

"That's that *niggaNan*...that *niggaNan* is back."

He had defeated their nemesis. The story of what happened in the courtyard quickly traveled like an uncontrollable wildfire.

When he got to the room Joe was still up waiting for him. Nan told him all about his run in with Shaborn and his crew. Joe had already heard the blow by blow from the other boys, but listened intently to Nan's first hand account in awe. Exhausted mentally and physically, they both drifted off to sleep shortly after midnight.

Poems is dope

῾Ʒhe summer days passed by quickly for the boys, most of their time being occupied by their training sessions. The days turned into months and the months had quickly passed by in the blink of an eye. Nan tried to see Latoya as often as possible, sneaking by her house whenever her stepfather was out drinking. He had become very strict on her recently, and would flip out whenever she went anywhere without his approval. Her curfew was six o'clock.

Joe had become accustomed to spending time alone in his room when Nan was out. A couple of months ago, one of his therapists had given him a composition book, that they wanted him to use to capture and document his thoughts. He discounted the idea at first, but slowly began to see that he had so many suppressed emotions built up inside of him, that he hadn't even realized.

Ever since that day, he had been faithfully writing in the book when he had time alone. The emotions just seemed to seep out of him like fluid. As he lay on his bed, he jotted down some words between the thin blue lines on the page.

Are you dead, or do you live on vicariously?
Everlasting, your soul's sustained through me inherently
If death spawns life, were you really murdered that night?
Or did the darkness spawn a new light in me?
Since I was only a few feet away in a room
when death chose to loom
I was spared for some reason... I'll assume

He paused in between sentences to admire his work, before thinking about the next line he wanted to jot down. He had become as passionate about writing as Nan had become with his martial arts training. It was his outlet. As his pen hit the paper, it felt soothing to his mind. He used his poetry to face his demons, and come to grips with his tragic past.

He rolled over on his back and stared up towards the flaky white paint on the ceiling, searching for just the right word. Nan walked in quietly while he was in deep thought. He had stayed at the dojo to train a few hours after Joe had left, and as he strolled into the room he looked noticeably tired and drained. Joe immediately closed his book, and rolled over now facing towards Nan.

"Wassup Zook?" Nan asked as he hopped on his bed. He pulled the armpit area of his tee shirt to his nose and sniffed it before saying, "Damn, is that you Zook?"

"Screw you Nan. You got the dragon."

"You ain't lying, G. I need a shower. What's up with you?"

"I'm just chillin'," Joe responded unconvincingly.

"You should have stayed a little longer man. Thaddeus showed me some new techniques for defending against melee attacks."

"I didn't really feel like doing that Bruce Lee stuff today," Joe responded sarcastically.

"Nah, plus we was messing wit guns. He showed me how to aim, load and fire a toolie."

"Word? That's cool. Maybe next time."

Nan stood up and reached towards Joe's book before saying, "What you writing in there?"

"Nothing. Just some thoughts."

"Let me see."

"Nah, it's just some notes, that's all."

Nan sucked his teeth and said, "So, let me see then."

"It's private."

"Private? Oh, it's like that Zook? As many times as I caught you reading the letters Latoya be writing me?"

"Nah, but this is different. It's my—well whatever. You can see it, but you can't say nothing about it."

"Ok. You got my word," Nan responded, as Joe threw the book over to him and walked out of the room.

After a few seconds passed, Nan started thumbing through the pages. More than half the pages in the book were filled with handwritten letters and poems. Nan skimmed through a few of them until he came across a poem entitled, "Who's really gonna love me?" It was a short poem, only about one quarter of a page that read:

I ain't got no house, I ain't got no home
I ain't even got me no Key—
The sign on my door reads "vacant inside"
So, who's really gonna love Me?
I ain't got no mom, no dad
but, a friend that's a lad
my eyes cry from the same pain as He-
Even though we survived,
both vacant inside,
Still wondering, who's really gonna love Me?

Joe's writing style was real simplistic, but effective. It reminded Nan of his own pain and sorrow, that he was unable to articulate to others. He never felt compelled to talk to anyone else about it. Always thinking, *"How could they know how I feel, unless they walked in my shoes?"*

Joe walked back into the room, startling Nan who was staring off in deep thought. As Nan closed the composition book, Joe looked at him and said, "So, go on, get it off of your chest. What you gotta say?"

Nan stared him in the eyes and asked, "How long have you been writing Zook?" His facial expression was very serious.

"About a month or so," he responded, still waiting for Nan to crack a joke.

"This is some deep stuff man. You got mad skills."

"Word, you think so?"

"Word up. The poems is dope. Mad deep man."

"Thanks, Nan. I got some other stuff too, but the stuff you read are like my pieces about me, you know? Personal stuff."

"I can relate to that. I just didn't know that you were writing poetry. You should let somebody see them. My English teacher, Mr. Carby is mad cool."

"Nah, that's ahiit. Why don't you try writing too? Have you thought about it?"

"That's not my thing. I don't even like writing answers to my homework. But, I'm serious man, you should let other people see some of your stuff. At least think about it, O.K?"

Joe nodded his head and said, "Ahiit, I'll think about it." He was surprised that Nan thought his writing was so good.

As Nan held the book out to him he smiled and said, "One thing, B. Don't get offended. But, why'd you call me a lad? Ain't no niggas call each others lads, B."

"Lad rhymes with dad," Joe said with a smile on his face.

"Fuck that. So does bad. *Just a friend that's bad.* Or, you could change it to comrade or some shit. I ain't no motherfuckin' lad. Lad is some old fruity Richard Simmon's shit," Nan said jokingly as he punched Joe in the shoulder. Joe laughed in return as he snatched his book from Nan's hand.

O.T.B.

*C*arson walked into *Sonny's Chicken N' Rib,* a hole in the wall soul food joint on Myrtle Avenue. He always smirked when he looked at the sign, wondering who would eat some chicken and one rib. The "s" at the end of "Rib" had fallen off the sign years ago, and no one bothered to repair it.

The interior looked like it had gone a long period of time without being cared for. A few older gentlemen were sitting at one of the square wooden tables scattered around the room, chomping down on a couple of pieces of greasy fried chicken.

Carson walked up to the counter and asked the young light skinned teenage cashier, "Where's Sonny at?"

She nonchalantly pointed to a door leading to the second floor, while blowing a bubble with the wad of pink gum in her mouth. Carson walked to the wooden door and headed up to the second floor.

Sonny was a clean cut brown skinned black man in his mid-fifties. He was always dressed to impress in an expensive Italian tailored suit, and matching shoes. Slight wrinkle lines were etched on his forehead, but his body was healthy and well preserved due to his strict vegetarian eating habits. He had been a numbers runner in his twenties, now he hedged bets, bankrolled loans, moved weight and got his hands involved in just about every other illegal activity that went on in the hood. Distinguished and extraordinarily powerful, he was definitely the man to see on the streets of Brooklyn.

He sat behind the mahogany desk in his finely furnished office, puffing on a cigar as he looked at various sporting events on three televisions positioned around the room at perfect angles for viewing. It was Friday night, so he had plenty to look at. Boxing, basketball and baseball.

Gunner, his right hand man and main muscle was looking out of the window through dingy white vinyl horizontal blinds. A

.45 was in a holster that hung around his massive waist. Gunner always wore an old black leather glove with the slots for the fingers cut off, on his shooting hand. As Carson walked up the steps, he nodded his head, recognizing his familiar face. Carson nodded back as he walked in to the room and enthusiastically gave Sonny a pound.

"What's shakin' baby?" Sonny asked, one eye focused on Carson as he tried to look past him and train his lazy eye on the boxing match taking place on a television screen behind him.

"What's going on with the Yankees—Red Sox series this weekend?" Carson asked.

"Oh, I thought you were here to get straight with me on the Sugar Ray—Hagler fight. What are you, like twenty five in the hole now, right? This shit ain't O.T.B nigga," Sonny said, focusing his full attention on Carson.

"Yeah, but you know I'm good for it. How you gonna come at me like that Sonny?"

"I know, I know. I just had to remind you baby, that's it. We cool with the series though. You read the paper and shit. You know what the spread is on the pinstripes playing the Bosox in the Bronx. Who you going wit, and what you talking?"

"Ten g's on the Red Sox. The Yanks is good, but not as good as they got em with that spread."

"O.K, then we good," Sonny said as he took a slow pull from his thick cigar, and dropped some ashes into the tray on his desk. "But, we gotta come clean after this one."

"Of course. You gonna owe me big," Carson responded as he laughed out loud confidently.

As he turned to walk towards the steps, Gunner called his name and in his deep voice said, "Do you think you can look into a couple of parking tickets for me? Motherfuckers hit me with an expired inspection and registration ticket last night."

"Yeah, call me tomorrow and I'll see what I can do," Carson said as he walked down the steps.

Gunner looked at Sonny and said, "That's a cool nigga."

Sonny smiled and said, "Yeah, a cool nigga. Cool as a ceiling fan," before focusing his attention back on the television screens.

Let me feel your pain

The summer was almost over, and Nan had spent most of his days working out both physically and spiritually. After the episode with Thaddeus, the topic of his parents became sort of like taboo. They let bygones be bygones and left the subject alone completely, without bringing any real closure to the situation.

Physically, Nan had grown considerably. He seemed to sprout upwards at least two inches, and his frame had developed nicely. Early each morning, he would stretch for at least a half an hour and perform all of his Chi-Kung postures before going out into the courtyard and doing one hundred handstand pushups followed by five hundred sit ups.

The other teens marveled at his physical conditioning, wondering where he got the energy. He referred to it as building up his *chi*, as Thaddeus had told him. Even Joe was amazed when he looked at him. With Latoya being confined to the house most of the time, he had truly committed to focused training, and it showed in the results.

Even though he was purposely consuming himself with training and conditioning, Latoya was still on his mind most of the time. They would find time to see each other when her stepfather would go out to the bar for a few hours, or whenever he would just wander off unexpectedly. Latoya would call the pay phone at *Saint Mary's*, and Nan would drop everything and jet right over. Just to see her face made him happy. He was looking forward to school starting up in a couple of weeks for that reason alone.

On this particular August morning, Nan was extremely excited when he woke up. Latoya had called him late the previous night and told him that her stepfather had finally found a new job. Nan was ecstatic. They hadn't spent a full day together in months, and his heart fluttered just thinking about being with her.

Nan had the whole day planned out for them. They were going to grab a bite to eat at *Juniors,* stroll through Prospect

Park and then spend some time at the dojo. Carson was generous enough to spot him some loot, and Thaddeus had given him the keys to his loft so he could train while he was out of town for a couple of days. The timing was perfect. Joe, who was blossoming into quite the wordsmith, even looked out by penning a nice little poem for him to give to Latoya.

After getting fresh dressed like a million bucks, he threw on his Nike sneakers and some fly tube socks. Today he was living large. He picked Latoya up in a cab, and they headed over to *Juniors*. The restaurant known worldwide for its tasty cheesecake was about half full when they arrived. They were immediately escorted to a booth with a wooden table in the back of the restaurant and seated. As they waited for the waitress to return and take their order, they sat across from one another, staring deeply into each other's eyes.

Latoya giggled lightly to herself, prompting Nan to ask, "What's so funny?"

"Nothing…it's nothing," she responded.

"Ah, you're corny. What is it?"

"It's nothing. I just can't believe how much you've changed since I met you."

Defensively Nan responded, "How you figure?"

"You've grown. You were a boy when I met you, and now you're a man."

Nan blushed, smiling widely and exposing both rows of teeth.

"I knew I could get you to smile," Latoya said as she started cheesing herself.

"I missed you so much, you know?" Nan said.

"I missed you too."

"You know, I never told you about when I called you a couple months back. I had so much on my mind. I needed to talk to you so bad, but when I called your house, your stepfather picked up the phone and was acting like a dick…as usual."

"What did you want to talk about? What was wrong?"

"I had got into a big argument with Thaddeus. I mean, things are cool now, but he had just pissed me off and I bugged out."

"What happened?"

"We was chilling at his dojo having a good time after we trained, talking and everything and then he just came out of his face and started telling me about how I need to face my demons or whatever. Trying to disrespect me."

Latoya looked downward, before she glanced up towards Nan and stared into his brown eyes.

"Nan, he's probably right. You have been through a lot of pain and suffering. Maybe you do need to deal with it in some way."

Nan sighed as he said, "Nobody knows what I've been through Latoya. Nobody can feel my pain."

Latoya reached across the table and grabbed his arm as she whispered ever so softly, "Let me feel your pain, Nan."

"It's my fault that my parents are dead. My mother would be alive today if it wasn't for me," Nan said, his voice trailing off as he spoke.

"Nan, it's not your fault. Some crazy lunatic killed your parents. There was nothing you could do about it."

"Nah, I killed them," he said, his voice cracking as he spoke, still full of emotion. "If I didn't—"

While Nan was talking, a shapely pretty young waitress who said her name was Tammy came to the table and interrupted him by asking, "Are you two ready to order yet?"

She was chewing a wad of bubblegum and full of attitude. Caught up in the moment, they hadn't even looked at the menus that sat on the table in front of them. The waitress offered to come back, but they told her to stay, and looked through the menus quickly until they came across some food that seemed of interest.

Latoya ordered a chicken cutlet hero and a coke, and Nan settled for a hamburger minus the French fries and a water. Thaddeus had told him that too much grease wasn't good for him, so he had stopped eating fries months ago. Latoya changed the topic after the waitress left, trying to lessen the tension. She could see the pain in Nan's eyes. She felt so in touch with his emotions, and wanted to share a part of herself with him.

"I don't even know why I'm sharing this with you, but I think I caught my stepfather staring at me when I got out the shower a couple of months ago," Latoya said.

Dumbfounded, Nan looked her square in her face and asked, "Are you serious?"

"Yeah. He gives me the creeps."

"Did you tell your moms?"

"No, I can't tell her anything about him. She loves him too much. I wouldn't want to hurt her. Besides, she's hinted to me that my real pops may have been cheating on her before he died. Some lady popped up at the funeral talking a bunch of crap, and that devastated her. I guess that's how it is. Love hurts sometimes."

"I still think you should say something. That nigga should be arrested or something."

"No, it's alright now anyway. Like I said, that was a couple of months ago. I barely even see him since he got a job doing security up at Albee Square Mall. They be having him work double shifts."

Tammy returned to the table and placed their beverages down in front of them. As she walked off switching, she told them that their food would be out shortly.

Latoya sucked her teeth under her breath and said, "You know she think she cute, right?"

Nan cracked a smile, and glanced at the waitress, purposely observing her every movement as she walked away.

"Word? I didn't even notice her. Why would you say that?"

Latoya reached across the table and punched him in his chest before saying, "You better watch it before I beat you down."

"What? I was just looking out the window."

"Yeah, whatever Nan. Don't play with me."

Their food was served to them a few minutes later. They ate slowly, enjoying the meal and the flirtatious conversation. When they finished eating, they caught a bus that took them into Flatbush, a few blocks away from the dojo. The sun's hot rays had pushed the temperature outside close to one hundred degrees, so they decided to go without the stroll through the park.

Latoya couldn't hide her excitement as she walked up the steps into the spacious dojo. Nan spent so much time there, and because it meant so much to him, she was happy that he felt compelled to finally share it with her.

The dark blinds were closed, allowing barely any light to filter into the room. Latoya followed closely behind Nan as he led her into the back room where he had sat with Joe and Thaddeus drinking sorrel. He told her to have a seat while he pulled a lighter out of his pocket and lit the candles that were placed around the room.

The yellow flickering light created a sensual ambience. They sat across from one another like giddy little kids. Their sexual attraction for one another created increased tension by the minute. They both knew how they felt inside, but they had no idea what to do.

Awkwardness prevented them from finding the right words to say, and inexperience caused them to hesitate without acting. Unprovoked, Nan took off his shirt, throwing it in the corner, as he dropped down to the floor and started doing pushups.

"Oh, you think you're *LL Cool J* now, huh?" Latoya said as she laughed out loud.

"You wanted to see how I train, right?"

"I really just wanted to see you," Latoya said seductively, while she stared at Nan. He stopped doing pushups and slowly crawled over to her. Without saying a word, their lips touched and they slowly slid their wet tongues into each other's mouths. Latoya felt his chiseled chest sensually with one of her hands, as she helped him slide his fingers up her shirt with her free hand.

Her nipple became hard beneath his fingers as he felt under her bra, and caressed her soft breast in his hand. He pulled her shirt over her head, and struggled slightly with the strap, before removing her bra and fully exposing her bare chest.

Nan observed her perfect body as she sat in front of him shyly, before he kissed her lightly on her neck and worked his way downward until one of her nipples were in his mouth. He sucked on it lightly, as he gripped her soft back with both hands. He didn't know if he was doing the right things, but he wanted to satisfy her. As he held her in his arms, she breathed in heavily, moaning in a fit of passion.

Straddling his lap, she could feel his manhood rubbing against her. They slow grinded while they tongue kissed sensually. Slipping deeply into a state of pure bliss, she laid back on the carpeted floor and slid her skirt and underwear down to her ankles. After taking off her sneakers, she placed all of her clothes in a neat pile, while Nan undressed in front of her.

She was filled with nervous excitement, as was he. He slowly laid on top of her, placing his torso in between her soft legs that were spread widely. As she gripped his muscular back, she whispered, "Please don't hurt me Nan." Not that she thought that he would, but it seemed like the right thing to say. He was her first.

In a soft whisper Nan said, "I won't," then he fumbled with his penis, trying to slide it inside of her. Using his fingers as a guide, he felt along until he could feel moisture. Latoya moaned loudly as he penetrated her, digging her nails into his back as she felt him inside of her. Her best friend Michelle had told her it would hurt the first time, but she didn't expect this. Hearing her moan scared Nan. He was awkwardly trying to push himself deeper into her, but stopped to ask, "Are you alright? We can stop if you want to."

"I'm ok. Don't stop," she responded convincingly, even though it hurt like hell.

A couple of minutes later, Nan let out a deep moan as he began to climax. As he came, Latoya exhaled and panted loudly. Both feeling exhausted now, they lay side by side looking in each other's eyes, while the candles still provided a sensual light in the otherwise darkened dojo.

"Did you like it?" Latoya asked in a childish whisper.

"Yeah, what about you?" Nan responded.

"It hurt, but it was good though," she responded as a thought came to mind.

"Did you pull out?"

"What's that?" Nan asked with a dumbfounded expression on his face. Latoya didn't really know what it meant either, but she tried her best to explain it.

"Well, Michelle said to make sure we use a condom, but if we don't use a condom to make sure that you pull out. It's so I don't get pregnant."

"Well, you can't get pregnant the first time anyway," Nan responded confidently, as if he had special knowledge on the subject.

"How do you know?"

"Cause the first time is when you bust the cherry." He said as he sat up. "But, next time we have to use a condom though."

Latoya smiled and in a soft tone said, "It hurt like hell, but it was worth it. I'm glad you were my first."

Nan kissed her softly on her lips, and held her in his arms.

"I love you, Toya."

She responded, "I love you too, Nan."

They lay next to each other back to chest for another hour, before they got dressed and made certain that they cleaned up the dojo, restoring it to its original state.

"I wanted to give you this," Nan said, as he held an envelope towards her.

"What is it?"

"A little something I wrote for you. Don't read it now though."

"O.K," she said, before kissing him lightly on his cheek.

Holding hands Nan walked Latoya to her house. They arrived shortly after seven o'clock. She had another hour before her mother came home, which was more than enough time to shower up and look innocent again. She blew Nan a kiss as she opened the front door to the brownstone.

Stepping inside, she closed the door and rested her back against its wooden frame. She cracked a slight smile, as a warm feeling came over her. She felt as if she missed him already.

Deadbeat Dad

*J*ames took a long swig from the pint of Jack Daniels hidden inside a wrinkly brown bag he gripped tightly in his hand. He bought it from the liquor store on his lunch break, and was almost through with it when his boss stumbled upon him lounging in the break room. After a heated argument, in which James called him, "A fat guinea bastard," his boss had him stripped of his security shirt and silver badge, before escorting him out onto the street.

Stumbling down Fulton Street, still drunk and disoriented, he headed towards home. His dingy t-shirt was drenched in sweat, with dark yellow stains encircling the armpits. It was a little past six, and the sun was still out, beating down on his forehead. The sweat that dripped out of his pores spewed out the stink stench of old stale liquor. He had capped off a fifth earlier, before his tour even began.

As he walked, he grew even more pissed off, thinking about the guinea bastard that had the audacity to fire him.

"I was a manager for the Port Authority, you fuckin' faggot!" He yelled out to no one in particular.

Pedestrians walked past him, ignoring his drunken rants, figuring that he was just another homeless derelict. He felt the watchful eyes on him as he continued stumbling along, until he reached Flatbush Avenue. The sound of the cars annoyed him. Big Daddy Kane's *Raw*, blared out of a huge boom box that a teen gripping the corner held on his shoulder. The rhythmic drums intensified his headache.

The heat beating down on his head caused him to blackout. Before he knew it, he was fumbling to get his key in the door to his house. He had no idea if he took a car, bus, train or just walked his dogs, but by the grace of God he had made it home somehow. It was a little after eight in the evening when he stumbled inside.

Hearing the door open, Latoya ran down the steps in her robe expecting to see her mother. When she got halfway down the shiny polished wooden staircase, she noticed that it was actually her stepfather, James. She hadn't expected him to be home so early.

"Oh, it's just you," she said disgustedly, as she sucked her teeth, turned around and headed back upstairs.

James rubbed his eyes, adjusting to the light in the house, before he scornfully yelled out, "Bitch, you better show me some respect. I'm the motherfuckin' man of this house!"

Latoya wasn't going to respond, but she couldn't let the moment pass without commenting. She thought back to the time James had smacked her after she told him off. When she told her mother about the incident, she actually defended him, telling Latoya that, "She shouldn't have been so disrespectful."

But, she just couldn't let it go. She giggled out loud and said, "A man? That's the funniest thing I've heard all day. My boyfriend, Nan is more of a man than you. As a matter of fact, when you become a man, let me know. But until then, just continue to mooch off of my mother."

As she walked up the steps towards her room, she felt a sense of joy and relief inside. Even though she talked back to him before, she had never spoken to him like that. Just thinking about the look on his face made her smile.

"Bitch?" She thought to herself. "I showed him how bitchy I could be. Damn, lowlife."

Opening the door to her room, she didn't even hear the footsteps that quickly crept up behind her. She was too deep in thought. The emotions that were guiding her behavior prevented her from hearing the creaking steps until it was too late. Startled, she turned around just as James's huge fist slammed into the left side of her temple, knocking her forcefully onto the hard floor in her room.

Her body was sprawled out on the floor for a few seconds, before she gathered her senses and attempted to scramble to her feet. She saw stars as her head throbbed and dizziness set in. She struggled to get up on one of her knees just as James threw another roundhouse bolo punch that blasted squarely into her mouth. Bloody mist sprayed through the air as she fell backwards. The back of her head slammed into the wooden floor.

James looked down at her through crazed pupils, as he admired his handiwork with a psychotic sense of pride. A sharp pain shot through her body, as she slipped into an unconscious state and her vision faded to black. She was awoken by the stink smell of alcohol, as she heard James yell, "Who's the man of the house now, bitch?"

She wondered if she was dreaming or not. His breath felt hot as he breathed heavily into her ear. She realized it wasn't a dream when she smelled the disgusting scent of his sweat dripping on her, as he roughly ripped her underwear off.

She could taste her own blood in her mouth, as she struggled to fight him off. Her arms were weak, but she managed to use one of her hands to gouge at his eyes. He delivered another vicious blow to her face, zapping what little strength she had left. With the fight beaten out of her, James cocked her legs wide open, and rammed his penis inside her. She screamed out in agonizing pain.

"You still think your boyfriend is more of a man than me now, bitch?" He yelled out, as he looked down at her bloodied face. Her soft body and perky nipples turned him on as he continued to ram himself into her, grunting as he started to erupt inside of her.

"James!" The voice startled him. His penis was still inside of Latoya, shooting semen into her while he climaxed.

"You motherfuckin' bastard!" Latoya's mother, Gina yelled as she slammed a butcher knife into the center of his back.

Hearing the ruckus when she walked into the house seconds earlier, she instinctively grabbed a knife from a drawer in the kitchen, fearing that an intruder had entered their home.

"Gina! It's not what—" He yelled out, as he attempted to turn around to defend himself. Undaunted, she plunged the knife deeper into him. The knife protruded from his back as he fell to the floor. A thick pool of blood began to pour out of his body.

"Baby, wake up! Wake up, baby," Gina yelled frantically as she pushed James's limp body off of her daughter. She lifted Latoya's head from the floor, and wiped the thick blood from her eyelids with her shirt. Blood slowly flowed out of the grotesque gashes on her face, caused by a huge ring James wore on his hand. Her lip was cut deeply, and the white meat was exposed through a deep wound under her left eye.

Latoya struggled to open her eyes. Her head was pounding and her vision was blurry. She struggled to focus in on her mother's face, as she was awakened by the sweet sound of her soothing voice. Her mother looked like two overlapping images, and even though she tried, she couldn't connect the blurry figures together. She peered outward through blood stained pupils.

"Ma," she mumbled in a weak tone.

"Yes, it's me Latoya. It's me," Gina said in an elated tone, relieved to see her daughter regain consciousness. "We've got to go Latoya. We don't have much time."

The windows were open in order to relieve the summer heat. James had let out a loud scream when the knife was plunged into his frame. She didn't know who heard. The police could very well be on their way.

As she glanced at the body lying in the pool of blood on the floor, panic and fear came over her. Her mind raced wildly. She thought about calling the police. Then she thought about his vicious beatings…the evil man he had become. Immediately, she made her decision. She had to flee the scene. Her motherly instincts told her to protect her daughter…to protect herself.

Gina helped Latoya to her feet, sitting her down on the bed before pulling a shirt and wrinkled blue jeans out of her dresser.

"Put these on," she said as she threw the clothes on Latoya's lap.

Gina walked out of the room and returned quickly with a small medical kit that she kept in the bathroom. After cleaning the wounds on Latoya's face with liquid iodine, and dressing them with first aid cream and gauze, she hurriedly left the room again. Under her breath she mumbled, "Hurry up, baby."

A few minutes later Gina returned. She had changed out of her work uniform into some capris' and a blouse, and now had a duffle bag draped over her shoulder. Quickly she rifled through Latoya's drawers and grabbed a few outfits and some bras and underwear. After closing the bag, she walked over to the bed and slipped some sneakers on her feet as she helped her daughter stand up.

Latoya placed her arm around her mother as she dizzily walked beside her, down the flight of steps that led to the ground floor. As they exited the brownstone, Gina discretely led her daughter to her car, not wanting to attract too much attention. After helping Latoya into the passenger's seat and throwing the duffle bag in the trunk, she pulled the car from the curb, thoughts of panic steadily racing through her mind.

Latoya looked over to her mother and mumbled, "Ma, I've got to see Nan. I can't leave Nan." Her words drifting off as she came to the end of her sentence.

Gina shook her head and said, "Baby, we can't. We have to get away from here. Away from this evil place"

Salty tears rolled down Latoya's cheek, burning her eyes and the cuts on her face, as her mother drove off. She cried uncontrollably for the next hour. Even though she was in pain, she wasn't thinking about herself. She was too concerned about Nan.

Love Lost

*N*an had been waiting for the first day of school with anxious anticipation, and it was finally upon him. He hadn't heard from Latoya since the day at the dojo a couple of weeks ago, and he was truly concerned. He walked the halls aimlessly, engaging in meaningless conversations with students vying for his attention. Word about his scrap with Shaborn and his click over the summer had spread like wildfire, and everyone and their mother was talking about it.

Heading to his first period class, he bumped into Latoya's friend Michelle. She was looking all fly in her new sneakers and outfit she picked out for the first day of school. Before Nan could open his mouth she asked, "Have you seen Latoya?"

"Damn, I was gonna ask you the same thing," Nan responded dumbfounded.

"I went to her house this morning to pick her up, but nobody answered the door. And, I've been damn near calling her for a week straight and the phone has just been ringing," Michelle said in a concerned tone.

Nan's heart dropped to the pit of his stomach. He had hoped that Michelle had at least heard from her. Besides him, Michelle was Latoya's best friend.

"Let me know if you hear anything," Nan said before walking off to class. The rest of his day painfully dragged on. The topics discussed during class were like a blur to him.

Joe's day on the other hand went rather well. After meeting with a guidance counselor and a psychiatric evaluator, they decided to let him attend regular classes with kids his age. His test scores and the documented observations they had made the previous year, no longer justified the need to keep him in special ed. He was elated. He jumped into his schoolwork with a newfound passion.

Walking home, the boys talked about school and the events that took place that day. Joe was ecstatic when he told Nan how his English teacher, Ms. Hawkins reacted when he shared his poetry book with her after class. Nan listened on, putting up a good front, but it was obvious that his mind was elsewhere.

Finally, Joe nudged him on the shoulder and said, "Let's go by there."

"Where?" Nan asked, with a perplexed look on his face.

"Latoya's crib," Joe responded.

"What about her stepfather? That nigga's an asshole," Nan said bluntly.

"I don't care. I'll ring the bell," Joe said confidently.

That was enough for Nan to hear. They headed over to Latoya's house, and Nan waited by the sidewalk as Joe walked up the steps that led to the door and rang the bell. He was on edge, as the butterflies fluttered around his empty stomach. The seconds turned to minutes as Joe rang the bell continuously and got no response.

Frustrated, Joe walked away shrugging his shoulders, as he glanced over to Nan who was staring back at him with a look of disappointment on his face. The door slowly opened behind Joe as he walked towards Nan. A sickly looking man in his mid-forties stood in the doorway and peered out onto the street. He had a shaggy un-kept beard. Nan knew who he was without any formal introduction.

"What the fuck yawl little niggas ringing my bell like you crazy for," James yelled out, wheezing slightly as he finished his sentence. Joe was taken aback and didn't respond. Undaunted, Nan stepped in front of him and asked, "Is Latoya home?"

"Who the fuck are you?" James asked annoyingly.

"I'm Nan. Is Latoya home sir?"

James let out a sound that resembled half laugh, half cough.

"So you're Nan, huh? Yeah, I heard about your ass. Well, Latoya's gone."

Nan bit his tongue, trying to remain composed under the circumstances. He let cooler heads prevail as he asked, "Can you tell me where she's at please?"

"If you don't know, than I guess you ain't supposed to know, you little nappy headed nigga," James said coldly, as he stepped back inside the house and slammed the door hard.

Nan started to walk towards the house, but Joe held him back and said, "It ain't worth it. If she was home she would have come to the door or the window or something."

Nan nodded in agreement, even though he wasn't fully convinced that Latoya was really gone. Latoya had told him that her stepfather was abusive. How did he know that he didn't do something to her? When they got home to *Saint Mary's,* Nan called Carson immediately. After pleading with him for nearly ten minutes, he convinced him to send a squad car over to the house to check and make sure everything was everything.

Later that evening, Carson stopped by to see Nan. He told him that everything checked out. He wanted to keep it real with him and say how he really felt. His motto was, "Bitches ain't shit." His wife had left him a few years back, and he vowed to never let that shit happen again. But, this situation called for compassion and sensitivity.

So, he calmly explained the details to Nan. Telling him that the stepfather's story about Latoya and her mother Gina leaving had checked out. To confirm that the stepfather wasn't lying, Carson even had someone swing by Gina's job. They advised that Gina had called and quit about two weeks ago, providing a forwarding address in South Carolina to send her remaining checks.

The stepfather being stabbed up was a little suspicious, but James had explained to the officer that he was drinking all day and some young niggas pounced on him and mugged him after he get fired from his job. His manager confirmed that he was loaded when they let him go, so anything was possible. He didn't really see any reason to suspect foul play.

Nan was deflated. He walked back to his room wondering why Latoya had left without at least calling him.

"South Carolina?" He thought to himself.

As he sat on his bed, he faced the realization that he would never see her again. Chaotic rumblings engulfed his inner being, as a cold unforgiving feeling came over him. He vowed never to completely trust anyone again.

Rebellious redemption

Three weeks quickly passed by in the blink of an eye. Joe continued to delve deeply into the books, embracing the newfound respect that he garnered as a result of his writing prowess. Meanwhile, Nan's prestige continued to grow as well, but for different reasons altogether.

He was no longer focused on school, nor did he have to be the comical storyteller in order to keep the vultures at bay. People gravitated towards him because they feared him. And those that crossed him got their ass kicked. In the meantime though, his schoolwork began to suffer. He couldn't focus. As he sat through the forty-five minute lectures, his mind was always on other things.

He was still very tight with Joe. Nan was actually very proud of the progress his friend was making. Every time Joe shared one of his poems with him, he was blown away by his talent. His favorite was a piece called, *"Brothers"* that described their relationship, documenting the bond that they shared.

Nan was sitting in his bed staring up at the ceiling, when Joe excitedly walked into the room. It was late Saturday morning, and normally Nan would have been training over at the dojo. But, today he decided to just chill and relax. Joe had a huge grin on his face. His facial expression compelled Nan to ask him, "What are you so excited about?"

"Bam!" Joe yelled, as he pulled out a white envelope that he had been hiding behind his back. "This is from Latoya."

A smile immediately came over Nan's face, as he snatched the envelope from Joe's hand, noticing the South Carolina return address before he ripped it open forcefully. He was still grinning as he unfolded the letter, causing Joe to laugh and say, "Damn, look at you cheesing it up."

"Whatever, nigga," Nan said, as he started reading the letter to himself. It read:

Nan,

     Words cannot express how I feel right now. I let you down, and in turn I let myself down. I can't explain why I had to leave to you in a letter, or why I couldn't reach out to you until now. You deserve more...we deserve more. But, you are still in my heart and I hope that I am still in yours. When my mom gets a phone hooked up down here, you will be the first person I call (I need to hear your voice so bad). Until then, I'll continue to read the poem that you wrote me over and over again. I love you, Nan...forever. Please find it in your heart to forgive me.

Yours always,
Latoya

     After reading the letter, Nan calmly ripped it up into little pieces and threw it into a wastebasket next to his bed. His elation was gone, replaced instead by a mean frown that matched his heart condition. Joe tried to feel him out, finally asking, "So, what was she talking about?"

     "Bullshit," Nan said as he laid back on his bed. "Just some bullshit."

     Joe read his body language, and decided to just leave him alone. As he walked out the room, Nan closed his eyes. Minutes later he drifted off to sleep. He felt like his energy was zapped from him, leaving him emotionally and physically drained.

     It was close to noon when he closed his eyes. Even with a full night's sleep the day before, Nan slept soundly. Hours passed by quickly, and before long it was almost eight o'clock in the evening and Joe was shaking him from side to side trying to wake him up. Looking outwardly, he saw Joe staring in his face. As he rubbed his eyes to focus, Joe said, "Carson is downstairs. He just got here. He wants to take us out."

Nan threw on some gear, and quickly joined Joe who was already waiting outside talking to Carson. They were standing next to Carson's new midnight blue 525. He had just picked it up from the BMW dealer, and wanted the boys to check it out. After giving each other the customary pounds, Nan hopped in the back seat while Joe rode shotgun. The sun had already set, but there were still people out on the streets. As they drove along, the young cuties hugging the corner eyed the whip flirtatiously. Carson had his window down, leaning with his elbow in the open space profiling.

Turning a corner, he looked in the rearview mirror at Nan. Joe had given him the 411, and he could tell by his demeanor that he wasn't his normal self. He turned down the *Debarge* song that was playing on the radio and said, "Thought that she was the one, huh?"

Nan just nodded his head in acknowledgment.

"Love'll do that shit to you. You know? You use half your wits, a bitch'll take half yo shit," Carson said bitterly, pausing as he looked out the window checking his surroundings. "I thought I had the one too, until that bitch flipped the script on me and served me papers and shit. Excuse my French."

After driving around for a while, Carson parked his car in front of an abandoned building in Brownsville. The sun was now replaced by a half moon. Two streetlamps in the vicinity of the building were broken, making it almost pitch black on the street. Fixing streetlamps wasn't really a priority in this part of the neighborhood that was overridden by poverty.

Carson facial expression became very serious. He turned in his leather seat facing directly towards Joe, but angled his body so he could also see Nan as he spoke.

"Yawl niggas ain't little kids no more. Yawl ain't little *Lemonhead and Bazooka Joe* that I took under my wings and raised like my own. You cats is fifteen and sixteen. You know?

You're practically men," he said in a stern tone, pausing to look out the window. "You know, I thought about this shit for awhile. Should I turn the nigga in, stomp a mud hole in his ass, or just off the motherfucker. All of that shit ran through my mind, but then I realized that this shit isn't my fight. It isn't my pain."

Joe looked towards the back of the car at Nan. Both boys had dumbfounded looks on their faces. Finally, Nan broke the silence by asking, "What are you talking about, Carson?"

Still looking at both boys, Carson said, "Jerome Reddy. What does that name mean to you?"

They looked at each other and shrugged their shoulders confused. The name didn't ring a bell. Carson had a look of intensity in his eyes as he pointed out of the window.

"The last place I would of expected to find a cold blooded murderer was in this abandoned building. But, after several years and no leads, I happen to see this perp jump a turnstile while I was waiting for the 2 train. I didn't really want to bring the bastard in and have to go through writing paperwork up and shit, but I figured I'd scare him a little bit," Carson said, his words growing more intense as he spoke. The boys listened on attentively, wondering where this was leading.

"So, I'm threatening him with disorderly conduct and all types of shit, and out the blue this nigga just drops dime. He just starts spilling his guts. Tells me how he knows the nigga who killed those two kid's parents a few years back. How he know where that nigga stays."

Anger immediately shot through Nan's veins as he realized the scope of what Carson was explaining to them. Instinctively he blurted out, "The motherfucker who killed our parents lives inside this building?"

Carson acknowledged him by nodding his head slowly, before continuing his thought.

"So, I came down here the last couple of nights with my burner ready to smoke this motherfucker. But, I realized that it's you two that need to get redemption. Not me." As he finished his sentence, he reached past Joe, who was still in a bewildered state, opened the glove compartment and grabbed a bag that was tucked inside.

Carson held the small nylon bag open and told Joe, "Take one," then he passed the bag back to Nan.

As both boys held .45 caliber pieces in their hands, an unshakable feeling of anxiety came over them. The handles were wrapped in plastic electrical tape, and the cold steel cannons felt heavy as they gripped the pieces tightly in the palm of their hands.

"He's on the second floor, probably getting high out of his mind. That's what he seems to do each night. It's dark in there, so take this flashlight, and go handle your business. I'll be just up the block. Drop the guns when you're finished, and walk slowly to the car. Don't be looking suspicious and shit. Nobody will say shit to you," Carson said firmly and without any compassion.

Before the words were completely out of his mouth, Nan had the flashlight in his hand and the back door open. Joe followed reluctantly, falling in a few feet behind him as Carson drove off down the street. The building's front entrance was boarded up with wood, but a milk crate was placed strategically beneath a window opening to the right of the doorway that had been knocked in, in order to allow entry. They stood on top of the crate and climbed inside through the window cautiously.

Light from the moon shined in through the spaces between the wood nailed on the windows, allowing some visibility inside. Nan turned on the flashlight that Carson gave him, and immediately eyed the floor, observing paper, discarded plastic vials and syringes that littered the building's interior. The smell of urine and feces seeped into their nostrils, as they walked cautiously towards a staircase in front of them.

Walking up the steps, a scent similar to that of candle wax burning became more intense. The sound of mice scurrying about could be heard. As they reached the second floor landing, they observed the wide open space. Since the windows weren't blocked by wood on this floor, visibility was much better. Scattered around the room they saw at least ten people with their lips wrapped around plastic dicks, or nodding out from the effects of the heroin that filled their veins.

As they walked around, they realized that the burning smell was from the crack mist that the feigns inhaled through the glass pipes. Nan carefully scanned the room, yelling out the name, "Jerome," as he walked around. There was no response, as he continued to scan the area slowly, with Joe trailing closely behind. Finally after he yelled his name out again, a bare-chested bony crack head propped up against a nearby wall said, "Why don't you motherfuckers stop yellin'! Jerome is right over there," as he pointed to a man lying down on the dirty floor directly across the room.

Nan and Joe walked hesitantly across the garbage strewn floor, stopping in their tracks once they were within inches of the man. He wore tattered clothing that emitted the disgusting scent of vile body odor. Nan used his foot to nudge him lightly, saying his name softly as he shook him. At first there wasn't a response, then finally the man looked up and mumbled, "What the fuck you want, nigga?"

"You Jerome? Are you Jerome Reddy?" Nan asked in a soft whisper.

In a drunken slur, the man responded, "It's according to who's asking. I ain't got no motherfuckin' money. And I ain't got no motherfuckin' kids either nigga. So, what the fuck you want from my life?"

Nan pulled the burner out of his pocket and pointed it at the man's head, holding it steady as Thaddeus had taught him. He stood emotionless as he coldly said, "Good, then I don't have to worry about anymore niggas growing up without their parents when I kill your ass. You piece of shit."

As the scathing words left his lips, his finger instantaneously pulled down on the trigger multiple times. At close range, the bullets ripped through Jerome's skull and chest, sending bloody fragments of brain matter onto the wall and floor.

The baseheads coherent enough to move scattered like project roaches, as the sound of the cannon reverberated throughout the building. Turning towards the steps, Nan looked at Joe, who was still holding his gun in his hand. His face reflected a state of shock. He hadn't fired one round.

"Toss the gun and let's get the fuck outta here," Nan said, as he walked at a quickened pace towards the steps.

Reaching the bottom of the staircase, Nan threw his gun in a corner and used the flashlight to get his bearings. He looked back at Joe, whose face looked ashen. Concerned, he patted him on the shoulder and said, "Yo, are you alright?"

Joe looked at him with a sickly look on his face. Before he could respond, he heaved a mass of vomit on the floor in front of him. Bile splashed on his sneakers as he bent over gagging on his lunch.

"Damn, are you O.K. Joe?" Nan asked again.

Joe gagged a couple more times, but managed to hold back additional vomit. Finally he said, "I'm sorry Nan. I froze up. I just couldn't do it."

"It's O.K. Let's get the hell out of here," Nan said, before grabbing Joe under his arm and helping him up. They climbed back through the window, and walked at a brisk pace in the direction Carson said he would be waiting.

Adrenaline continued to rush through Nan's veins, as he felt the rise that comes along with pulling a trigger and taking someone's life for the first time. While he emptied his gun, he thought about the death of his parents. He thought about the emptiness that he felt with the loss of Latoya. It was nothing to him to take that bastard's life. He was bereft of any feeling.

Both boys looked around making sure nobody followed them as they climbed into Carson's car. After they sat down and closed the door, Carson pulled off slowly down the street.

"How'd it go?" he asked no one in particular.

"He's dead," Nan said coldly.

"Yeah. Any problems?" Carson asked.

"Nope," Nan responded.

"Both of yawl let off in that nigga?" Carson asked, as he looked over to Joe. Joe didn't respond, still tasting the acidic tinge of vomit in his throat, as he looked out of the side window.

"Yeah, we both took him out," Nan responded confidently.

"Good. Good. And yawl tossed the guns, right?"

"Yeah, of course," Nan responded.

"Good. Yawl niggas did good." Carson said proudly as he continued driving.

"We can pick up some chicken from Kennedy's before I drop you back off at *Saint Mary's*."

As they drove down the street, Nan thought about what just transpired, feeling the same rush that came over him when he pulled down on the trigger. He yearned to grip the cold steel once again. No longer would he let his emotions become his weakness. He had tasted what it felt like to deliver death, and wouldn't hesitate to do it again if need be. He left a piece of his soul in the crack house that night. His rebellious redemption had made him cold and heartless.

BETRAYAL: 3

A PLEASANT AROMA SIMILAR to that of a country kitchen, filled the apartment as Kimba did her thing in front of the gas stove. Using three burners, she had skillfully fried eggs, beef sausage and prepared some creamy cheese grits all at the same time. Nan grew even hungrier as he inhaled the inviting scent of the food. His stomach churned uncomfortably.

Impatiently, he walked into the kitchen and put both of his hands on Kimba's waist, caressing her as he looked over her shoulder at the food.

"Damn, that smells good as hell," he said excitedly.

"It'll be done in a couple of minutes. Go wash your hands in the bathroom, and I'll make your plate. You remember where it is, right?"

"Yeah, of course I remember. Don't be silly," Nan responded, as he turned and walked out of the kitchen and headed towards the bathroom.

Kimba listened intently as Nan walked down the hall. After she was certain that he was in the bathroom, she hurried into the living room. Scrambling through the pockets of his leather goose, she finally came across the black 9mm she had seen earlier. Grabbing the gun, she hurriedly hid it under some food stamps inside a drawer in the kitchen.

With Nan still in the bathroom, she focused back on cooking. She turned her eggs, carefully keeping the yolks intact, before reaching into an overhead cabinet in front of her. Roaches scurried off of the ceramic plate she grabbed, as she placed it on the counter and nonchalantly spooned some grits onto it. After putting some eggs on the plate as well, she walked back towards the bathroom. Standing outside the door she asked, "Nan, do you want toast?'

"Yeah, that's cool," he responded, his voice straining as he spoke.

"O.K," Kimba said, as she walked away from the bathroom.

She was betraying her heart, trying her best to sound nice and come across as being accommodating. On her way back to the kitchen, she paused to unlock the front door, and unlatch the chain lock.

Nan's stomach continued to grumble in anticipation of eating a home cooked meal. He walked back into the living room and patiently sat down on the sofa. A thought seized his mind, as he heard the faint sound of a police siren off in the distance. Instinctively, he grabbed his leather goose and rifled through the pockets. Not finding what he was looking for, he searched beneath the sofa cushions, still unable to find his burner.

He felt uneasy. If Five-0 came for him, he could only do so much without a gun. They would undoubtedly come for him with a death squad, even more prepared than the one he faced earlier. He threw on his jacket and zipped it up, figuring he'd head back to the car to retrieve his piece. At least he could take advantage of the darkness that still engulfed the city.

Yelling towards the kitchen he said, "Kimba, make me a plate. I'm a be right back."

The metal spatula she held in her hand fell to the floor, as she felt a hot flash come over her. Nervousness was setting in. She didn't know what to do.

"Where are you going?" She asked, while she picked up the spatula and reached back into a drawer in the kitchen.

"I'll be right back. I left something in my car," he responded.

Melquan was gonna be there any minute. He had firmly told her to keep Nan there, and now she didn't know what to do. Wrapping her hand around the cold steel of the 9mm, she stepped out of the kitchen, and called Nan just as he was about to grab the door handle.

Turning around, he saw Kimba standing there pointing a four pound at him. It was shaking uncontrollably, as she struggled to steady the heavy gun in her weak hands. Her face was ashen, and her mind was full of conflicting emotions.

"You motherfucker! Why the fuck did you do this to me? You fuckin' bastard," she yelled out. Bitterness filled her voice. Her eyes looked menacing.

Looking closer, Nan noticed that it was his own piece she was pointing at him. He was only five or six feet away from her. He inched forward hesitantly, but stopped in his tracks when he saw Kimba's finger tighten up on the trigger.

Pleadingly he asked, "What the hell are you talking about, Kimba? This shit is crazy. Put the gun down and lets talk."

"Oh, let's fuckin' talk! Yeah, *let's fucking talk, nigga!* Why'd you kill Power motherfucker, huh? Why'd you have to take him away from me?"

Nan didn't know what the hell she was talking about. Through word of mouth, he had heard that Power got shot up, but he didn't have nothing to do with it. Wasn't his style. But, looking at Kimba's face, the sadness in her eyes, he knew she had already made up her mind and couldn't be convinced otherwise.

"Kimba, why the hell would I kill that man? I'm the one who told you to get back up with him. That shit don't even make no sense."

"Just like niggas in Fort Greene tried to rob you, right? Then I see your ass on T.V. wanted for multiple murders and shit!"

"What are you talking about?"

"The cops. The fuckin' grandmother and her grandson. Power and the other niggas. You even killed your girlfriend you sick motherfucker," she spewed out venomously. The anxiety that existed earlier was replaced with intense anger and confidence.

Nan tried to remain calm. Looking deep into her eyes he said, "I'm being set up. You know that's not me. That shit don't even sound like me. These niggas is trying to—"

"Fuck you, Nan," she interrupted him. "You took away my heart. That nigga loved me. That nigga wanted to spend the rest of his life with me. You deserve what you're about to get. You—"

Her sentence was interrupted by the apartment's front door being kicked in forcefully. It swung open wildly behind Nan, slamming loudly against the wall on its hinges. Reacting out of fear, Kimba squeezed down on the trigger.

"Boom! Boom!"

Two shots whizzed through the air. One slammed into a picture of Power, Kimba and her sons hanging on the wall, shattering the glass. The other round sailed past Nan's right ear. He felt the heat against his face, as it passed him and plunged into the figure that had just emerged behind him. It caught him in the neck, piercing his carotid artery.

It was Melquan that took the slug. On impact, his massive frame fell to the floor , as he grabbed his neck with both hands, gasping for air. His eyes bulged out of his head displaying shock and shear terror. His facial features were just like his brothers. It brought back bitter memories for Kimba. Seeing him lying there dying caused her to lose it. Thoughts of Power ran through her head. She felt light headed and weak, before her body gave way and she fainted.

Nan moved swiftly, grabbing the gun out of her limp hand. He glanced at her beautiful face, still disbelieving the fact that she could think he was capable of what she had accused him of. Crouching to the floor, he turned around just as another gunman in an Adidas sweat suit entered the apartment. He came through the door shooting wildly, holding his piece sideways like thugs on the street with no experience do.

When the young gunman noticed that his intended target was actually crouched down on the floor, it was too late. Nan sent a hot slug ripping through his shoulder and another through his thigh, causing the young gun to spin around in his tracks before he collapsed to the floor in a heap. Nan upgraded his weaponry by grabbing the nine out of the young killer's hand.

The sound of gunfire had awoken Kimba's children. Nan heard them crying, calling out their mother's name, before the door to their room slowly opened up down the hall. He looked towards their room and saw two sets of sad looking eyes staring back at him. The boys recognized his familiar face. Their dejected eyes were innocently wanting for some direction. There was chaos going on all around them.

Nan put one of his fingers to his mouth, urging them to be quiet. Then he motioned them back into their room, mouthing, "It's gonna be o.k."

Surprisingly, the boys listened, as Nan crept forward towards the apartment's door, listening for movement. As he got near the doorway, he put his back to the wall. The footsteps he heard in the hallway had ceased. The gunmen had positioned themselves at both ends of the hallway. They waited anxiously for him to exit the apartment, so they could ambush him. Nan knew they were amateurs, confused and scared. It was the perfect time to attack.

Quickly, Nan placed his body between the doorway's frame with his back towards the hallway. He listened studying the movements on the other side of the frame. Coolly he took a deep breath before he allowed his body to fall backwards freely, emulating a man bungee jumping without a cord. The moment played out as if it was in slow motion. He extended his arms fully, like Jesus nailed to the crucifix with a burner in each palm. As he fell slowly, his fingers worked the triggers on the 9mm that he held in his left, and the 9mm he grasped tightly in his right palm, as he targeted his would be assassins positioned in the hallway on both sides of the doorway peripherally.

They returned fire, lighting up the dimly lit hallway with orange flashes, as bullets sailed over Nan's head, hitting the walls, hitting apartment doors and hitting each other. Horrific screams of agony and confusion filled the hall. Nan landed with a thud on the hard floor, holding his head up and angling his back so his shoulders absorbed the brunt of the impact. His lower body was halfway in the apartment still, and his upper torso was completely in the hallway. Still lying on his back, he put three bullets into the lower extremities of the only killer that remained unharmed, crippling him as one of the bullets ripped off his kneecap.

Reflexively, Nan hopped to his feet in a crouched stance (*Pubu*). After surveying the area, he cut through the obstruction caused by the five or six bodies lying in a bloody path, and jetted down the nearby steps. His hand scraped against the cheap peeling paint on the concrete walls, as he braved the urine filled stairwell, taking three steps at a time until he reached the lobby.

Walking through the lobby slowly, he expected to encounter some more killers, but surprisingly there was no one. Continuing to walk forward, he tucked the guns in his jacket pockets, still gripping them tightly.

Outside, the young shorty named Dee that said, "What's up," to him earlier was still scrambling in front of the building.

"Peace," Dee said as he observed Nan closely.

Nan nodded his head and said, "Peace out."

Their eyes met briefly, before Dee looked downward. The cold early morning breeze felt refreshing against Nan's skin as he walked. Strolling along, he tried to plot out his next move. The puzzle pieces slowly came together in his mind. He thought about getting his hands on another car. Making it to his dojo before sunrise. Then he thought about Dee's shifty eyes.

Instinctively, Nan spun around gripping his 9mm in his right hand as he aimed it at the young thug he just passed. He caught the shorty by surprise...luckily. A second later and he would have twisted Nan's cap off. Instead, he was caught fumbling with his gun, and was now staring down the barrel of a four pound.

"Drop that shit nigga," Nan spewed out through clenched teeth, exhaling white vapor into the cold air. Dee obliged, as Nan walked over, picked up the pistol and removed the clip, before throwing it as far as he could.

"Yo, my bad, Nan. Niggas told me that you had killed Power, and that was fam. I don't got no problem with you god. Me and you is cool," Dee pleaded.

"Where's that beat up Accord you be whippin' around?" Nan asked, while looking around his surroundings cautiously.

"My whip? Oh, that shit is right over there," he said, pointing towards the street.

"Give me your keys."

Dee pulled out a key ring with the initials "DW" on it and handed it to Nan.

"Now get the fuck outta here shorty," Nan yelled out.

Dee walked off in a slow bop, prompting Nan to kick him squarely in the back on his ass. "Don't be cute, nigga. I said, get the fuck outta here."

Dee didn't need any more convincing. He jetted off, disappearing into the darkness while Nan made way to his whip. As soon as he started the car, BDP's *I'm Still Number 1* blasted through the speakers.

"Fifty years down the line we can start this, cuz we'll be the old school artists. And even in that time I'll say a rhyme, a brand new style ruthless and wild. Running around spending money having fun, cause even then I'm Still number one..."

As he drove, Nan's head nodded to the infectious beat for a minute or so, before he popped the cassette out and turned the radio to 1010 WINS. A commercial was playing. Since the sun would be starting to rise within the next couple of hours, Nan knew that he had to get off of the streets soon. The commercial came to an end, and Nan heard the news he had been dreading.

"1010 WINS ALL THE TIME. POLICE ARE STILL ON THE LOOKOUT FOR NATHAN JONES. HE'S WANTED IN A MULTIPLE HOMICIDE IN BROOKLYN IN WHICH SEVERAL PEOPLE WERE EITHER KILLED OR INJURED. POLICE WERE INVESTIGATING THE GANGLAND SLAYINGS OF SEVERAL DRUG DEALERS, IN WHICH JONES WAS A LEAD SUSPECT WHEN THEY WERE AMBUSHED..."

Nan turned down the radio, as he drove the two-door Accord down a side street, not needing to hear anymore. He was being set up and he didn't know why. In any case, he had to get off of the streets, and find some place to hide. He wasn't worried about the car he was driving in being reported stolen. Hustlers don't get down like that. But, he was more concerned with being out on the street once the sun started to peek through the clouds.

He headed towards the naval yards, taking the scenic route, consciously avoiding any main streets where the police might have roadblocks set up. He found a place to park a few blocks from his destination. His stomach grumbled as he walked. He thought about the breakfast Kimba was preparing, wishing he could have just ate a little something before the drama set off. Then he chuckled to himself thinking, "If she really thought that I killed Power, she probably put rat poison or some other shit in the grits."

It was deceivingly cold outside, but Nan took his time walking to his makeshift dojo, being sure not to draw any attention to himself. As soon as he got inside, and made his way down to the basement, he unlocked a gray steel lockbox he had bought to stash his belongings. Inside, besides the guns and ammo and other paraphernalia, there was a bag of stale Doritos. Nan tore them open, savoring the scent of nacho cheese, before he quickly finished them off within seconds. The pains within his stomach immediately started to subside.

Sitting in the middle of the dirt floor, he began meditating, concentrating deeply to free his mind. He stayed this way until the sun came up and the morning rolled in. Nan could hear the workers in adjacent buildings. The normal hustle and bustle that comes along with any workday was taking place around him. Things were starting to get busier around this part of town over the last few months. With buildings being renovated, and new companies moving in, Nan knew that it was only a matter of time before he would have to move his hideout.

Fractured rays of sunlight always managed to make it into the basement, but overall it was still dark and serene. There was just enough light for Nan to see that he had caught three rats in the traps he set up around the room since he had last been here.

He yawned and stretched his arms, before he laid on top of a table in the corner that he had often used for a bed in the past, and fell asleep. He thought about Joe, wondering what he must be thinking seeing his best friend on every news channel. Then he thought about his parents, Leslie, and oddly enough Latoya.

Waking up out of his sleep hours later, he felt relaxed and focused. He stretched for a little while, before grabbing a shoe box that he kept securely inside the lockbox. He pulled out some rubber band wrapped envelopes, figuring that he'd read them to pass time until the sun went down.

These were letters from Latoya that he never read. He unsealed the first one in the stack and started to read it, squinting his eyes as he tried to make out the words written on the loose-leaf paper. It read:

Nan,

Hello sweetheart. I hope that everything is well with you. I didn't want to write this, I really wanted to tell you face to face or at least hear your voice. But, I can't come up there now, and I've tried to call you numerous times and they always tell me that you're gone. I know *they're lying to me. I know that you're bitter, but please find it in your heart to forgive me once you hear me out.*

I don't know any other way to say this, so I'm going to just put my heart on this paper. The night that we made love was the best and worst night of my life Nan. Of course being with you was the best part, but when I got home later that night, my stepfather raped me.

The letter slipped out of Nan's hands, falling slowly to the ground. His face revealed his disbelief. His hands shook uncontrollably. Gaining his composure, he picked the letter back up and continued to read on through watery eyes.

That bastard tried to kill me Nan. I don't want to go into details, but that's why I left. I had to leave. I had no choice. I hope you find it in your heart to forgive me. Please answer my next call, or at least write me back. I need you as much as you need me. I love you, Nan...forever.

Yours always,
Latoya

He couldn't stomach the thought of reading any of the other letters. The anger that filled his heart could not be described. It fueled him, gave him energy that he didn't know he had. He paced the room like a mad man, with delusional thoughts filling his mind. All of this shit he was in, was because Latoya was gone. Everything spiraled out of control after she left. His heart had become so bitter. From killing Jerome Reddy, to all of the drama he was caught up in now...all of it stemmed from that one event. He had given her his heart and she betrayed his trust...or so he thought. He was upset with himself for doubting her. But, deeply embedded inside of him was pure hatred for the man that truly stole her innocence.

Nan loaded clips, and readied his guns. Channeling his energy, he did crunches, push ups, chin ups, and stretched before he did his Chi-Kung postures. Anything to pass the time until the sun went back down. He was fueled by the energizing rush of pure adrenaline. He loved her even more for surviving the troubling ordeal she had described. She was concerned about him, while he was selfishly only concerned with himself.

As soon as the sun settled, Nan was on the street in the raggedy Accord. The darkness made his heart even more bitter and frigidly cold. As he thought about Latoya, he became even more determined. He drove quickly, weaving in and out of traffic, not giving a damn about his wanted status as a fugitive. Once he got in the area of the building, he took the first space he could find, pulling into it crookedly with one tire up on the curb.

Exiting the vehicle, he wrapped his hand around the 9mm that was concealed in the pocket of his leather bomber. He walked swiftly and with purpose. There were plenty of people on the street, which he ignored as he pushed open the gate and headed up the steps leading to the front door of the brownstone. It had been so long since he had been to the building. He could remember the bastard's face, his bitterness, the sarcastic grin on his face when he asked him where Latoya was and he responded, *"If you don't know, than I guess you ain't supposed to know, you little nappy headed nigga."*

Ringing the doorbell with his left hand a couple of times, he impatiently waited for the bastard to answer. Cold vapor escaped his mouth as he exhaled deeply.

Seconds later, he saw the curtain that covered the glass on the wooden outer door move back ever so slightly, as an eye peeked out before unlocking the deadbolt. He pulled out his burner, gripping the cold steel tightly, just as the door swung open. Overcome by evil intentions, he slowly pressed his sweaty finger against the trigger.

THE DIARY OF ~~DESPAIR~~:

Winter - Summer of 1988

Your money or your life

_Be_ntleys nightclub was crowded as usual. The local radio station KISS was in the house, and one of their popular female radio personalities was hosting the affair. The mid-sized dance floor was packed, and the liquor was flowing steadily. Carson was dressed to impress in an Italian tailored suit and matching gray gators. The sharp creases on his slacks could cut a steak. Like a smooth operator, he was playing the bar draped by two shapely cuties. He rubbed on their asses, as they sipped from the margaritas he bought them only minutes earlier. Both hoes giggled real giddy-like, while he placed a twenty that he pulled from a 14-carat gold money clip on the bar for the female bartender.

Looking outwardly, he observed all of the people enjoying themselves on the dance floor. There were a sea of guys with flat tops and females with some fly hairstyles dancing in front of him. He liked Bentleys because of the nice mixture of young and older cats, and the music selection was usually on point. There were more than enough hoes, and the dress code limited the amount of knuckleheads that could get in.

After taking a shot of warm Hennessy to the head, Carson walked from the bar into the bathroom, telling one of the giggly chicks that he'd be right back. The place was crowded, but he found a way to navigate his way to the men's room, taking his time to rub up on the fine women as he squeezed past them. A _Frankie Beverly_ song was blasting out of the speakers, and the dance floor was packed.

He felt a nice buzz off of the liquor, but he was still fully cognizant of his surroundings as he strolled into the smoke filled bathroom. The scent of weed was so strong, that he felt himself getting a contact as he stood at the urinal. Two guys dressed in sharp suits were leaving the bathroom, just as a six-foot something muscular black man walked in. He had shifty brown eyes, which Carson noticed immediately.

The burly pock faced man stood in front of the urinal next to Carson, and they nodded at each other politely. Carson finished urinating, and went over to the sink to wash his hands. As he looked up to grab some paper towels, he noticed the muscular man was now standing in front of the door leading out of the bathroom. Light reflected off of the nickel-plated .45 caliber pistol he gripped in his hand.

Instinctively, Carson started to think like the police officer that he was. Fear slowly came over him. Frantically, he reached into his pocket feeling for his piece. The muscular man at the door grinned sarcastically as he saw Carson reach into his jacket pocket to search for a weapon. He knew he wasn't packing. He was the bouncer that searched Carson when he entered the club.

Carson contemplated his next move. The bathroom was so small. Not much space for evasive movement. In his peripheral vision, he saw the door of a stall to his left open slowly. Sonny's right hand man Gunner walked out, smoking a thick *Phillie* blunt stuffed with weed. He put the blunt out on the side of the stall, slowly making his way over to Carson with his hand extended.

Carson gave him a pound before asking, "What the fuck is going on Gunner?"

"Damn, Carson. What happened to how's the family? What you been up to? Now we just on some, what the fuck is going on Gunner shit?"

"Nigga, you got a motherfucker standing at the door with a gun in his hand and—"

Gunner rudely interrupted him, extending his hand as he said, "Carson, shut the fuck up before I put two bullets in yo head and stuff your pussy ass in the toilet with the rest of the shit."

The bouncer at the door laughed, nodding his head at Gunner who was standing less than a foot from Carson now.

"Nigga, you owe Sonny one hundred and fifty g's. I need that shit by tomorrow night," Gunner spewed venomously.

"How the fuck am I supposed to come up with that type of cash by tomorrow night?" Carson asked pleadingly.

"Nigga, sell your cars. Sell your motherfuckin crib. Nigga, what I look like a fuckin' financial planner? I don't give a fuck what you do, but you better have that shit by tomorrow."

"Tell Sonny to give me a week. I can—"

Gunner interrupted him again and said, "Nigga, I ain't telling Sonny shit. Have the loot tomorrow. It's your money or your life, nigga."

Gunner pulled out a lighter and relit his blunt, as he waved his gloved hand letting the bouncer know to move away from the door.

Carson started to walk towards the door, as Gunner pulled a piece of paper out of his pocket and said, "Oh yeah, I almost forgot nigga."

Carson turned around as Gunner walked over and handed him a folded up ticket. "Your boys gave me a ticket the other night for parking illegally or some shit. Said I was less than twelve feet from a hydrant or something. Take care of this shit for me. Also, get me another one of those police parking permits too, nigga."

Carson grabbed the ticket and walked out of the bathroom deflated. The buzz he had off of the Hennessy shots was gone, replaced by a pounding headache. He felt like he needed another drink, but decided to leave the club and head home instead. He had less than twenty-four hours to figure out how he was going to come up with that money.

He walked into his apartment feeling sick to his stomach. The weight of his predicament came down on him like a ton of bricks. The gambling and the poor spending habits had finally caught up with him. Years ago his wife left him for the same reasons, and now his addiction had placed him in harm's way. He sat on the side of his bed the rest of the night thinking. Unable to sleep, he struggled to come up with a plan. Time definitely was not on his side.

Devils pie

"Freeze motherfucker," Carson yelled as he ran through the doorway of a small apartment on Saratoga Avenue, shortly after he and two other officers knocked the door off of the hinges with a battering ram. His piece was aimed at the chest of a light skinned teenage boy sitting on a raggedy couch in his boxers. He held a lit joint in his hand. A kilo of coke, measuring pot and some plastic crack vials were spread out on the coffee table in front of him.

The sound of glass shattering could be heard. It originated from the kitchen, which was off to the right. One of the officers quickly moved in, finding a scared brown skinned female in her panties and bra, visibly petrified out of her wits. Pieces of a ceramic plate, some eggs and fragments of uneaten bacon were on the floor by her feet.

"All clear, just a bitch," the young officer yelled out as he kept his gun trained on the girl.

"Is there anyone else here?" Carson asked the teen on the couch.

"Nah, just me and my girl," the teen responded with attitude.

"O.K. Gomez, keep these two covered while I check the bedroom," Carson said, as he slowly began to walk towards the rear of the apartment with his gun still drawn. When he reached the bedroom door he kicked it open forcefully. His eyes scanned the room and there was nobody inside. After checking under the bed and in the closet, he rifled through the drawers in the dresser, uncovering nothing.

He was growing frustrated. Finally, he pulled a pocketknife out and sliced the side of the mattress and box spring exposing the guts. Reaching his arm inside the incision, he searched around until he came across what he had been looking for. The devil's pie.

Carson placed three bricks of cocaine on top of the bed, before pulling out four stacks of hundreds and quickly placing them in a pouch on his waist. It was hidden beneath his oversized nylon NYPD jacket. He paused, looking over his shoulder cautiously. The hidden loot made his stomach look a little bulkier, but it was barely noticeable.

"Bingo! I found the shit," Carson yelled out, as he walked back into the living room. The girl was now sitting next to her boyfriend on the couch, both of them staring down the barrels of the two officer's guns.

"I'm a go outside and call the precinct for back up. Jimmy, you go to the back and see how much coke and loot is actually in the mattress. Gomez, cover the perps," Carson said as he quickly headed out of the apartment to his unmarked cruiser.

As he sat in the front seat, he pulled a nylon bag from under the driver's seat and unzipped it. The sun was out and there were plenty of people outside, looking at him suspiciously. Nobody likes a pig, especially in Brooklyn. When Carson felt the coast was clear, he took the money out of the pouch beneath his jacket and stuffed it in the bag. He knew that he was way short on what he owed Sonny, but at least it was something for now. He securely hid the bag beneath his seat, then he called the precinct and told his commander the good news.

After making the arrests, booking the evidence and filling out the tedious mounds of paperwork, Carson headed home and showered up. It was around three in the afternoon, and he was running late. He had promised the boys that he would pick them up to go to the shooting range. He had been taking them to the range with him at least once a month for the past few months.

After scooping the boys up and putting in an hour at a shooting range right across the Verrazano in Staten Island, Carson headed back to Brooklyn. Nan and Joe were starving, so he drove over to *Sonny's Chicken N' Rib,* parking directly across the street from the establishment.

He handed Nan a twenty and said "Go get a bucket of chicken, some fries and a two-liter of coke or something."

Nan said, "O.K," and grabbed the car door handle.

As he stepped out of the car, Carson said, "Nan, do me a favor and tell the cashier to give this to Sonny." He was holding a small nylon bag towards him, which Nan grabbed without hesitation. "Tell her it's from Carson. We go way back."

Nan walked off, returning about fifteen minutes later with two white plastic bags in his hand. Carson held the door open for him before asking, "Did everything go cool?"

Nan nodded his head and said, "Yeah, she said she'll give it to him."

"Cool," Carson said, as he pulled away from the curb and headed towards *Saint Mary's.*

After dropping Nan and Joe off, he pulled over by a pay phone and called Sonny. The phone rang a couple of times before a gruff voice answered asking, "Who is it?"

"It's Carson, let me speak to Sonny."

"Carson? Man, Sonny don't wanna speak to your dead ass, Gunner responded coldly.

"Did he get what I sent him?"

"Yeah, I got the parking permit."

"What about the money?"

"Yeah, we got that shit too. Twenty five g's, which leaves you one hundred and twenty five short, which means that you gonna owe one hundred and thirty five g's tomorrow."

"One hundred and thirty five. Come on man, you gotta cut me some slack," Carson said pleadingly.

On the other end of the line, Gunner laughed out loud sarcastically.

"Slack? That's funny. But, since I like you, I'm a make this real simple. Today is Sunday. You've got until Saturday to come up with one fifty. If you don't have it then, you's as good as dead."

Carson was about to respond, pleading his case, but the phone went dead. After spewing out his convincing threat, Gunner had hung up.

Do the write thing

𝔍t was more than half way into the school year, and Nan was just hanging on by a thin thread, very close to being expelled completely. He rarely attended class, and when he did it was usually only on the days that he had exams, which he always aced. That was partly the reason why the teachers were willing to work with him. They knew he was extremely smart, and he caught on to new things quick. And even though a few years had passed, he was still getting sympathy because of the highly publicized murder of his folks.

Joe tried his best to encourage Nan, but he was very bogged down himself. They were in two entirely different predicaments. Joe was in twelfth grade, and Nan was in eleventh. Joe's English teacher and guidance counselor were working closely with him, helping him fill out applications and other paperwork required by the different colleges he was aspiring to attend. He was really interested in attending Howard, if only because of the fact that his father had gone there.

His guidance counselor, Mrs. Adams had become his advocate. She was proactively calling schools and letting them know about Joe and his writing prowess. She also wanted to explain his plight to them, so they wouldn't be turned off by the fact that he had to take some remedial courses the previous year. She wanted him to have the best opportunity to get a scholarship.

Joe was in the middle of his Biology class, when his teacher advised him to go down to the principal's office. His stomach began to churn immediately, as he wondered if it had something to do with Nan. He hadn't been to school the whole week, and he thought that either something had happened, or they wanted to question him about his friend's whereabouts. In his mind he tried to think of a few good lies in case they planned on questioning him.

Walking into the principal's office, he immediately knew something was up. There was a middle-aged white lady, in a conservative gray business suit that he had never seen before, sitting in a chair in front of the principal's mahogany desk. After spotting Mrs. Adams sitting in the corner, he felt a slight sense of relief. Catching his eye, she cracked a huge smile and assuredly said, "Relax Joe, we called you down here for good news." He smiled back in return. They were close, and he knew Ms. Adams had his back.

The lady sitting in front of the desk stood up and introduced herself as Ms. White, ironically.

"Finally I get to meet Joseph Hayes. Joseph, your writing speaks volumes about you," Ms. White said, pausing to shake Joe's hand before continuing. "I was compelled to come down here in person to meet you, and to also advise you that we are interested in offering you a full scholarship to attend our school and participate in our creative writing literary arts program."

Joe smiled widely before intuitively asking, "What school are you from?"

"I'm sorry," Ms. White said politely as she grinned sheepishly. "New York University. Joseph, we don't accept many people into our program, only those we deem to be truly exceptional."

"Well Joseph is exceptional," Principal Johnson responded, adding his own two cents. Joe smiled, finding it amusing that the principal had never said one word to him before today, and now he was giving him props.

Joe heard about the writing program at NYU, and knew that the institution only considered accepting the top few applicants. He felt ecstatic and extremely honored just thinking about the opportunity.

"So, are you interested Joseph? I know that you were kind of leaning towards Howard." Mrs. Adams asked with a smile on her face. She already knew what Joe's response would be.

"Howard? What's that?" Joe asked sarcastically, as everyone in the room broke out into laughter. His humorous response was right on time.

Ms. White shook his hand again, as she stared directly in his eyes. In a serious tone she said, "Joseph, we know about your past, and quite frankly it creates sort of a risk for us. I'd be lying if I told you that I wasn't a little concerned. But, I'm willing to take that chance. You're very talented, and you have some good folks in this room that have gone to bat for you. All I ask is that you keep your grades up and your nose clean, and please don't let us down. Just do the right thing."

Still holding her hand, Joe smiled and said, "I appreciate the opportunity, and I won't let you down."

"Good. Well, I look forward to seeing you in the fall."

Hands in the cookie jar

*C*arson was completely consumed lately, barely finding the time to stop by and see the boys. They didn't take it personally though, realizing that he had a lot on his plate. That's why they were surprised when he popped up at *Saint Mary's* less than a week after his last visit.

It was Friday evening, and Carson seemed overly excited, to the point that he looked jittery as he greeted Nan and Joe with gifts. He had two boxes of new Nikes and Champion hoodies that he had picked up from Kings Plaza.

It was almost time for dinner at the home, but Carson told the boys that he'd take them out to get a bite to eat. He didn't have to make his offer twice. The crew in the kitchen had been replaced about a month ago, and they jumped at the chance to avoid eating any of the sorry meals the new staff prepared.

Carson took them to *Juniors*, and they talked over some saucy chicken cutlet heroes. Carson's mind was noticeably wandering. He maintained a conversation with the boys, but his eyes constantly veered off looking outside and around the restaurant as they conversed. Finally Joe spoke up asking, "Is everything alright?"

Carson quickly stared him in the eyes, realizing that he had been looking out of the window daydreaming for the past few minutes.

"What was that, Zook?" He said in response, acknowledging that he wasn't paying attention.

"Nothing, nothing. Yo, you know that NYU accepted me into their writing program, right?" Joe said excitedly.

Carson's eyes lit up as he responded, "Yeah, Nan told me. Congratulations, man. You deserve it. I know you're happy."

"Yeah. I can't wait."

Just then a car backfired loudly outside, startling Carson. He jumped in his seat, clumsily knocking over a glass of water.

"Shit!" Carson yelled out in disgust as he stood up from the table.

A little water had spilled on his trousers, but it wasn't enough to cause such a reaction. Patrons that were sitting close by enjoying a meal with their family, looked on in disapproval.

Walking off, Carson mumbled, "I'll be right back," under his breath as he headed towards the bathroom.

Nan and Joe looked at each other with bewildered expressions on their faces, before Nan finally said, "Yo, that nigga's bugging out."

They both laughed out loud, and then Nan said, "Your man is shaking and shit, like he's smoking jumbos or something."

Joe giggled again and said, "It's probably the job stressing him out."

"If it's like that, quit. *Knowwhati'msaying?*" Nan said, before taking a sip from his ice water. "Ain't no job worth that."

After a few minutes, Carson came out of the bathroom and stopped by a pay phone that was hanging on the wall right outside the door. He grabbed the handset and quickly keyed in seven digits, still looking around apprehensively. It was obvious by his facial expression and body language that he was becoming agitated, as the conversation went on.

Finally, after a couple of minutes, he slammed the phone down and walked back over to the table.

"We gotta go," he said, as he pulled out two crumpled tens and a five and placed them down on the table.

Joe and Nan got up disappointedly, before following behind him slowly. They looked at each other curiously, both wondering what was going on. When they got outside on Flatbush Avenue, Carson stopped mid-stride and faced the boys.

"Sorry about this shit. They don't give me much time to myself anymore. I got a lot of open cases and shit. And they keep shoving more bullshit down my throat," Carson said unconvincingly.

"It's cool," Nan said, as he started walking towards Carson's car slowly.

Carson was still standing in the same spot. Looking downward he said, "I gotta run over to the precinct, so I can't drop yawl off. But, I need yawl to do me a favor."

"What's up?" Nan asked, now facing towards Carson.

Carson walked to the trunk of his car and unlocked it, before pulling out an oversized black duffle bag.

"I need you to drop this off at *Sonny's* for me. You know, that place where we got the chicken from last time," Carson said, pausing to grab two twenties out of his pocket. "Here's some loot to catch a cab back to *Saint Mary's*."

Joe grabbed the money and took the duffle bag out of the trunk, placing the strap over his right shoulder. The bag was heavier than he anticipated.

"Damn, what you got in here a body?" Joe asked Carson, as he adjusted his feet to support the weight of the bag.

Carson forced himself to grunt out a laugh before saying, "Nah, but don't drop it though."

He glanced quickly towards a street vendor that was loading his merchandise into a van close by before saying, "There's um, glass frames, and a few small paintings in there too. They wrapped up tightly, that's why it's so heavy."

"Can we have a couple for our room? Help jazz it up a bit, *knowwhati'msaying?*" Nan asked with a twinge of sarcasm in his voice.

"Nah, don't go sticking your hands in the cookie jar. I promised those to someone else. I'll get you a couple later, if yawl really want some," Carson responded.

Joe nodded his head, as he put his right arm under the bag to support it. Carson's eyes looked glassy. The excitement that existed when he picked them up was long gone. Joe felt sad as he looked at him. The wear and tear of his job was physically taking its toll on him. He looked like he was withering away.

"We'll take care of it Carson," Joe said confidently.

Carson mustered up a slight smile before saying, "I know yawl will. I'll make it up to you guys next time. I promise."

As Carson drove off slowly, light rain began to fall, sprinkling the ground with a wet mist. As the boys walked down Flatbush towards Dekalb, they looked around wondering if he was going to double back and pick them up. Once they reached Dekalb, it became an afterthought. The rain had begun to come down heavily, and Carson was nowhere to be found. They took refuge underneath an awning in front of a corner store.

"Damn, that nigga couldn't even come back? That's fucked up man," Nan said disgustedly.

"He's on a mission, B. Work got him all out of wack," Joe said pausing to spit some phlegm on the sidewalk, as he attempted to change the subject to a more positive topic.

"I can't wait to go to NYU. Ms. White called today to check up on me. She's mad cool, but I think that she really feels like I'm a mess up or something."

"She probably heard about me," Nan said jokingly.

"Yeah, you the one always getting in trouble anyway," Joe responded smugly, as he placed the duffle bag on the wet ground in front of him and said, "That bag is heavy as hell."

"Picture frames? What the hell does he do, run a flea market on the side? What's this nigga an art collector or some shit now?" Nan said sourly, his voice filled with disbelief as he bent down on the ground next to the bag. There were two zippers that were zipped together and secured with a small suitcase lock.

"What's up with this? Don't nobody lock up no picture frames in a duffle bag," Nan said suspiciously, as he pulled a small Swiss army knife out of his pocket.

Joe bent down concerned and said, "Whatchu doing?"

Nan was already cutting a small hole in the front of the bag, right along the seam, so the incision would be hidden. He ignored Joe's question and stuck two of his fingers in the hole.

He frowned up his face while he fished around annoyingly, until he was finally able to grasp on to a plastic bag. Pulling slowly, he got a piece of the bag through the hole.

The rain had let up, and the light that lit up the corner store sign provided a decent amount of illumination. Nan and Joe both looked at the small piece of plastic protruding out of the hole in the bag. It was filled with white powder.

Nan poked a small hole in the plastic and dabbed his pointer finger in the powder, before placing his finger on his tongue. He had no idea what he was doing, but he had seen Crockett do this on *Miami Vice* before. As the acidic taste hit his tongue numbing it slightly he whispered, "It's coke."

Joe shook his head in disbelief before asking, "How do you know?"

"It is trust me," he responded, as he pushed the plastic back into the duffle bag and stood up. He put the straps on his shoulder, relieving Joe by carrying the bag himself.

Without talking, they started walking off down the street again, trying to take advantage of the break in the weather. Both of their brains were numbed by an intense feeling of betrayal. The streets had become very bare once the rain started, and now there were only a few stragglers out.

"I can't believe that Carson would have us out here doing this shit," Nan said.

"There has to be some reason for this, Nan. He wouldn't just have us dropping off drugs," Joe responded in a weak tone.

Nan shrugged his shoulders and said, "The way he was acting. It makes sense now. I just thought he was buggin' out, but deep down I knew sumthin' was up. I could just feel it."

Just then, a dark blue Chevy Impala pulled up alongside them. It was creeping at a snail's pace, slightly slower than they were walking. Nan noticed it first, and whispered, "DT's," under his breath to Joe. Unknown to the boys at the time was the fact that the car had been following them since they left *Juniors.*

A feeling of tenseness came over them both, as the seconds that followed seemed like an eternity. Nan thought about the contents of the bag that he held on his shoulder.

"This shit can't be happening," Joe whispered aloud, as sweat beads began to form on his forehead.

"Just stay cool Joe. Just stay cool," Nan mumbled under his breath.

"Poppi. Come over here for a second," a female with a Spanish accent said as the passenger's side window on the sedan rolled down.

Coolly, Nan turned towards the car. He stood his ground defensively, not wanting to get any closer.

"What's up?" Nan asked, holding his hands out animatedly for further emphasis as he spoke.

"Whatchu got in the bag, huh?" The female officer asked, as she slowly pulled on her door handle stealthily.

"Nothing, just clothes," Nan responded unconvincingly. He looked at the female cop's eyes. They looked shady. Nan observed her partner's movements next to her. One hand was on the steering wheel, and the other was down by his waist. Nan figured that he was reaching for his gun. He knew that they were about to make a move.

Joe was disillusioned. He saw his future passing by in front of his eyes. Ms. White's words of caution played over and over in his head.

"All I ask is that you keep your grades up and your nose clean, and please don't let us down."

His mind was in a fog as he stood looking outwardly, comprehending nothing.

"Run Zook!" Nan yelled, as he jetted in the direction they had just walked from.

Joe quickly followed Nan's lead, hearing the car door slam and the footsteps hitting the wet pavement behind him as he ran. Nan headed across the street, causing a car to swerve in order to avoid him, as he briskly ran towards the steps leading into Fort Greene Park. He took three steps at a time, quickly scaling them and reaching the top.

Nan could have kept running, but he stopped to see where Joe was. He saw him running up the steps, but the male officer was quickly closing the gap between the two of them. Joe had stopped training with Thaddeus months ago. He was visibly out of shape, laboring as he ran up the steps.

"Run Zook! Hurry up!" Nan yelled, trying to urge him on. Joe tried his hardest to scale the steps, but his muscles burned. His weak lungs felt winded as he breathed.

Reaching the final flight of steps, he felt a strong tug on the back of his shirt. He struggled wildly as the officer wrestled him to the ground, slamming him against the hard concrete. He could feel the officer trying to restrain his arms. He was stronger and much bigger than Joe.

Joe struggled in vain. His arms were too weak to fight off his stocky opponent. Just as he had given up all hope, he heard the cop painfully yelled out, "Uhh...you motherfucker!"

The grip loosened on him as he felt the officer scramble, defending himself from Nan's vicious blows. The officer climbed to his feet and gathered himself, forgetting about Joe as he focused on Nan.

Nan's attack wasn't well planned out. The wild bolo punches that he threw didn't cause much damage, but they were enough to get the officer's attention. Now they were standing within a few feet of each other, both of them sizing up their opponent.

"Go Zook," Nan yelled, as he planted his feet on the pavement and balled up his fists. Joe took a couple of steps before hesitating in his tracks. He didn't want to leave Nan behind.

"Go, motherfucker!" Nan yelled out angrily, compelling Joe to heed his advice and run through the park at full speed. When he reached a section of trees about fifty yards away, he stopped to catch his breath. His throat was parched, and the sweat that ran off of his forehead burned his eyes.

Officer Digangi planted his feet in a defensive stance that he had learned in the Judo class that they teach you on the force. For a quick second, he thought about pulling out his glock on the young punk in front of him. But after sizing him up, he knew that he could easily handle him physically.

Nan noticed the positioning of the officer's feet, and immediately smirked to himself. His legs weren't planted correctly. His whole style looked very suspect.

"It's that bullshit self defense stance," he thought to himself.

Thaddeus had shown him how to attack an opponent practicing Judo before, and he immediately recognized the chinks in his armor. He was bigger and most likely stronger than Nan. But, the awkwardness that came along with his size could be exploited as a weakness.

Digangi attacked first with a lunge punch, followed by a short thrusting punch. Nan easily blocked both, as he bounced on his feet emulating Bruce Lee's style from *The Game of Death*. Patiently he feinted with his left, causing Digangi to cover up as he expected, before delivering a front slap kick *(Caijiao)* to his chest and a fist punch *(Chongquan)* that landed flush against his jaw.

Digangi reeled backwards, rubbing his thumb against the side of his mouth, confirming that he was bleeding from a cut caused by Nan's aggressive attack. He angrily reached for his gun, and Nan lunged towards him grabbing his hand. Digangi used his upper body strength to push Nan backwards forcefully.

With his arms restrained, Nan head butted him on the nose, immediately causing blood to stream down his face. Nan knew that he had him where he wanted. He focused all of his attention on his wounded prey. He readied his attack, raising his fists just as a sharp pain shot down his spine. Weakened considerably, he turned around to face the steps behind him just as the female officer delivered a crushing blow with her nightstick to his temple.

"Nan!" Joe yelled out, as he watched his boy being plummeted by the nightstick. He started walking towards the steps involuntarily, giving in to his sense of concern.

Nan's vision was blurry. He struggled to get to his feet just as the hard nightstick came down one final time to the back of his head, leaving him temporarily paralyzed.

Teary-eyed, Joe willed himself to run back into the park. He disappeared into the darkness as Nan collapsed on the wet pavement. Coldly, the police officers dragged his limp body away, before throwing him into the back of their unmarked car.

Stand up guy

*W*hen Nan awoke, he was sitting in a hard metal chair in an empty room that resembled a cellar. His hands were bound tightly behind his back. A fluorescent lamp in the middle of the floor lit the otherwise darkened room. His head and back were throbbing with pain. The result of the vicious attack he had suffered in the park.

The air smelled damp, and from what he could see, the walls around him were unfinished concrete slabs. As he looked around, trying to get his bearings, he saw three mice scurrying across the floor. He figured that he was either in the basement of a tenement building or possibly a warehouse.

He started to struggle with the rope behind his back, just as the Italian cop he fought with earlier walked into the room.

"Rodriguez! It looks like sleeping beauty has awoken," Digangi said in a sarcastic tone. The bridge of his nose was bandaged, and he had a thick gash on the side of his lip. Nan felt happy that he at least went out like a trooper.

Rodriguez walked in and looked him up and down. She was a little chunky around the midsection, with a cute face hidden beneath her hardened features. Nan thought about the attack with the nightstick. She didn't seem like she was capable of being so brutal. Apparently, he had underestimated her.

Looking at both cops in front of him, he thought about the police shows on T.V. He wondered who was going to be the good cop and who was going to play the role of the bad cop.

"This motherfucker got you pretty good Digangi," Rodriguez said sarcastically, as she stood in front of Nan with a slight grin on her face. "You better be happy that I caught up with you when I did."

"I was just about to put a bullet in his ass," Digangi responded harshly. He was holding a revolver in his hand, removing the bullets from the cylinder.

"So, listen Poppi. We got the bag and the cocaina. All we want to know is who you work for," Rodriguez asked, in a non-aggressive tone.

Nan shrugged his shoulders before confidently saying, "I don't know what you're talking about."

"Poppi, I don't wanna play games. Who gave you the coca, and where the fuck were you taking it motherfucker!" She yelled out angrily at the top of her voice. A vein was visible in the middle of her forehead.

She was obviously not the "good cop", Nan thought to himself as he observed her growing visibly agitated. Unfazed, he looked directly in her eyes and said, "I don't know what you're talking about."

Impatiently, Digangi walked over to Nan and stood by Rodriguez's side. He placed a bullet in the revolver he held in his hand, spun the cylinder, before placing the pistol flush against Nan's head and pulling the trigger.

Nan fearfully jumped in his seat, when he heard the sound of the hammer clicking. He was nauseous from fear. His throat was dry, and his pants were wet from urine.

"You wanna play fuckin' games nigger!" Digangi yelled out loud. The words sounded even more scathing being spewed out of the mouth of a white man.

Nan tried to gain his composure under the circumstances. Thaddeus had told him stories about how he had been tortured, and the psychological games that the enemy will play with you. He thought about those stories and tried to regain his confidence.

Rodriguez pulled out her nightstick and forcefully jammed the pointy end into Nan's crotch, causing him to double over in pain. As he struggled to deal with the pain, Digangi held the gun to his head again and pulled the trigger.

"Click!"

"You're one lucky motherfucker. But, you're luck will run out soon. Last week another motherfucker heard the gun go click six times before he got his brains blown out," Digangi said as he cracked a sinister grin.

Nan was still trying to figure out who was the "good cop." Both of them seemed vicious and unfeeling. Thaddeus's torture stories seemed a lot different when you're actually living through it. It was easy to say that you, "welcomed death", when it wasn't staring you in the eyes. Nan struggled to free his hands from behind his back unsuccessfully.

"Give us a name Poppi," Rodriguez said, as she twirled her nightstick around impatiently.

"Nathan, my name is Nathan," Nan said in response.

Rodriguez twirled her nightstick a few times before viciously hitting him in the stomach with it. On impact, Nan let out a scream of anguish, as sharp pains shot through his midsection. Digangi and Rodriguez laughed at his agony. They were enjoying every minute of it.

Digangi spun the cylinder again, and pulled back on the trigger twice "Click! Click!"

Nan closed his eyes and braced himself in anticipation of being shot. Digangi squeezed Nan's cheeks with his calloused hand, until he forced his mouth open. Then he shoved his revolver between his teeth, scraping roughly against the roof of his mouth.

"I don't give a fuck who you worked for before. You work for us now. You understand motherfucker?" Digangi asked in a harsh tone.

Nan nodded his head in acknowledgment. The fight was visibly out of him.

"That's what I fuckin' thought. You fuck with us, and we'll kill everything close to you," Digangi said, as he pulled the gun out of Nan's mouth. Bloody saliva drooled down his chin, as he coughed a few times struggling to get his breathing right.

Digangi held the gun next to Nan's head once again. He pulled down on the trigger slowly, pointing the pistol past him at the last second.

"Bang!" The sound resonated and echoed throughout the cellar.

"Damn, Rodriguez. He's one lucky motherfucker," Digangi spewed, as he looked towards his female partner.

"Well, Poppi. If you follow the rules you won't get hurt. Fuck around, and you'll be getting a dirt nap like your fuckin' parents!" Rodriguez yelled out venomously, before she turned to walk out of the room. She used her nightstick to break the dim fluorescent light as she passed it.

Digangi followed behind, laughing as he said, "See you later, Nan. Get home safe."

Nan waited until he was sure that they were gone, before he struggled with the rope binding his arms behind his back. His eyes burnt intensely as he blinked, which only increased his anger. Across the room, he could hear mice still running on the floor, and the sound of water dripping.

As he struggled with the rope, he thought about what the cops had said. Digangi called him Nan and the female cop knew that his parents were dead. Even still, he said that they would, "kill everything close to him." That meant that they knew about Joe, and they must have also known about Carson.

Fueled by anger, he mustered up the strength to free his hands. Skin prickling he stood up cautiously, fumbling in the darkness. He felt on the concrete walls as he tried to find his way out of the building, not sure if he was headed in the right direction.

Darkness engulfed him, as his footsteps echoed with each stride. He faintly saw a small ray of light, about thirty feet in front of him. He subdued his urge to rush, not knowing what lie ahead in his path, continuing cautiously towards the fluorescent beacon. Reaching the light source, he found a steel ladder that he used to climb up to a floor that appeared to be street level.

He quickly adjusted his eyes to the light that filtered into the room from the moon, as he tried to get his bearings. The room was cluttered with old machinery, plastic bags filled with garbage and other debris. He located a doorway leading to the building's exterior and walked at a quickened pace towards it.

When he got outside, he looked around and realized that he was over by the old Brooklyn Naval Yards. He walked the streets aimlessly, until he noticed a payphone on a corner. After fishing a quarter out of his pant's pocket, he called *Saint Mary's*. One of the other boys answered, and Nan told him to get Joe. A few seconds later, Joe was on the phone. He had been standing close by waiting to hear something.

They spoke briefly, just verifying that they were each alright. Nan told him that he would give him details later, and asked if he had heard from Carson. Joe advised that he had called his crib a couple of times earlier, but got no answer. His answering machine didn't even pick up.

After talking a few more minutes, Nan hung up and tried Carson's house himself. He waited patiently, as the phone rang about fifteen times before it busied out. He desperately tried one more time, before he started his long trek home.

Every muscle in his body seemed to be in agonizing pain, but he continued walking, looking fearfully over his shoulder each time he heard a car pass. Latoya came to his mind briefly, but he forced himself to block thoughts about her out. She had left him when he needed her most, and now he had to focus on how to deal with the shit he was going through.

After walking twenty blocks or so, Nan saw another payphone in front of a gas station that was closed for the night. It was after midnight now, and not much was open. He picked up the receiver and dialed Carson's number again. After two rings someone answered the phone, catching Nan by surprise.

"Hello." It was Carson's voice on the other end of the line.

"Carson, it's Nan"

There was a brief pause, and then Carson said, "Nan, where are you? Is everything o.k?"

"Two cops beat the shit out of me and took the bag. They said that they are going to kill me. Why didn't you tell me there was cocaine in the bag, man? How are you gonna have me and Joe out there transporting coke?"

The phone went quiet for several uncomfortable seconds before Carson responded. He seemed to be sobbing as he said, "I fucked up Nan. I fucked up. I needed cash. Motherfuckers was after me, and I had to get some money quick. I don't know what to say."

Nan was tongue-tied for a moment. He never saw Carson shed even a tear, and hearing him cry on the other end of the phone caught him off guard. His anger turned to compassion.

Nan broke the silence by saying, "The cops said they were gonna kill everything close to me Carson. They're not playing around."

"Nan, I'm getting the hell out of here now. I'm heading out of town, man. I…I don't know what else to fuckin' do. Do you want me to turn myself in? Did you tell them it was my coke?"

"No, I didn't mention your name. But, I think they might know it already."

"They probably do. My captain has been acting funny. I think somebody set me up Nan. Somebody set me the fuck up," he paused mid-sentence before asking, "Just tell me what you want me to do?"

"What do I want you to do?", Nan thought to himself. He wanted him to step up and take responsibility for this shit. Take him and Joe out of town with him. He wanted him to handle his shit, "One on One," like he had told him when he had his run in with Shaborn. He wanted him to be the father figure that he thought he was.

He was fuming inside, but not with hatred. He still loved Carson. But, he was more disappointed than anything. He realized that he was going to have to deal with this shit on his own.

"Go. Bounce out of town, man. It's cool. I'm a be alright," Nan said grudgingly.

"Are you sure, Nan? All you have to do is say the word," Carson replied, his words sounding unconvincing.

"Nah, I'm straight. You better get going though. They may be on their way to come see you."

"Nan, I'll call you as soon as I get situated out of town," Carson said. He mumbled something else incoherently, before hanging up.

His words had fallen on deaf ears. Deep down Nan knew that he would be forced to take care of this drama on his own.

Wise words being spoken

The next few weeks became a complex game of cat and mouse for Nan. Rodriguez and Digangi were on the prowl, stalking him daily. Nan was moving stealthily like a well trained ninja avoiding his hunters. They were persistent, but ultimately ineffective in their pursuit.

Everyday Nan got up in the wee hours of the morning, leaving for school before they staked out *Saint Mary's*. In the afternoon, he would leave school without attending his last period class. He developed several distinct routes to return home, always staying a step ahead of them.

On this particular Saturday morning, it was a little after nine, and he had already been training with Thaddeus at the dojo for three hours. After Nan told him about his run in with the cops, he started stepping up their sessions, helping Nan develop more advanced skills and techniques to enhance his perceptive abilities. As always, Nan was a willing and very fast learner.

Thaddeus purposely closed all of the blinds in the room, allowing minimal light to enter. He told Nan to stand in the middle of the dojo, before securely blindfolding him with a black bandana.

"When faced with an opponent that is equally skilled, perception is often the only exception. I've already taught you how to attack and defend, with or without weaponry. I've shown you how to break the extremities of your enemies," Thaddeus said, as he walked around the room circling Nan. "When death approaches, you may not have a moment to think, *seen?*"

"I understand," Nan responded.

"I can't teach you to hear what is often not heard, to see what to most would go unseen. Do you hear that?" Thaddeus asked.

Nan paused briefly, listening intently but hearing nothing but a car honking its horn outside.

"Are you talking about the car horn?" Nan asked confused.

"No, listen for what isn't easily heard. I know it sounds confusing, but you must learn to block out those things. Differentiate between sounds requiring a reaction, and those that are just a distraction."

Still confused, Nan asked, "What am I listening for?"

"The sound of your opponents footsteps echoing as he moves in for the kill. *His hesitancy...his aggression.* The sound of his heart as it pounds behind his chest plate. *Is he fearful and confused, or is he calm and determined?* I can't teach you these things, you have to learn it on your own."

He was standing behind Nan now. As the words left his lips, he planted his feet and delivered a quick jab to Nan's lower back. Nan winced in pain on impact. He turned to face Thaddeus, but he had already repositioned himself.

In a soft whisper Thaddeus said, "You have to listen to what's not easily heard."

Nan stumbled forward, slowly trying to reach him. As he inched ahead, Thaddeus delivered another jab to his lower back. Hearing the punch travel through the air, Nan reacted by attempting to block the blow, without much success. He reacted too slow. As the kidney shot connected, he winced once again, causing Thaddeus to laugh out loud.

"You can take off the blindfold now," Thaddeus said.

As Nan pulled the blindfold from off of his eyes he asked, "How did I do?"

"You've got a ways to go, but if you keep practicing you'll get it."

They both sat down on the mats to stretch, which was what they normally did before and after their workout sessions. With his legs spread wide, Thaddeus bent over, touching his chin to the floor in front of him. Nan wasn't that flexible, but he made it more than half way down. His chin was about two inches from the floor.

"I'm only going to be able to train you a *likkle* while longer, and then I must set you free young one," Thaddeus said, as he stood up and looked directly at Nan.

Nan nodded his head in acknowledgment. This didn't come as a surprise to him, he had actually expected this to happen sooner. Thaddeus was a recluse, whose past demanded that he attract as little attention as possible. It would only be a matter of time before the police trailed Nan and discovered the dojo, and Thaddeus couldn't have that.

A look of seriousness came over Thaddeus's face, as he folded his arms in front of him.

"Nan, you and Joe have to get the hell out of New York immediately," his accent was deeply pronounced as he spoke.

Nan listened intently, giving him his complete attention. He was taken aback, because he was used to Thaddeus talking in riddles instead of just being straight up.

"Those cops are corrupt, Nan. Whatever their intentions are, the end result is not going to be in your best interest. You need to get as far away from them as possible," Thaddeus said, his voice cracking from emotion as he spoke.

"Where am I gonna go? What am I supposed to do, Thaddeus?"

"You go as far away from here as you can and don't ever come back...ever," Thaddeus replied.

"Thaddeus, I don't have nobody. Where am I going to stay? I can't go nowhere."

"I'll give you money, Nan."

"Money ain't gonna help me. That shit would do nothing for me. Plus, Joe can't go nowhere. He's about to start school. He can't just give up on his dream. It's easier said than done."

"Nan, listen to me closely. I've thought deeply about this. You have to leave. The police soon find you and ya have *likkle* choice then," Thaddeus paused mid-sentence, his right eye welling up with tears.

Nan shook his head, poised to interject with his own rebuttal, but Thaddeus interrupted him soundly.

"Please listen *yout*. Get out of town now. Your life depend on it. I'm begging you. You must listen to me. You have to get out of here!"

Nan finally nodded his head, acknowledging that he heard what Thaddeus said, even though he knew that it wasn't an option. He refused to take the money that Thaddeus had offered him earlier, instead telling him that he'd think about it and get back to him. He knew that they would never discuss this topic again. And he also knew that this would be the last time they trained together.

Thaddeus's words sent chills down his spine. His one good eye seemed to look deeply into his inner soul. When he spoke he seemed so intense. But, Nan knew that he had no choice. He had to find a means to handle this. He couldn't just run away like Carson. Not only for the sake of himself, but even more so for the sake of Joe and his future aspirations.

The owners

*N*an's lucky streak ran out after only a month or so. Rodriguez and Digangi grew impatient with trying to track him down, realizing that he was too swift for them. Instead, they just took a trip over to the principal's office at *Boys & Girls* high school, and told him that they needed to question Nan regarding an armed robbery that took place in Fort Greene. With Nan's rep, it didn't take much to convince the principal to send security down to third period English to get him.

They put up a good front in the school, but once Rodriguez and Digangi got him outside in the unmarked car, they immediately showed their true colors.

"I guess you thought we were fuckin' around with you, huh?" Digangi asked. He was sitting in the backseat, directly behind Nan, while Rodriguez drove.

Digangi giggled to himself, as he patted Nan on the shoulder from the backseat. He was leaning forward in his seat, and Nan could feel his hot stink breath on his neck. The smell alone turned his stomach, making him think about the day they tortured him in the naval yards.

"Listen, maybe we got off to the wrong start, beating the shit out of you and all. But, you don't have to worry about that anymore. We're partners now. Right, Lisa?" Digangi asked.

Rodriguez looked at him through the rearview mirror and said, "You know it Digangi."

Nan sat quietly, looking out the front windshield as they drove along. Digangi broke the silence by passing a manila envelope over the seat to Nan.

"Take a look inside."

Nan opened the envelope and pulled out four 8 X 10 glossy black and white photos.

As he looked over them, Digangi said, "Pretty good quality, huh?"

Two of the photos were pictures of Carson, taken the day they caught Nan with the duffle bag. The other two were of Joe. Nan recognized the clothes he had on as the outfit he had worn to school yesterday.

Digangi giggled as he smacked Nan lightly on the back of his head before saying, "We could easily touch everything that means something to you in a heartbeat. That coward Carson may be on the run, but he'll show up at some point. And when he does, if shit ain't kosher between us, he may just go to sleep somewhere and wake up dead."

Rodriguez laughed out loud, repeating Digangi's words, "Wake up dead? Ha ha! That's funny as hell. How you gonna wake up if you dead?"

Defiantly, Nan turned around halfway in his seat and asked, "What do they have to do with this? Why you getting them involved?"

Digangi retorted scornfully by saying, "Because we can. Plus, I know all about Joe's scholarship to NYU. I'll bring those dreams to a halt in less than a New York minute motherfucker!"

"So, what do you want from me?"

"See, now we're talking. I knew that he would see it our way, Lisa."

After driving a bit, Rodriguez abruptly pulled the sedan over to the curb. They were parked in an area of East New York that Nan wasn't familiar with. He glanced out the tinted window, observing the hustlers that were scrambling on a nearby corner. They froze up and acted as if they were just hanging out, when they saw the unmarked DT car pull up.

"You see that building over there?" Digangi said, pointing from the back seat towards a three-story building diagonally across the street from where they were parked.

"They get a shipment of coke in at least three times a week. In an apartment on the third floor, an old lady named Ms. Daniels and her two daughters cook and bottle that shit up, for most of the petty street corner pharmacists in a three block radius of here. Her sons Roach and Chaos take care of distribution when the motherfuckers need a re-up."

Nan heard of Roach and his brother Chaos. Back in the days Roach used to run with the Juice Crew, carrying crates and opening up for them at local shows. When that didn't work out, both brothers turned to the drug game. Over the years, they both had developed reps on the street for being ruthless killers.

Nan shrugged his shoulders before saying, "If you know all of this, why don't you get a warrant and arrest them then"

"Cause we don't want to arrest them Poppi," Rodriguez said, chiming in to provide her own two cents.

"Right, we just want their shit. And I don't mean no crack vials," Digangi said.

"Yeah, we want all of their uncooked raw shit, Poppi," Rodriguez said, one eye looking at Nan and the other on the street.

"And how am I supposed to do that?" Nan asked, with a dumbfounded look on his face.

"Good question. I really don't know. But, if I were you, I'd come up with something quick. They have a shipment coming in tonight, and we want that shit," Digangi said in a harsh tone.

"But, how am I—" Nan started to ask once again, before being rudely interrupted mid-sentence by Rodriguez.

"But, nothing Poppi. No chingas. We fuckin' own you puta. Get us the bricks, or your fuckin' dead maricon."

She pulled off down the street, quickly driving a couple of blocks before stopping by a curb, where there was no one around.

"You can get out here and walk the rest of the way home," Rodriguez spat out venomously.

"Yeah, give yourself some time to come up with a plan," Digangi chimed in.

As soon as Nan was fully out of the car, Rodriguez sped off down the street. As he walked, he thought about the pictures, and their venomous threats. They were right…they owned him.

Kick in the door

"*B*ang! Bang! Bang," was the sound the crackhead's hard ashy knuckles made, as they pounded against the reinforced steel entry door at the base of the apartment building. Her wild hair and dark complexioned skin made her resemble Flavor Flav, as she fidgeted around on the darkened stoop. The lights in the street lamps were out, purposely broken by the local hoods, in order to create the eerie atmosphere that existed on the block.

As she was just about to knock again, an eye level slot in the metal door slid open. Two bloodshot eyes peered through the small slit, as a voice from behind the door yelled, "What the fuck you want bitch?"

"I need that jumbo. I need some rock," she pleaded, as she tried to push a crumpled ten dollar bill through the opening.

"Bitch you better get the fuck outta here," the deep voice from behind the door spewed out, before sliding the slot closed.

Undaunted, the crackhead knocked on the door even harder. She was feigning. Determined to get that next hit, no matter what it took.

As her knuckles rattled the door again, a sound of dead bolts and chain links could be heard unlocking on the other side. Finally, the door cracked open slightly, and a twenty something dark skinned thug stuck his head out.

"Bitch, what the fuck did I say? Do you want me to put my foot up your—"

"*Smash!*"

Nan, who was bent down hiding on the opposite side of the door, forcefully smashed the thug's head between the steel door and the metal frame. Stricken by pain, and barely coherent, the thug stumbled back into the building. Nan moved in quickly. Grabbing him from behind, he threw him into a cobra clutch choke hold. Instinctively, his flawless moves were executed precisely as taught by Master Thaddeus.

Within seconds, the battle was over, as the man lay in an unconscious heap. The crackhead began rambling demands in a slurred manner, but quickly zipped her lips when Nan pointed the Tec-9 at her, that he had just lifted off of the thug laying on the floor. Staying true to his word, he slid her the twenty dollars as promised, motioning her to get lost.

Nan lightly closed the steel door behind him, avoiding any unnecessary noise as he surveyed the area. The interior lobby of the building was deathly quiet. Nan listened intently, trying to capture the sounds of his environment. He was keenly aware that there were more enemies within his midst. He noticed two apartments, but no noise could be heard from behind any of the doors. Nan recalled hearing rumors about Roach and Chaos having a couple of buildings on lock down, but had never actually been inside a tenement that was completely overridden by drug dealers.

He dragged the limp body across the dingy white tiled floor, leaving it in front of one of the apartment doors, so it couldn't be spotted from the landing at the top of the staircase. Then he pulled a black stocking cap out of his pocket and slid it over his face. Quietly he slid the Tec-9 in one of the pockets of his long black trench coat.

"Yo, Tahleek. Why don't you make a run to the Chinese food store?" A gruff voice asked from the second floor, startling Nan. Clutching a sharpened knife, he crept towards the base of the steps, studying the shadow on the upstairs wall as it moved. Nan's footsteps echoed in the darkness, causing the man hovering at the top of the steps to become weary.

"Tahleek, what you doing nigga?"

Fortunately, he didn't notice Nan crouching down at the bottom of the steps, as he lurked within the shadows. Nor did he hear the whistling sound of the knife that was thrown at him. The blade sliced through his skin, lodging itself in his right bicep. The young soldier lost grip of his pistol, letting it fall to the floor as he doubled over in agony.

"Fuck!" He yelled out, anguishing in pain as he scrambled to pick up his gun with his one good arm.

Reacting swiftly, Nan charged up the steps taking three at a time. The old wooden stairs creaked loudly as his weight came down on them. His eyes locked with the young stocky soldier at the top of the staircase, who was bent down on his knees with his hand just inches away from his weapon. Before he could grip his sweaty palm around the gun, Nan leapt on top of him.

As they struggled on the floor, Nan pushed his knife deeper into the wound on his shoulder, while muffling his victim's screams of anguish. Grunting, he twisted the knife until his foe unwillingly surrendered.

Nan rose, yanking his opponent to his feet. In one swift motion he pulled the knife out of the shoulder, and tossed his one hundred and fifty pound frame down the staircase like a rag doll. As it plummeted down the steps, the dead weight of the young soldier's body came down awkwardly on his neck, snapping it like a twig.

The second floor was identical to the first. Same dingy white vinyl tile and two apartment doors. Both were closed and quiet inside. As Nan neared the banister, he expected another soldier to be at the top of the landing guarding the third floor, but no one was there.

He cautiously climbed the steps, and listened attentively outside of each apartment door. On this floor, there was an extra door leading up to the roof. Realizing that he didn't have much time, he kicked in the door of the only apartment that he heard noise emanating from.

The inside was gutted out, so it gave off the appearance of a wide open studio styled apartment. Six square card tables were pushed together in the middle of the room, creating a big rectangle. There were bricks of coke and measuring pots spread out across each of them. He startled two chicks in their late teens that were standing around the tables measuring the coke. An older lady was standing off to the side by a gas stove, mixing a batch of the white powder with baking soda.

Without talking, Nan pulled the book bag off of his shoulders, all the while pointing the Tec-9 towards the girls. He unzipped it and pulled out a huge duffle bag that he had folded up inside, before throwing both bags towards the girls.

Both of the females were pretty, with light complexioned skin and curly shoulder length hair. Their actions betrayed their appearance. The younger of the two was noticeably more brash and outspoken than the other. She walked towards Nan with her hand in the air yelling.

"Do you know who the fuck my brothers are, nigga? You's a dead motherfucker. You know that? Do you fucking know that?"

Nan angrily back slapped her, sending her tumbling to the carpet and quieting her down considerably. She crashed into a radio that had been playing some old Smokey Robinson song, before the plug was jarred out of the socket by her leg.

"Fill the bags up bitch," he grunted angrily to the other sister. The older lady was fidgeting suspiciously by the stove, seizing Nan's attention.

"Get over here old lady."

She walked over slowly, standing next to her daughter who had filled the book bag up with bricks and was now filling up the duffle bag.

"Hurry the fuck up, and nobody has to get hurt," Nan said in a stern tone. After the girl finished stuffing as many bricks into the bag as she could and zipped it up, Nan threw the book bag back on his back. As he reached down to grab the duffle bag, the old lady spat on him before saying, "You piece of shit."

Nan raised his hand, tempted to pistol whip her, but instead resisted. He spotted a phone on a coffee table against the wall. Wisely, he yanked it out of the wall. While exiting the apartment, he paused to grab a wad of cash he saw lying around, before backing up towards the door.

"If any of you come outside, you're dead," he said convincingly, as he opened the door and backed his way into the hallway.

His confidence was immediately shattered and replaced by a sense of fear that came over him as he heard noisy commotion downstairs.

"Roach, come inside! Niggas is up in our gate! They up in our gate nigga!"

For a second, he thought about going back into the apartment, but then he tried the door leading up to the roof. It opened when he turned the knob, and he quickly ran up the steps hearing the creaking sounds of feet hitting the stairs leading up to the floor he was just on. Reaching the roof, he forced himself to slow his pace, feeling his heart pound in his chest.

Darkness surrounded him, but the moon looked so serene in the clear sky. He surveyed his surroundings quickly. A tinge of fear crept through him, as he suddenly realized that he didn't have any place to go. He walked past a pigeon coop, stepping on some discarded Trojan wrappers as he reached the waist high stone edge of the roof.

Looking downward over the edge, he saw a wide alley that housed a pair of metal trash bins. There was no fire escape, and he knew that he couldn't make the long drop without injuring himself gravely. He peeled the stocking cap off of his face and tossed it. As his eyes glanced towards an adjacent tenement building, the pieces of a plan seemed to come together in his head.

The building was a two story, and it was at least twenty five to thirty feet away. Nan heaved the heavy bags, tossing them one by one across the alleyway and onto the roof of the other building. Then he followed by tossing his Tec-9. He backed up about eighteen feet, to give himself some room for take off, as he got into a sprinter's stance and prepared to leap to the other building. He breathed in deeply, preparing himself to run, just as the door to the roof opened behind him.

"That nigga's up here! He's on the roof," a stocky figure yelled as he ran outside spotting Nan immediately.

Nan stopped in his tracks, turning around in a crouched stance just as a bullet whizzed past his head wildly. The loud blast startled him. He refocused his mind in order to conquer his fears, as he sized up his formidable foe. He could sense the danger that lurked within him as he stared into his dark eyes.

Nan dove forward towards his foe, now crouched down within two feet of him. This move surprised his opponent, who had instinctively expected him to flee. He raised his gun trying to lock in on Nan, but his action happened too late…his target was hovering too close.

Nan delivered a powerful tornado kick *(Xuanfengjiao)* to his opponent's arm that sent his pistol flying through the air. His muscular foe reacted quickly, throwing a wild haymaker with his left hand. Nan's eyes followed his opponent's balled fist mindfully. He planted his feet firmly as he absorbed the forceful blow to his abdomen. Still focusing, Nan delivered a vicious chop to the fully extended arm, separating the bone on impact. As his opponent shrieked in anguish, Nan threw a swinging fist punch *(Baiquan),* that sent him reeling backwards. His arms splayed as he collapsed onto the roof with a thud.

Taking advantage of the moment, Nan replanted his feet and ran full speed towards the roof's edge. He clearly heard the distinctive sound of the door opening behind him, but forced himself not to look. He heard a man's voice yell, "Sic em, Butchie," but still, he remained focused on his objective. The pitbull's footsteps and heavy pants seemed so close as he leaped forward like a hurdler, sailing towards the adjacent building.

The distance between the buildings was greater than Nan anticipated. He failed to time his jump correctly. As he sailed through the air, he willed himself forward, barely making it across the divide. Nan landed awkwardly on one foot as he tumbled forward on the tar coated roof. Pain immediately shot through his left ankle as he sprained it on impact.

Scrambling to his feet, he grabbed his Tec-9, which was lying a few feet away from him, before glancing to his rear. The pitbull that was chasing him was midair. Its legs were still running in mid-stride, moving wildly as if it was searching for a surface to plant its feet. Nan watched as it made a sickening dive, landing in a loud thud as it crashed into the alleyway below.

Within seconds, Roach was at the roof's edge, anguishing as he looked down at the lifeless body of his favorite pet and prized fight dog. Those few seconds he spent glaring down at the carnage cost him dearly.

Refocusing he glanced towards the roof of the adjacent building, leveling his 9mm as he blindly searched for his target. Amidst the darkness, he finally spotted Nan. But, it was too late. Just as he trained his gun on him, three well-aimed bullets ripped through his chest, sending him reeling backwards.

Nan gazed down at his injured ankle, before gathering the bags and hiding against a brick wall concealing himself. His heart was beating so fast, he thought that it was going to explode out of his chest. Trying to calm himself down, he listened closely, waiting a few minutes for someone else to come onto the roof...but no one came. Limping, he put the bags back on his shoulders and headed downstairs through a door on the roof.

When he reached outside, to his surprise the streets were empty. He walked on the sidewalk cautiously, but at a quickened pace, easily blending into the shadows as he headed away from the building.

As Roach's crew ransacked every apartment in the tenement looking for Nan, he slipped off into the darkness unnoticed.

BETRAYAL: 4

OVERWHELMING ANGER CAUSED NAN'S trigger finger to shake slightly as he heard the locks disengage on the front door. A cold sweat slicked his forehead and intense hatred filled his blood. He wasn't fearful, but instead he was extremely focused and determined. Murder was on his mind. He channeled his energy.

The door slowly opened inwardly, the moment seeming surreal. He looked around to make sure no one was within earshot, gripping the pistol tighter in his palm. As a figure appeared through the crack, Nan kicked the door forward, aggressively pushing himself into the apartment. The door slammed into the female's chest, causing her to fall backwards as she screamed out hysterically at the top of her lungs.

"Nan! Stop...Stop!!! It's me."

There was dead silence, as the pistol fell out of his limp hand. He looked downward in disbelief, wondering if he was dreaming. His heart dropped to the pit of his stomach as tears welled up in his eyes.

"Latoya," he managed to mumble in a sort of childlike whisper. By now she was getting back on her feet, looking at him through untrusting eyes. He stood in front of her dumbfounded. She closed the front door behind him, but only after checking the streets to make sure no one had witnessed what just took place.

With composure that seemed uncanny under the circumstances, Latoya looked him in the eyes and said, "Nan, you're all over the news. They're saying you killed a bunch of people. What's going on? Why did you bust in here with a gun in your hand? What has happened to you?"

He didn't respond. He just stared deeply into her eyes in a trancelike state. Through the features that were more defined with age, and a scar that was about an inch long under her left eye, he could still see the young girl that he fell in love with a few years ago...the one that he still loved.

"Mama...mama wan' juice. Wan' juice mama," a small boy said as he walked over to Latoya unsteadily.

Nan studied the toddler as Latoya picked him up, holding him in one arm against her waist.

"Ok, boo boo, Mama gonna get you some juice," she said, repositioning him in her arms as she looked towards Nan.

"He looks just like you, right?"

"What?" Nan asked, snapping out of his trance.

"Just like I told you in the letter, Nathan looks just like his daddy."

"That's...that's my son?" Nan asked incredulously, while looking closely in young Nathan's face and seeing a reflection of himself as a youngster.

"You didn't read my letters Nan?" Latoya asked in a hurtful tone, her voice cracking.

Embarrassed and at a loss for words, Nan looked downward. His facial expression revealing the shame he felt regarding his own actions and selfishness. He cleared some phlegm that had formed in his throat before saying, "No, I didn't. I...I couldn't. I just read the second letter you sent me earlier today."

Her facial expression immediately changed, as the hurt and pain she felt inside became visible. Nathan was toying with her face. Due to his childish innocence, he was not cognizant of the significance of the tears that streamed down his mother's cheeks. Her heart felt heavy. She wiped her eyes with her free hand.

"Nan, do you know what I've been through these last couple of years? Do you know how many times I reached out to you, the only man that I felt I could trust, the only man that I truly ever loved? Do you know how many nights I spent crying, wondering why you wouldn't write me back? Praying to God that I would just be able to hear your voice, but not being able to reach you on the phone...wondering what I did to deserve that from you. What did I ever do to you Nan? Just tell me what I did?"

Her words cut through him like a bushido blade. She was crying uncontrollably as all of her emotions came to a head, causing her to explode. Growing restless and still wanting for juice, little Nathan squirmed around in her arms.

She mumbled, "I have to get him something to drink," walking towards the kitchen while Nan stood by with a depressed expression etched across his face.

A few minutes later, Nan joined them both in the dining room. Latoya was sitting at the table, and Nathan was in a highchair drinking out of a plastic sippy-cup. On the table, there was a copy of the *New York Post*, opened to page three. The headline read, "Crazed Gunman Ambushes Cops in Brooklyn."

Nan pulled a chair from beneath the table and sat down next to her. She wiped her eyes and pointed to the article before bluntly asking, "Well, is it true?"

Nan shook his head from side to side slowly, shrugging his shoulders as he looked down towards the white ceramic tile on the floor.

"No it's not true. I can't even believe that you would ask me that. You should know me better than that," he replied in a weak tone.

The tears had stopped flowing. With composure and increased confidence she said, "I thought I did, but apparently I was wrong. The Nan I knew wouldn't have abandoned me when I needed him most. Shit...you busted in my house waving a fuckin' gun at me. You're on the news every half an hour. I guess I don't know you."

Nan's eyes welled up. He stared off towards a corner in the far end of the kitchen, looking at nothing in particular. His tone was soft as he started to speak, his words full of emotion.

"I remember sitting down at *Juniors* with you that day when we went out to eat and I told you about my parents. I mean, I started to tell you about them.

About how I killed them and you said that there was nothing I could do. You told me that it wasn't my fault," he said, as he forced himself to swallow in an attempt to moisten his parched throat. After making a few attempts in vain, he continued his thought. "I can see my parents now, almost like it was yesterday. Their faces are still so vivid in my mind. We didn't have a lot. But, we weren't poor though. But, we was just, I guess almost middle class. But, my parents would do whatever they could for me to make sure I didn't go out looking bad. You know, new clothes or whatever. Not as much as the other kids but enough so I wouldn't be embarrassed at school. *YouknowwhatImean?*" Latoya nodded her head in acknowledgment, as Nan stopped focusing on the wall and looked in her face.

"Well, on Christmas eve we would always go out as a family tradition. And that year I wanted Nintendo. It was dope then and everybody wanted it and I was begging my moms everyday giving her little subtle hints leading up to that day," a slight smile came over Nan's face, but disappeared quickly as he said, "I was a momma's boy, and my mom's would do anything for me. My pops was more of the money manager—disciplinarian. He thought things out more, always thought about our future and saving up to get us a better place."

He paused uneasily, looking towards the floor and then off into the far corner of the room again. His leg moved up and down, tapping the floor with the heel of his boot uncontrollably.

"I remember them arguing in the store about getting the Nintendo. My pops said that it cost too much, but my moms bought it anyway. She wanted her baby boy to be happy. I still remember my father and mother not talking as we started to go home. I remember the smug look I had on my face. I was spoiled and unappreciative of shit. Just happy that I got my way. When we crossed Atlantic Avenue, my father was a few paces in front of us, and me and my moms trailed behind," Nan's eyes drifted downward, his leg still tapping and his hands now shaking as well.

"He saw the car first. The bright lights, shining and bearing down on us so quickly. My mother ran towards him pulling me along, but in the confusion I...I dropped the bag with the Nintendo. I don't know how, but it slipped out of my hand. I forcefully pulled my hand away from my moms, escaping her grasp and running back in the street towards the bag. I knew I could get it before the car came...I had to get it. But, my mother being the protector that she was, ran back for her baby. And even though my father was heated with my moms, he also ran back to save us. I wrapped my hand around," he paused as he sobbed, tears were streaming down his face now.

"I...I wrapped my hand around the bag and looked up. It was so bright. The headlight was right in front of my face. I squinted from its brightness. I could feel the heat. I knew that the car was about to run me down. But, at the last minute, my moms pushed me out of the way. *She pushed me out of the way!* My pops grabbed my moms. I turned around just as the car slammed into both of them, mowing them down. Blood was everywhere. They'd both be alive if it wasn't for me! *I killed them. If I wasn't so selfish, so concerned about myself...about a fuckin Nintendo, they'd both be alive!*" Nan screamed the words out in shear anguish, as he cried uncontrollably. Tears ran in a steady stream down his face, and his nose was running.

He had never shared this story with anyone. Never faced his demons. He had never even shed a tear up to this point. It had eaten away at the soul that embodied him all of these years. The same soul that had been fleeing from the nightmare of guilt, sadness and death since his innocence was lost at the tender age of thirteen. Mentally and emotionally drained, he slumped in his chair with his elbows on his knees, head buried in the palms of his hands. Latoya hugged him tightly, kissing him on his wet cheek and whispering in a calming tone, "Nan, it's ok. It wasn't your fault. You didn't know. You were a kid." Her outer shell was harder with age, but she still had a soft inner soul.

He hugged her back tightly. Remembering how good she felt in his arms, and feeling as if she was the only one that ever belonged there. He felt ashamed by his emotions. Leslie hadn't even been buried yet, and he was in the arms of another woman, feeling the way that his heart couldn't deny he was feeling. But, this wasn't just a woman. Latoya was undeniably his heart. He loved Leslie dearly, and quite frankly he even loved Kimba in an endearing way. But, with her in his midst, he couldn't deny his true feelings…and neither could she.

She felt Nan's face lightly, running her fingers across the light stubble on his cheek before kissing him slowly with her soft lips. They shared a brief romantic moment, before they unwillingly broke from each other's embrace, both thinking about the gravity of the situation at hand.

Little Nathan's face was lying flat on the high chair's plastic tray, sound asleep. Latoya got Nan's attention, pointing at little Nathan as she said, "Look at him. You know, all the time I was pregnant I didn't know whose baby was inside of me. I thought it was that bastard's child, until I saw his eyes. When I saw his eyes, I knew he was yours."

Nan stared at his son with a wide grin etched across his face. He was full of pride.

"Man, and I thought that you couldn't get pregnant your first time."

"Yeah, I don't know who you got that one from," Latoya responded laughing lightly.

Nan's facial expression changed, as a thought came to mind. "Whatever happened to your stepfather anyway? Where's he at? That's who I came here for. I wanted to hurt him for hurting you."

"You don't have to worry about him anymore, he's dead. God took care of him." She paused and mushed Nan's forehead with her hand, before sarcastically adding, "You would know this if you read my letters."

"I know, I know. My bad," Nan responded defensively.

Latoya shrugged her shoulders and smiled as she said, "It's alright Nan, you've been through so much."

"We both have," he interjected.

"Yeah, but I forgive you. Ironically, James died a couple of months back. Liver gave out. It was cirrhosis or some shit. Whatever it was, his ass is dead as dirt and I came up here to get some of our belongings and some paperwork for my mother. This was her house you know. All in her name, paid off and everything."

"Word?"

"Yeah, it became hers when my real pops died. After we got news that the bastard died, she asked me to come up here. Too many bad memories. She couldn't even stomach the idea of stepping in this house again."

"I can't blame her. I'm surprised that you were able to do it."

She looked in his eyes, and in a soft and very sincere tone said, "I only came up here because I hoped that I would get the chance to see you again."

For the next couple of hours they caught up on lost time, sharing stories with one another. Nan held nothing back, sharing his complete soul with her, as he told her about the murder of Jerome Reddy, Rodriguez and Digangi, the robberies, Kimba and Leslie. She listened on intently, filling in the gaps on her end as well. They only took a break when Latoya pulled out some leftovers, satisfying Nan's famished body.

Things had been hard on her and her mother after they went south. Latoya was noticeably harder and more vocal. She even cursed quite a few times, which was something Nan had never heard her do before. Like him, she was forced to grow up faster than any teenager should have to, but she handled her business. She took care of their son, without the help of a man and only asked her mother for assistance when she was in dire need.

But, something had kept her from becoming intimate with another man. She struggled with this, not knowing if it was her longing to be with Nan, or the after effects of experiencing a torturous rape. But, as she sat in his midst, she knew the answer. She didn't care about the other women he had been with. That was insignificant now. They were meant to be together, and she wasn't going to abandon her man again in a time of need.

Still in the dining room, Latoya was now sitting on Nan's lap with her back to his chest as he held her in his arms tightly.

"What are we gonna do Nan? If these cops are trying to set you up, there has to be something we can do," Latoya said in a concerned tone.

Nan glanced at a clock that hung on one of the walls in the kitchen, and it read ten thirty. "I have to go see somebody. I have to find out what's going on…find out how I can get out of this shit."

Latoya hopped up from his lap, with a determined look on her face.

"I'm coming with you."

"Nah, I need you to take care of our little man. I can't risk something happening to both of us."

A tear slowly ran down Latoya's face, as an uneasy feeling came over her.

"Nan, just come with me. We can go down south now. My car is right outside. No one will know to look for you with me. Please, let's just go," her voice cracked from emotion as she spoke.

He pondered the thought for a second, but his gut told him that it was too risky. Pulling her close to him he said, "If I don't find out what's going on, this shit ain't never gonna end. They'll be looking for me countrywide. *They'll be looking for us.*"

"So, what are you gonna do, Nan? I don't want to lose you again."

Master Thaddeus came to mind. He knew that he could assist him.

"Let me just make a quick run, and visit an old acquaintance that may be able to help us out. He may be able to help me disappear. Once I go see him, I'll come back and we can go."

"Well, why don't you just take me with you?"

"I can't. Five-0 is looking for me in every borough. I'm on the news every five minutes...I gotta do this alone," he paused to wipe away the tears that had begin to stream out of her eyes. "I'll be back at midnight for you and little man and then we'll go."

"You promise, Nan," she asked in a weak voice.

Nan used the palm of his hand to lift up her chin before saying, "I promise, I promise. But, if I'm not here by five after twelve, you have to promise me that you'll go on without me."

She looked in his eyes and hesitated before saying, "I can't promise that."

"You have to promise me that. If I'm not back by five after twelve, you have to go for the sake of our child."

Reluctantly she mumbled, "O.K, O.K," as she buried her head in his chest.

Nan kissed her lightly on the forehead, before heading over to little Nathan who was still sound asleep. He kissed him on the cheek as well, blushing as he looked down at him proudly. Seeing the rotary phone hanging on the wall made him think about Joe. He knew he must be going crazy, with everything on the news. He thought about calling him, but decided that he would reach out once he got to the dojo.

"I'll see you at twelve," he said, before he turned and made his way out of the house.

Once outside, Nan made way to the Accord and quickly ducked inside. He turned off the radio, not wanting to be disturbed. Driving along, his thoughts were filled with visions of Latoya and little Nathan. The buildings and lights that he passed were a blur. No matter what he tried to focus on, his thoughts continued to come back to them. He had to make things right somehow, so they had a chance to be together. A chance to be a real family.

Before he knew it, he was pulling into a space around the corner from Thaddeus's dojo, parallel parking on autopilot. Cautiously he surveyed his environment. He purposely waited in his car for fifteen minutes, to observe anything out of the ordinary. He hadn't been here in well over a year, but he didn't know if Five-0 had been tipped off to this spot. At this point, he wasn't taking anything for granted.

After being assured that no one was staking out the place, Nan discreetly walked to the side of the West Indian bakery and rang the bell. The buzzer quickly went off allowing him entry inside, sooner than he expected. *Almost too soon.* But, Nan brushed it off, thinking that perhaps Thaddeus was expecting someone. Maybe a new student he took on. Or, maybe he had been watching the news and knew that his former protégée was in need of assistance. In need of refuge.

Nan pushed open the metal door and hesitantly climbed up the narrow steps, all the while engulfed in darkness. He was used to this. His eyes adjusted to the lack of light, as he reached the landing, using his ears and perception in the same manner as a blind man navigating instinctively.

As usual, the blinds in the dojo only allowed minimal light to enter from the street lamps outside. To Nan's right he also noticed that light from a candle was flickering in Thaddeus's back room. He started to walk towards the room on the balls of his feet, as he heard a familiar sound. The soft whistling sound that accompanies a projectile as it cuts through the wind. The sound is ever so slight, but in most cases the result being ever so deadly to an unsuspecting target.

Nan reacted swiftly, turning his torso around his waist (*Fanyao*), as the two throwing knives flew over his head, vanishing into a sea of darkness as they missed him completely. In one motion, he had turned to face the direction of his attacker, his body in a defensive stance.

The words that followed echoed throughout the dojo, sending chills through Nan that reached deep into the bowels of his inner soul.

"I begged you to leave before it would come to this. But, you didn't listen," Thaddeus yelled in a harsh tone and deep accent. He was within ten feet of Nan standing bare-chested, muscles pulsing and exposing the veins in his arms that extended down to his hands that wielded two bushido swords. Calmly, he tossed the sword he held in his left hand towards Nan, and it landed on a pad within inches of his feet.

As he relaxed into a crouched stance (*Pubu*), with his sword at waist level, Thaddeus menacingly stated, "Fate has brought you back into my presence, and now regretfully I must return you to your essence."

THE DIARY OF ~~DESPAIR~~:

Spring-Winter of 1989

Around the way girl

The sun was out and the temperature was just right on this beautiful spring day. Nan had gotten up early and drove a little hooptie he picked up earlier in the year, over to the naval yards to work out. This had become an early morning ritual for him. It had seemed like ages since he last visited Thaddeus's apartment for training. Instead, he built his own makeshift dojo, practicing and meditating in the same decrepit basement that the pigs had tortured him in almost a year ago now.

He grew to embrace the rundown building, because he knew no one else would venture into its depths. It was also the perfect place to focus his thoughts, hone his skills and stash his small cache of weapons.

Besides some guns and a change of clothes, he stored the Kevlar vest that Rodriguez gave him as a "gift" here. He never wore it because it made him feel too stiff and rigid. She told him that she was concerned with his health, which basically meant that she just wanted to take proactive steps to protect her investment. He was bringing in a pretty good supply of product, which increased their revenue stream. They wanted him to keep it coming.

Nan also kept a shoe box stashed in the hideout, where he kept all of his keepsakes. Inside, there were some old pictures of his parents and a few of him when he was an infant. Also, he had some stacks of paper that he had been saving up from the robberies he had done over the past several months. Mostly though, the box was filled with unopened letters from Latoya.

Initially, she had started out writing him once a week. Then it decreased from twice a month, to about once every six months. Nan just rubber band wrapped the letters in order of receipt and stored them in the box. He never read any of them, since her initial letter that he tore up in disgust.

With Joe off at NYU, Nan found that the time he was spending in the doldrums of the basement was increasing considerably. Joe was in his second semester, holding it down with a 3.5 GPA and balancing a part-time job. Still in all, they spoke often enough, even though Joe stayed in a dormitory on campus. Every time they conversed, he sounded so excited that it brought a smile to Nan's face. He had even bagged up a girlfriend and everything, in his short time at the school.

Nan lived vicariously through him, listening intently to all of his stories about college life. He himself had lost interest in school, and rarely attended. He had already made up his mind that he was gonna just get his GED, but he didn't tell Joe though. Just like he never told Joe what Rodriguez and Digangi threatened to do to him, if he didn't cooperate with them. He knew that Joe would give up everything in a heartbeat if he knew the sacrifices Nan was making on his behalf. But, it was second nature for Nan. He'd do anything for his brother.

After working out, Nan headed over to Red Hook. He discretely parked his whip on Henry Street by Carroll Gardens, and started walking towards the projects. Rodriguez and Digangi told him about some dealers that ran a distribution ring throughout the projects, and Nan was peeping them out trying to see their routine and determine how they re-up.

He was hugging a corner trying to blend into his environment, when a fly around the way girl pushing a stroller and holding a little boy's hand walked past. She was wearing a white Benetton shirt and a pink Guess skirt. The outfit highlighted her firm thighs, nice well-defined calves and voluptuous breasts. Their eyes locked as she walked past rocking her bangle earrings and Reebok 5411's. Her slow confident strut was sexy as hell. She looked a few years older than him, but very youthful.

After passing by, she took a few steps before saying, "You just gonna look, or you gonna say something?"

Nan laughed, caught off guard by her directness. He rebounded quickly by saying, "I could ask you the same thing."

"Well, why didn't you?" She asked with a smug grin on her face. She blew a bubble seductively, licking her lips to get the pink bubblegum off of them when it popped.

"What's your name cutie?"

"Kimba, and yours?"

"Nan."

"Nan? That's fly. I like that."

Her skin was flawless, and her features drop dead gorgeous. Looking into her beautiful hazel eyes, Nan saw some things that words seldom say. Her beauty masked her pain, but her eyes revealed it all. Actually, they reflected his own pain. He looked her up and down studying her body closely.

"I'm not really one to waste words or time, *knowwhati'msaying?*"

She smiled before saying, "No, not really. Why don't you explain?"

"I'm just saying, we should get to know each other."

"I agree," she said as she pulled a paper out of her wallet and wrote her number down quickly.

Nan took the paper and asked if she wanted his digits, but she refused saying, "No, I'll wait for your call."

He smiled, digging her style as she walked off telling him that she had to get her kids home to feed them.

He watched her perfect frame as she walked off, her round bottom jiggling noticeably under her skirt. She stayed on his mind the rest of the afternoon, occupying his thoughts as he continued to finalize his plans for the robbery he was going to perform later that night.

Digangi and Rodriguez

Rodriguez wasted no time slicing into her thick Porterhouse steak, cutting a juicy piece off of it as soon as the waitress served her food. Digangi was sitting across from her savoring over a seafood platter. The huge shrimps alone were as big as the palm of his hand.

It was Friday evening at *Valentinos*, the most popular and expensive Italian restaurant in downtown Brooklyn. As usual, the place was packed with people that had made their reservations weeks in advance. Digangi and Rodriguez on the other hand always dropped in unannounced. Just showing their faces guaranteed them the finest table, and they never saw a bill. It was just one of the perks of being a cop on payroll.

"Jose and I are planning on taking the kids to Disney in a couple of months," Rodriguez said, pausing to chow down on some fettuccini alfredo.

Digangi laughed out loud before saying, "Don't you think they're a little too young for Disney? Do they even know who Mickey is?"

"I guess it's more so for us. We never had a honeymoon, you know?"

"I got you," Digangi said, as he wiped some lobster bisque off of his mouth with the sleeve of his shirt.

"You know, the money coming in from redistributing the product is copasetic, but I still think we could be doing better for ourselves."

He had Rodriguez's full attention now. She put her fork and knife down on the table and asked, "What do you mean Poppi?"

He looked around making certain no one was in earshot before saying, "The bagged up white lady that we get our fucking hands on, we give to the motherfucks who repackage and redistribute it, right?"

"Si. I mean Uh, huh."

"They give us our cut, which we split amongst ourselves making a decent profit for doing little to no work."

"Uh, huh. I'm following you."

"But, fucks like Sonny, are double dipping. They sell the coke initially, then we take it back. Then they sell it again. We're getting a little piece of the pie, but we're taking just as much risk, if not more."

"Ay. I got you Poppi. So, what are you saying, we should try to negotiate a bigger cut?"

"Nah, we diversify our interests," Digangi said, laughing out loud. "I sound like my wife's brother. He's a stock broker, always using big words and shit."

He paused to take a sip of the double shot of Jack Daniels that he had ordered earlier, savoring the taste of the liquor.

"We know who Sonny distributes to. We still give him his share of the product and get our cut from him, but we also set up our own little network of dealers that buy directly from us. We supply the coke and the protection. Then *bada-bing bada-bang*, we are making some major doe-ree-mi."

"I like how that sounds," Rodriguez said. Her eyes were twinkling, as if she was being turned on by the topic of money.

"*Fuh-get-about it*. We all could be millionaires in six months."

"Don't even tease me like that Poppi. Jose can barely help with the bills, with the crumbs they pay him at the bodega."

"Well, shit's about to change."

"Yeah, we just need to run it past the boss."

"Yeah, we can go see him after we finish up here. I'm sure he'll approve. You know how much he loves money."

What's it gonna be?

"Ohhh, shit. Ooh my god. You're hitting my spot! Fuck that pussy, nigga! Fuck that pussy," Kimba screamed. Her voice shuddering seductively between her sexual pants. Her thick toned legs were spread eagle, with her chunky ass hanging just slightly off the side of the bed, allowing the perfect angle for him to get deep inside of her. She gripped the cotton sheets tightly in her sweaty palms, moaning while he banged her ass out.

"How's this pussy baby," she asked in a soft whisper. The question was rhetorical...she already knew the answer. So many niggas had been up in it, getting turned out momentarily. She had incredible pussy control. Using her inner walls to grip onto the hardened manhood of any cat she blessed with the honor of sliding up in her.

She knew how to turn a man out, and would do anything sexually to place her name on a dick. After Kimba freaked a nigga, their thoughts always came back to her when they were running up in another chick. Since her first sexual experience at sixteen, she had become a true freak. She was very in touch with her body, and not afraid to experiment and try new things.

Her only problem was that the cats she dealt with were not willing to be on lock just because she was an exceptional piece of tail. Hustlers weren't looking for ready made families, nor were they interested in sporting a chick up at the Rooftop or the Fever that half the dealers up in the piece had already ran through.

The only nigga that treated her different was Power though. He didn't care about her reputation, and went out of his way to always make her feel like a queen when they were together. She birthed his seed shortly before he got locked on a possession charge. Even though she slipped and got knocked up while he was away, he still wrote her each week religiously. In his letters, he always let her know that he wanted them to be together as a family once he got out.

She told Nan to let her stand up, and he grabbed her hands in order to help her to her feet. She walked slowly over to the side of the room, and placed her hands on the wall, arching her back while she placed one of her feet on a chair nearby. With her ass poked out she said, "I know you wanna hit it from the back."

Nan slid inside of her, pulling her back to his chest as he gripped her healthy breasts in his hands. She moaned in his sweaty arms, slightly pushing off of the wall for leverage.

"Pinch my nipple while your fucking me," she urged him in a seductive whisper. Nan obliged causing her to moan passionately.

Bending over further, she pushed her ass out, rhythmically moving in unison with his body to meet him with every stroke.

"Let me know when you're ready to come so I can suck your dick. I want to swallow your babies."

Just as Nan started to climax, there was a loud disturbance that could be heard from the apartment building's hallway. They would have ignored it, but what followed was the undeniable sound of gunfire. Kimba screamed loudly. The bullets gave off the sound of firecrackers, followed by two loud booms, similar to M-80's. It sounded like it was happening right inside her apartment.

Like a protective mother, Kimba grabbed her robe and ran into her children's bedroom. She scooped her youngest two up before frantically placing them in the bath tub. Nan followed closely behind, tripping over toys scattered on the floor, as he carried her oldest son. All three of them were crying hysterically. Scared by the gunfire and their mother's reaction. This had become the drill for them. It happened at least once a month, but this was the first time that it happened right in front of her apartment door.

When the shooting let up, Nan opened the door slowly, clutching a 9mm in his hand. He stepped outside wearing a t-shirt and boxers. The hallway was clear by now. A trail of blood could be seen on the floor leading towards the door to the stairwell.

A neighbor in an adjacent apartment came out a few minutes later and explained how she had heard some young boys arguing before the gunfire. Nan noticed that bullets had actually struck Kimba's door in the crossfire. There were three holes, most likely from shotgun birdshot he assumed.

When he returned inside, Kimba had the boys calmed down and back in their beds. Seeing Nan walk back inside made her immediately feel safe, but she was still visibly shaken. After closing the door to the boy's room, she ran into his arms.

"Is anybody dead out there, Nan?"

"Nah, nobody's out there now. But, I think someone got hit. There's blood on the floor, and some holes in your door."

She hugged him tightly as warm tears began to run down her cheeks. She was at her wits end, wearing her emotions on her sleeve.

"We need to talk," she said in a hollow voice, as she lead Nan into the living room and sat on the sofa.

He sat down besides her as she looked at him and said, "Nan, I need to know what's it gonna be?"

He looked deeply into her hazel eyes. They were full of so much hurt and pain. "What do you mean?" He asked.

"I can't live like this Nan. I deserve more than this shit. Throwing my kids in a tub because niggas is shooting outside of my fuckin' door. The place where I lay my head to rest at night. I can't fuckin' deal with this shit!" Her voice cracked from emotion as tears ran in a steady stream from her eyes. Nan reached over and grabbed a napkin that was lying next to a plate on the coffee table, before wiping her tears for her. She blew her nose lightly and looked in his eyes.

"Power is getting out this summer, and he's asking me what's up, wanting to know if I'm a still be here for him. I need to know the deal, cuz I don't know. We've been messing around with each other for a while now, and I need to know something."

Nan gulped down some saliva. His mouth was dry. He felt hollow inside. He cared about her a lot, but she could never be his girl. He knew her pain, and didn't want to hurt her anymore by giving her false hopes. Selfishly, he wanted to lead her on, so he could still hit it when he wanted to. Sexually, she was undoubtedly the best piece of ass that he ever had. But, he had a heart. And his compassionate side wouldn't allow him to feed her dreams he knew would never materialize. She deserved better than that.

He had heard her make references to Power before, and he knew she had feelings for him still. He ran his fingers through her hair and said, "You need to be there for your man when he gets out."

She bit her lip and looked downward, before looking back in Nan's face. He was young she thought, but so much different than the other so called men that she messed with. He was mature beyond his years. She wanted more from him…more for them. His emotionless response wasn't what she wanted to hear.

"So, you're willing to throw away what we have just like that?" She asked in a whisper, her words trailing off towards the end of her sentence.

"I know what's best for you, and what's best for your kids right now, and it ain't me. Before everything else, we're friends. I wouldn't be a friend if I wasn't honest with you, *knowwhati'msaying?*"

Their relationship ended like so many of the others that she had in the past. When she asked a man to commit, they were Audi 5000, pulling as many lame ass excuses as they could conjure up out of their ass. The only difference with Nan, is that she could feel the sincerity in his voice, which is what made it hurt even more.

After he left, she lay in her bed looking at the ceiling, wondering if she made the right choice by asking him, "What's it gonna be?" More importantly, she hoped that Power was gonna finally be the man he promised to be in all of the letters he had been writing, once he came home in a couple of months.

Love is a house

ℰvery time they spoke or got up with each other, Joe had to constantly deal with Nan teasing him about his grades. He was on the Dean's list, still worked a part time job and was recently recruited as a tutor for other students. Nan constantly rode him, jokingly saying that he must be part Jamaican because he had so many jobs.

Beside juggling so many jobs, it also didn't help that his girlfriend, Shedanka was a white Yugoslavian. Nan really got a kick out of that one. Joe didn't have a girlfriend in high school, so Nan would jokingly tease him saying, "The chicks at Boys n' Girls were a little to dark for Mr. Joey. Mr. Joey don't like anything too ethnic. Mr. Joey likes plenty of cream in his coffee."

Joe would grab him up, and they would still slap box like the young teens that used to horse around walking home from school. That seemed so long ago. But, the time and even the distance between them only seemed to make them closer. Nan would pop up on campus and try to kick it to what he referred to as, "the good girls." He even managed to make it to a couple of college parties with Joe, borrowing a student ID to get in.

The subject of Nan and school had become just about as taboo as the deaths of their parents. Joe purposely left it alone. He knew that Nan wasn't at *Saint Mary's* anymore, and he had an apartment in Crown Heights, which meant that he had to be getting money from somewhere. Joe didn't know where, and he didn't ask, figuring that Nan would tell him when he was ready.

On this particular afternoon, they sat in Joe's small dorm room, kicking it, when Shedanka popped over. She was undeniably pretty for a white girl, but she dressed real reserved. Her blue eyes lit up behind her thin spectacles when she saw Nan. Holding her hand up for a hi-five, she said, "Whassup homie," in your signature accent.

"Shay-Love," Nan said, cracking a huge smile as he got up and gave her a warm hug. They got along well. As he told Joe on numerous occasions, "She's the coolest white girl I ever met."

Nan hadn't meant many white chicks in high school, but Shay was indeed one of a kind. She by no means tried to act "black", unless she was joking with Nan. But on the contrary, she was very much in touch with herself and confident as well. That's what drew Joe to her, and the reason why Nan accepted her. Even though he cracked mad jokes when she wasn't around, deep down he knew she was good for his brother.

Shay's mother was still in Croatia. She saved up and sent her daughter to the states via a student visa, in hopes of her obtaining a better life than she had. Shay didn't see skin color like everyone else, but she felt the disapproving eyes from the sisters around campus. These same girls wouldn't have paid Joe any mind before, but they definitely didn't want to see him with a white chick.

"So, did Joe tell you the good news?" Shay asked, as she sat down on the edge of the bed next to Nan.

"Nah, what's up?" Nan asked inquisitively.

"I didn't get to say nothing yet. But, now's as good a time as any," Joe said.

"Well what's up?" Nan asked impatiently. "You pregnant?"

"Nah, don't even put that on us," Joe said, shaking his head from side to side animatedly. "We're getting an apartment together."

"Word? That's fly," Nan said, before giving Joe daps.

"We'll be moving this summer," Shay said excitedly.

"Word? Yo, that's dope. Yawl need help moving or anything, you know I'm there," Nan said assuredly.

"Thank you, Nan. You are so sweet," Shay said, as she hugged him warmly.

"Don't worry about it. You know how I do," Nan responded.

"I'm a run out and grab something to eat. Do you guys want something?" Shay asked, as she walked towards the door.

"Nah, I'm good." Nan replied.

"Me too," Joe responded as well.

After Shay left, the boys chilled in the room and caught up with one another. They reminisced, laughing about everything, including their run ins with Shaborn and his crew. Time had flown by, and they had both grown up so fast. They were so much different now, than when they first met in the courtyard that cold wintry day.

"Yo, you ever think about everything that happened? I mean, it had to be fate what happened to our parents that night. And for us to end up growing up together. That happened for a reason." Joe said.

"That's bugged, cuz I was thinking about the day me and Carson met you just last week. You should have seen your haircut, B."

"Ha! I was zoned out man. I didn't want to live. All I wanted to do was join my parents. And then yawl came through."

"Yeah, and Carson with his candy and shit. Like it was Halloween three hundred and sixty five days of the year. That nigga musta had a sweet tooth or some shit," Nan said, as they both laughed aloud.

"Word up. But for real, I felt like I was in the lost and found. Like I was waiting for someone to come retrieve me."

"Look at you. Always the introspective one. That's why you're such a good writer man," Nan said.

"Thanks, B. I appreciate it. I appreciate all the times you had my back."

"Come on man, you ain't gotta thank me for that. You know I always got you. We brothers."

Joe's eyes scanned the room, as his thoughts drifted momentarily. Finally, he decided to speak what was on his mind.

"Nan, have you thought about what we did to Jerome Reddy at all?"

Nan bit down on his lip, shaking his head before saying, "Nah, not really."

"The other day I couldn't sleep. I kept thinking about that day at the building," Joe said in a weak tone.

"Yo, don't trouble yourself with that man. That nigga got what he deserved. Besides, you didn't do nothing. I did. Don't lose sleep over that nigga Joe, cuz I don't."

There was an uncomfortable silence momentarily, as both boys thought about the ghosts that haunted their past. Finally, Nan decided to change the subject to something of a lighter note by saying, "Yo, I think you found the one."

"Who, Shay?"

"Yeah, no doubt. She may not be able to fry you no chicken or bake macaroni like your moms used to. But, she's good peoples," Nan said sarcastically. He effectively lightened the mood, and caused Joe to laugh.

They talked for a few more hours before Nan hopped in his hooptie and headed back to BK. When he turned on his Aiwa radio, Frankie Crocker was on. The song he was introducing was, *Force MDS*, "Love is a house."

"How fitting," Nan said to himself, as he thought about Joe and Shay.

It ain't hard to tell

It was the beginning of the summer and things couldn't be better. The sun was out, there was a nice breeze outside, and more importantly Kimba had her man by her side.

Power had been home a few weeks, and true to his word he was back living with Kimba, making her the happiest girl in BK. He had gained a few pounds while he was locked down, but was still muscular and solid like a NFL running back. His coal complexion complimented Kimba's lighter skin tone. He had a flair for clothes, always keeping a fresh pair of Nikes and Guess jeans on, like he was rocking on this particular day.

Kimba never knew what it was that always kept Power coming back. He loved his son, but he treated all of her kids as if they were his own. For lack of a better explanation, she figured that it had to be the sex. But, actually, Power just loved her for her.

When he was at the top of his game, he could bag any chick. But, he saw in Kimba what so many other dudes didn't. She just wanted to be loved. She wasn't a hoe in his eyes. She didn't just sleep with any dude, she slept with cats that she thought would really care for her.

Unfortunately, Power was the only dude that really did care. And if he had it his way, he would finally get a chance to make an honest woman out of her.

Things had been a little tough for him since he got out. Like most cats, he was gung ho initially, filling out job apps, hoping to land a legal gig somewhere. He knew how the system worked, and figured that it was only a matter of time before his PO would start questioning him in regards to employment.

His brother Melquan had held shit down for him while he was locked, so he didn't really have to worry about loot. Quan would hit him off with whatever he needed. But still and all, he wanted his own. He wasn't used to relying on no niggas. He had always been his own man.

After spending a day at Prospect Park with Kimba and the kids, Power picked up some ice cream cones and headed back towards Red Hook. He was pushing a blue 89' beemer, everything legit with the paperwork in his uncle's name.

The car was so clean, that he didn't even get nervous when the blue Ford Crown Victoria pulled him over on Flatbush Ave. He had signaled, plus the car was registered and insured. He had nothing to worry about he told himself. But, once he realized who the two cops were walking towards him, he became slightly concerned.

"Well, well, well. If it isn't Power," Rodriguez said, as she stood next to the driver's side window. Pedestrians were nosily looking on, anticipating an arrest about to happen. Digangi was on the other side of the car looking in the windows. When Kimba saw him she said, "Why don't yawl leave us alone? We didn't do nothing. Yawl always fuckin' with somebody!"

"Shh, baby. It's alright. I didn't do shit, so I ain't worried," Power said calmly as he looked at Rodriguez.

"Yeah, just chill out Mami. We just wanna talk to your man in private for a second," Rodriguez said.

"I'll be right back," Power said, before opening his door and walking towards the back of the car where Digangi was waiting.

"So, it's good to see you back on the streets. You enjoying the fresh air?" Digangi asked.

"Yeah, it's better than being locked down, *knowwhati'msaying?*" Power responded, while sitting his two hundred pound frame on the trunk of the BMW.

"How long you think it will be before you end up back upstate, Poppi? Two, three months at the max," Rodriguez said in a harsh tone.

Power calmly responded, "Nah, I'm not going back." He was looking around at the pedestrians, that had resumed their daily routine, realizing that an arrest wasn't imminent.

"How many people do you think are gonna hire a two time felon with a ninth grade education?" Digangi said harshly.

"I don't know, but I guess I'll find out soon," Power responded smugly, unfazed by their comments.

"Shit has changed since you got locked up. We run the streets out here. We provide product and protection. If you don't roll with us, you don't roll at all," Digangi said.

"Well, I told yawl already, I ain't rolling with no one. Besides, you two clowns are the ones that locked me up in the first place. What the fuck would make you think that I would trust you?"

"Because when shit starts getting rough, which it will soon Poppi. It ain't hard to tell. You're going to go back to your old ways. And you know that we're gonna be fuckin' watching you," Rodriguez said, before Digangi interrupted her.

"And if you're not rolling with us, you'll be on a one way bus trip back up north. So, if I were you, I'd think about it," Digangi said.

Power laughed out loud.

"Yeah, I'll do that. Are yawl done? Can I go?"

"Yeah, we'll be seeing you Poppi,"

Power climbed back in the car and drove off, barely getting a few feet before Kimba said, "What did they want Power? Why they harassing you? You not dealing again, right? You told me it was gonna be—"

Power interrupted her saying, "Damn, would you relax. Chill out, everything is cool. They just testing me, that's all."

She immediately felt at ease, resting her head on his muscular shoulder. She gripped his dark skinned hand and closed her eyes. Her man was back home. Things were going to be different this time.

Shoot to kill

Coco's was a little nondescript West Indian spot in the middle of Flatbush. Supposedly, it was renowned for "specializing in beef patties and roti", as the writing on the yellow awning proudly proclaimed. But, the people in the hood knew that it was really one of the best spots in Brooklyn to get a thick dime of seedless chocolate tie weed. Digangi and Rodriguez had informed Nan that somewhere behind the storefront, there was plenty of coke being cut up. That was the reason he was there on this particular night, blending in with the shadows as he looked on from across the street.

He was draped in green camouflaged army fatigues, Timberlands and a fisherman's hat pulled down low enough to almost hide his eyes. As he begin walking across the street, the harsh sound of tires shrieking shot through the air, as a car skidded to a halt at an intersection up the street. A middle aged mother rushed to the aid of her young child, that had aimlessly ran into the street seconds earlier. Nervous energy caused her body to shake uncontrollably, as tears streamed down her face. She hugged the young girl tightly, while lovingly scolding her as they embraced.

Nan looked on closely, from afar observing everything as it transpired. Emotions ran rampant through his mind, as his thoughts slowly began to drift back to Christmas Eve, 1985. He stared at the woman's face as she glanced in his direction, their eyes seeming to meet for a split second. As he examined her face, he saw his own mother's eyes looking back at him.

Nan fought back his painful memories, struggling to refocus his mind. Taking advantage of the sparse traffic, he slowly crossed the street, walking into the small West Indian shop just as a patron was leaving. It was a young black female. She had a soda in her hand, a Phillie blunt and two bags of weed tucked in her pocket.

Nan held the door open for her, keeping his head tilted down low. He consciously made an effort to try and disguise himself lately. He had robbed numerous spots over the past few months, and mistakenly let a few dealers catch a glimpse of his features. By now, even those that didn't know the face, were very familiar with the name, and nobody wanted a run in with that *niggaNan.*

Nan looked through the dirty glass in the small food warmer that sat on the countertop, and pointed while saying, "Let me get a pat-tea an coco bread brethren." He didn't know what it was, but whenever he was in a West Indian spot, he felt compelled to test his bogus sounding accent.

The skinny dred retrieved some plastic tongs, while Nan waited patiently. As he bent down to get the coco bread from underneath the counter, Nan quickly locked the metal deadbolt on the front door. By the time the dred stood back up, he was back at the counter looking innocent.

"Any ting else brethren?" The dred asked.

"Yeah. Where's the coke?"

The dred just stared at him defiantly without responding.

With a tinge of anger in his voice, Nan repeated, "Where's the fuckin' cocaine, nigga?"

"Wha ya say, rude boy?" The dred asked, while trying to discreetly press a button under the register.

Nan caught his movement, and in one swift motion, pulled his hand out of his pocket and pistol-whipped the bony Rasta. The blow connected squarely to his temple, knocking him unconscious as he fell to the floor with a thud.

Nan quickly catapulted the counter and lightly pushed open the shoddy wooden door that led to the back room. His eyes surveyed his surroundings thoroughly, as he channeled his mind in order to pick up any sounds or movements. He could feel the presence of someone else in the distance. Crouching down, he cautiously walked forward. Nan failed to notice the surveillance camera hidden perfectly inside a brown ginger beer delivery box on top of a refrigerator in the front room. The dreds had purposely made a minute cutout on the side, just enough for the small lens to fit through.

The rear of building looked like an empty warehouse. There was no oven or any of the appliances needed to store or prepare food. Nan walked quietly on the balls of his feet, between the tall gray metal racks, juxtaposed throughout the room. The shelves that lined the racks extended from the floor to the ceiling. A middle aged Rastafarian spotted him as he reached an opening at the end of the row of empty racks. Instinctively, the dred jumped up from a small black table in the corner of the storeroom and started tossing a bag filled with weed into a plastic can that was nearby.

Nan pointed his gun at the man, fearfully stopping him in his tracks. As he started to cop a plea, Nan put his finger to his lips, invoking silence. The dred quickly put his hands over his head without resistance. Nan noticed that the can was filled with acid. Fearing a police raid, the panicky dred had wasted a brick of weed, and Nan wasn't even there for that.

"Where's the coke dred?" Nan yelled, while pointing his piece in his face.

"Me don't know," the dred responded in his thick accent, but his eyes glanced suspiciously at a door in the rear of the room as he spoke. It was a quick movement, but Nan caught it.

"Let's go!" Nan yelled, pushing the man in the direction of the door. With his hands over his head, he walked to the back of the storeroom, pausing to open the door that revealed a staircase leading upstairs.

With the door ajar now, he looked to Nan for direction.

"Go up the stairs," Nan said, while pressing the gun's cold barrel up against the back of his neck. The dred walked up the wooden steps, still cooperating. At the top of the stairs there was a gray reinforced metal door. He looked back at Nan, through fearful eyes. His facial expression gave Nan an uneasy feeling that he couldn't shake.

The door opened with ease as the man twisted the brass handle, surprising Nan. The massive door looked so intimidating, that he had kind of expected it to be locked. Things were looking easier than he expected. Almost too easy, he thought.

The area upstairs had obviously been renovated at some point, and was now an immaculate oversized office space and boardroom. It spanned the full length of the building. In the center of the room was a long mahogany table surrounded by at least twenty high backed Italian leather chairs. Pictures of various Jamaican posses and cartel members encased in solid gold frames adorned the walls. The room seemed so out of place.

Nan expected to see workers bagging up product, but as he scanned the room, he became a little concerned. There were brown cardboard boxes stacked on one side of the room, and three closed redwood doors directly on the opposite side. He began to wonder if there was even any cocaine in the building.

A curly haired light skinned man with chinky eyes, resembling the reggae star, Supercat sat at the far end of the table. Even though Nan didn't know it, the man was James Chin, the leader of the Jamaican drug syndicate in New York. He paid little attention to Nan when he first walked in. Sharply dressed in a flawless white linen suit and brown sandals, his eyes remained focused on the huge bay window that was facing the street. The thick black drapes that engulfed it allowed no visibility from outside.

Chin slowly took a long pull from a fat spliff he had just rolled, taking his time to inhale deeply. Thick smoky haze filled the room as he exhaled. His cockiness pissed Nan off. Nan repeated his mantra.

"Where's the coke at?" This time sounding more desperate.

"There's coke all around you," Chin responded nonchalantly, pausing to take a tote from the weed. "Best of the best, nuttin less. All dem package good n' plenty in de boxes gainst de wall."

Still holding the gun to the dred, Nan took the book bag off of his back. After following his normal routine of taking the folded duffel bag out and throwing both bags across to the far end of the table he said, "Fill them shits up!"

The man at the head of the table laughed aloud before saying, "Pack it your ras clot self. Me don't do manual labor, bumba ras."

"Well you gonna do that shit today nigga, or I'm a put a hole through your man!"

"Do as you will. Easy come easy go. He only a helper. Dem come a dime a dozen. Lick a shot," Chin responded, still smoking steadily.

Agitated, Nan knew that he didn't have much time. This was taking too long. He had only pistol-whipped the dred downstairs into submission. He could be awake and calling for help at that very moment.

"Bag the shit or I'm a kill this motherfucker!" Nan yelled out angrily.

"Shut your ras-clot lyin' and get out mi face,pussy clot yard—boy," Chin said with a sarcastic grin on his face.

Angrily, Nan moved his gun from the dred's back, and shot him in the back of his thigh. The dred let out a scream of anguish as he collapsed to the floor. Blood slowly begin to flow out of the wound.

Chin pulled from his spliff, laughing out loud again as he looked at Nan.

"Real bad boy shoot to kill, or they don' shoot ah-tall"

As the words left his mouth, Nan heard a creaking noise behind him. He instinctively turned around and saw the metal door that he used to enter the room slam shut, followed by the distinctive sound of a lock engaging. He turned back towards Chin, but he was gone. As Nan scanned his surroundings, the room went pitch black, as all of the lights were suddenly shut off. An eerie silence came over the room, followed by a sinister laugh.

Anxiety gripped Nan's insides, causing the pit of his stomach to churn. The room was dark and still. His eyes frantically gazed into the darkness, attempting to pick up any sudden movements. He heard a noise behind him, so he spun around quickly, but failed to see anything. Another sound forced him to spin back around towards the table, only noticing the red circular light on his chest a second before the bullet blasted through his left shoulder searing his skin. He fell to the ground absorbing the powerful jolt, as the sound of muffled gunfire exploded around him. The assassins were using silencers.

The sound of doors opening could be heard, breaking the uncomfortable silence that existed only seconds earlier. More red laser lights pierced the darkness in search of their target. Trained killers wearing infrared goggles and packing glocks began to pour into the room from the redwood doors Nan had noticed earlier. They were well equipped, and Nan was extremely out of his league. He crawled to the side of the table as he thought out his next move.

The dred he had shot in the leg earlier was sprawled out on the floor next to him. Nan pointed the pistol that he gripped in his hand towards the dred and shot him again. As he screamed, red dots trained on him quickly.

"Whoosh…whoosh…whoosh," could be heard as the muffled sound of bullets pierced the air and ripped into the dred's limp body. Nan tracked the source of the gunfire. As the dred screamed in anguish, Nan knelt down under the table and sent two bullets sailing through the air. A loud scream at the far end of the room let him know that he had hit his target.

He followed the red lights, trying to guesstimate how many killers were in his midst. He heard the faint sound of their footsteps as they filled the room, and lessened the distance between them and him. Realizing that time was not on his side, he had to seize the moment.

Nan swiftly hopped to his feet with a spring jump *(Tantiao)*, before delivering a punishing hook fist *(Gouquan)*, to the throat of an unsuspecting killer that had just stumbled upon him. The blow sent him stumbling backwards, gasping for air as he fell into the assassins closing in behind him. Their red laser light beams waved wildly in the air, as they stumbled over their brethren.

Nan was surrounded. The assassins were closing in from both sides of the table. He had to react quickly. Rising to his feet, he jumped up on the tabletop swiftly, the bottoms of his boots slipping on the polished surface momentarily before he gained traction. After steadying himself, he started running full speed towards the far end of the table. Orange blasts flickered from his cannon as he shot wildly in the air.

Red lasers pierced the darkness, tracking his movements and locking in. Silence overtook him. He breathed in deeply, focusing as he ran off of pure adrenaline. He knew his objective, and concentrated his mind solely on his goal. A small ray of light, visible through the bay window, served as his beacon. As the red beams engulfed him, he sprinted faster.

As he ran, a bullet whizzed past his head, missing him by less than an inch. The assassins were talking to one another, whispering orders and coordinating their attack. He heard two more silenced gunshots, but they missed their mark, lodging into the far wall. As Nan neared the edge of the table, his body jerked violently as a round pierced his chest, sending burning flesh blasting out of his back.

Excruciating pain and awareness of his own impending death, darkened his eyes and weakened his inner soul. Still, he kept running forward undeterred. Reaching the end of the table, he sent two shots from his cannon sailing through the window, before leaping into the air. He felt the drapes first, followed by the impact of the shattering window. Glass shards flew through the air, as the window broke into a thousand pieces.

The drapes that engulfed his body actually prevented him from getting cut by the jagged glass. He landed roughly on top of the roof of an old Lincoln Town Car parked 20 feet below, and rolled into the street just as the dreds sent multiple bullets ripping through the car's metal frame. Screaming pedestrians, shocked and confused by the violent outbreak ran for cover amidst the gunfire.

Badly wounded, Nan stumbled around the corner in search of his car, bleeding profusely from his wounds and coughing up thick foamy blood. As he walked, he looked towards the intersection where the accident had nearly occurred earlier, desperately searching for the eyes that belonged to his mother. They were nowhere to be found.

Slipping in and out of consciousness, he had no idea how he made it to Beth Israel Hospital. All he remembered was a nurse grabbing his bloody hand tightly as he struggled to breath.

He couldn't see her face, but she whispered, "Don't give up. You have to fight," over and over to him. Her voice was soothing. It sounded angelic.

Operation Falcon

After the usual morning roll call was finished, the officers that were gathered around began to dissipate as they headed off in various directions to conduct their scheduled tours. It was two months into autumn, and there wasn't much to talk about. Most of the drama was going on in Brooklyn with the investigation following the Yusef Hawkins murder, and they were happy to have the microscope off of them.

This was the 44th precinct. Corruption ran rampant in these parts, and they were trying their best to stay off of the radar screen. They had enough negative press with films like *Fort Apache The Bronx*, and they were desperately trying to steer clear of the negative press.

That was the reason Lieutenant Wilkes asked two of his Sergeants to stay behind after the roll call. Wilkes was an older black man in his late fifties, who had seen his fair share of street drama during his time. His hand shook noticeably and his left eye twitched when he spoke. No one really knew why, other than assuming that it was due to the stress that came along with the job. But nonetheless, it was even more noticeable when he became agitated.

He told his two Sergeants to sit down, as he stood in front of them with his arms crossed beneath his chest. His left eye twitched as he asked, "How's everything going?"

"Good," both Sergeants answered at the same time.

"That's good. I asked both of you to stay behind, because I needed to talk to you in private."

They nodded as they looked on, giving him their full attention. Wilkes wiped sweat off of his brow before he began to speak.

"I got a tip that IAD is about to come down hard on a few rogue cops in Brooklyn. Some stupid motherfuckers dealing crack and robbing drug dealers," he said, pausing mid-sentence to light a cigarette. His hand holding the lighter trembled, before he finally got it lit.

"I don't know what precinct, and quite frankly I don't really care. What I do care about is that this shit isn't going down out here. I'm giving you two forewarning that I'm not fucking around. If any of your guys are dirty, you better get them clean before IAD catches wind of the shit. I don't want any goddamn excuses."

Both Sergeants nodded their heads acknowledging that they fully understood what he was saying.

"Operation Falcon has these motherfuckers out there losing their goddamn minds. Robbing drug dealers and all other types of underhanded shit. But, this bullshit is about to end," Wilkes stated.

They both knew that if Wilkes took the time to pull them aside for this discussion, it was not to be taken lightly.

After the brief meeting, one of the Sergeants quickly headed out of the stationhouse and drove a couple of blocks to a payphone on the side of a bodega. He got paged a few minutes earlier, from a seven digit number followed by a familiar code that identified the caller. He made it a practice to never return coded pages from the station.

He push dialed the seven digits on the keypad, and waited while it rang a few times before a male picked up on the other end of the line and said, "Digangi."

"It's Carson," the Sergeant said.

"Hey, boss," Digangi responded, pausing to gather his thoughts.

"We need some more candy. The runaway slave still hasn't returned home, and the candy store is running dry. Is it possible to get more supplies from out there."

He was talking in code, but Carson knew exactly what he was saying. Nan had been missing for a few months, ever since the Jamaican robbery went bad. Shit was drying up in Brooklyn. He had been compensating by providing coke from robberies he had some kids doing locally in the Bronx. But, now he'd have to shut that down as well.

"No go. The candy's no longer kosher, it's starting to cause cavities. The dentist is about to pay a visit. Countdown to shutdown should begin," Carson said in response.

"Understood. We'll speak later."

"Later," he replied before hanging up.

Carson had the jitters as he hopped back into his car. His mouth was dry and he felt clammy under his arms from prespiration. He had been in the Bronx for awhile now, after accepting a promotion to Sergeant and agreeing to the subsequent transfer that followed shortly thereafter.

Everything seemed to fall into place so perfectly. He had masterminded the successful operation in Brooklyn, forging a partnership with Sonny that had gotten him out of debt, and made both of them very wealthy. This had prompted him to start a similar operation in the Bronx. It was in its infancy, but the young thugs that he recruited were working out well. They weren't Nan, but they got the job done nonetheless.

Speaking of Nan, Carson still marveled at how well things had worked out with him. He had been reluctant to deceive him at first, but the situation offered no other alternatives. But, even he was surprised at Nan's love for him and Joe. That love had turned him into a skilled thief and a ruthless assassin, all to protect those that he held close to his heart.

Carson was himself an orphan. Tossed in a dumpster as an infant and left for dead, he never knew his parents and never really learned how to love anyone but himself. His wife recognized this, by exposing the shallow interior that existed beneath the façade exhibited by his fraudulent exterior.

When he saw Nan standing in the intersection the night his parents were murdered, he saw a reflection of himself. The story of both boys losing their parents on the same night only helped to make things even more compelling. He sincerely wanted both of them to grow up together, and he planned on playing a huge role in their lives. But, the novelty of fatherhood quickly wore off, and his selfish motives overwhelmed him. Love was so overrated. Long ago he accepted the fact that he didn't need anybody but himself.

The day dragged on while Carson performed his regular job duties mindlessly. His thoughts were constantly drifting elsewhere. After the sunset and his tour ended, he headed over to a small hole in the wall bar in Coney Island, with much anticipation.

Rodriguez and Digangi were already sitting at a table in the corner, downing some shots of 151. Carson grabbed a bottle of Jack Daniels at the bar before joining them at the table shortly thereafter.

A few minutes later, Dickson walked through the door looking disheveled and wild eyed. He was a short brown skinned cop in his mid-thirties. You'd never think that he was that young with his pock face and the deep wrinkled craters that ran through his forehead like an interstate map. Life hadn't been easy on him, and his body provided visual proof. He scanned the room until he spotted his partners in crime at their usual spot in the corner. Hurriedly he walked over to the table and said, "Sorry Boss."

"No biggie," Carson replied, his words betraying his true feelings. Dickson worked in the Bronx just like him. He should have been at the meeting on time. Showing up late was blatant disrespect.

Chugging down a shot glass of JD, Carson quickly glanced at Digangi, Rodriguez and Dickson. All of their lifestyles put them in situations where they needed money. Whether it was kids, bad credit, mortgages or rent, they each had obligations. So, they all counted on the loot they were making on the side. That's why they were each perfect for the operation. But, with things about to get shut down, Carson knew that they would each take the news extremely hard.

"Listen, the gravy train has dried up. IAD has cracked down on Operation Falcon, and they're going to be focusing their internal investigations directly on Brooklyn and probably the Bronx shortly thereafter," Carson said, cutting right to the chase.

"How do you know. I mean, do they know about us?" Dickson asked, while frowning up his face disgustedly.

Carson glared at him like he was an idiot. Dickson's ignorance pissed him off.

"Listen, I heard it from a credible source, and that's all the fuck you need to know. I don't know what they know, but I know what the fuck we need to do."

"Whatever you say boss, just let us know what's what," Digangi responded.

Carson looked over his shoulder to make sure no one was in earshot. The bar was buzzing with the regular after work crowd. After he confirmed that no one was paying them any attention, he finished his thought.

"You need to start cleaning up shop. Trust no one. The dealers we fuck with, take em' out. Make it seem related to the game."

Rodriguez shook her head from side to side. She had a stunned facial expression as she said, "I can't go down for this Carson. My kids. I mean, I can't even imagine Jose raising my kids. And—"

"Look, save the tears for a nigga who cares," Carson said, while holding his hand up and interrupting her rudely.

"If we do this shit right, nobody goes down. We close up shop, lay low, and maybe we can be back in business in a year or so. But for now, cut your loose ends and shut down shop. Understood?"

Everyone nodded their heads in agreement. Carson took a couple of swigs directly from the bottle of JD, before leaving the bar. The rest of the crew left shortly afterwards, one at a time. All going in separate directions as always.

On bended knee

It was approximately 9 o'clock in the evening and a light drizzling rain was sprinkling the ground, covering it in a light mist. It was only the middle of October, but winter's cold breath had began to blow its way into town, making the air feel cold as a witch's tit. Kimba placed her hands in front of the heat vent, rubbing them together as she tried to warm them up. The BMW's leather seats felt so frigid when she sat down. Even with a full length leather coat with lining on, she could feel the coldness permeate through her skin.

Power laughed when he sat in the driver's seat next to her.

"Damn, it ain't even that cold out here yet and you shivering. Imagine when it really get cold."

He only had on a Champion hoodie, but he was just fine. Kimba just sucked her teeth, barely paying him any mind as she kept her hands glued to the vent.

They were headed out for a night on the town. The kids were at Shawnika's house, a sixteen year old that lived two floors up from Kimba. She watched the kids from time to time, but only when her mother was home to supervise. Shawnika was trustworthy, but she was just at that age when boys start coming around. Kimba knew about those times all too well.

Power glanced down at his watch a few times catching Kimba's attention, but when she asked him what was going on, he just brushed it off. He was running late. Dipping in and out of traffic, he did his best to make up for lost time, but he knew that he was still going to be late. He cursed himself for spending so much time at the jewelry store earlier that day. But, he had to be sure. Everything had to be just right.

Kimba's patience was running thin. Her stomach was grumbling, and their reservations for Copelands were for nine thirty. They were late already, and judging by the direction Power was driving in, they weren't headed towards Harlem.

"Where are you going Power? I'm hungry as hell and you driving all the way to west bubblefuck," Kimba spat out, unable to contain herself any longer.

Already frustrated, Power angrily lashed back, "We gonna get something to fucking eat. Why don't you just be patient? Damn!"

"Fuck you, nigga! You can take me the fuck home."

"Yeah, whatever. Fucking bitch," he mumbled under his breath.

"What?" Kimba asked, but he didn't respond. He knew that she heard what he said, and he already regretted saying it. He was stressed out and he always had a problem dealing with tense situations. But he didn't mean it. Tonight was supposed to be a beautiful event. Everything was supposed to be perfect.

Glancing over at Kimba's face, he knew that he had to do something to salvage the night. She was glancing out the side window, and her whole grill was screw faced. Her arms were crossed in front of her and she had that, *"Nigga please,"* look on her face. She definitely wasn't having it.

It was around nine twenty when Power pulled the car over on a street somewhere in East New York. He was twenty minutes late, but he knew that the people he was meeting with never arrived on time. Kimba hadn't even been paying attention anymore. She was too pissed off to give a damn. She was ready to go home, and make herself a fried bologna sandwich or something.

Power glanced out the window before he began fidgeting around, fishing in his pants pocket. When he finally came across what he was looking for, he turned and faced towards Kimba.

"I planned on doing this later tonight, but if I wait any longer I may not get the chance," Power said, pausing to clear his throat from anxiety. "I'm not perfect, you know. I got a lot of shit that I need to get straight in my life, but I'm working on it."

Kimba turned towards him. Her face was still frowned up.

"I know that I told you that I was gonna stop hustling and I ain't been true to my word, but word is bond I'm ready to give all of this shit up for you. If you take me for me, as is…through motherfuckin' thick and thin, I'll give this whole shit up after tonight."

Kimba shook her head disgustedly and looked away from him, focusing on nothing in particular as she sucked her teeth.

"I've heard it all before Power. When you was locked up you said you wasn't gonna deal no more. Then you come home and you told me you was gonna find a job. Then you tell me you can't find a job, but you just doing a little bit of shit on the side, and you can't really get into it but there's no chance that you could go back to jail dealing with the cats you rolling with. I'm sick of this shit Power. I can get dick from any nigga. I want a family. I want someone to be there for me."

The street was so dark that Kimba barely saw what was in the box Power held in his hand. He grabbed her by the chin and gently turned her towards him nervously.

"I'm wearing my heart on my sleeve right now. On da real, I'll give it all up for you. I may have to work at Pathmark or some shit, but I want to spend the rest of my life with you. Will you marry me, Kimba?"

Kimba's jaw dropped as she stared at the princess cut diamond engagement ring that he was holding in his hand. She was speechless. She wondered if she was dreaming. Finally, the kids would have a real daddy that was there all of the time. Finally, she would have a man to claim as her own. She didn't care if they were rich or poor, as long as they were together.

"Well?" Power asked, as he smiled patiently waiting for an answer.

"Oh my god, oh my god. Of course I'll marry you. I love you so much Power," She replied ecstatically as she hugged him tightly. He hugged her back, basking in her warm embrace.

After a couple of minutes passed he said, "I hope you're not mad that I didn't do it on bended knee. I can do it again if you want."

"Nah, you don't have to do nothing again. I can't wait to tell Dawn and Michelle. Are we gonna have a big wedding? Cuz you got a lot of friends and so do I and—"

Power interrupted her, smiling as he said, "Don't worry baby, we gonna do it up. Horse and carriage and everybody and they momma gonna be there. Then after that we gonna have to move down south or sumthin, cuz if I gotta get a real job I ain't gonna be up around the way where everybody could see me."

The whole time he was talking he stared into her eyes deeply, wondering why she no longer seemed excited.

"We don't have to move down south," he thought to himself. It was just a suggestion. He didn't expect it to damper the mood. But, he noticed that her eyes were no longer focused on him. She seemed to be looking through him, off to his side. The look of excitement in her eyes had suddenly changed into a panic stricken gaze.

Sensing something was terribly wrong, he glanced towards his side window just as a 9-millimeter slug shattered the window and blasted through his skull at point blank range. Chunks of his brain and skull fragments showered Kimba's face, as she screamed out at the top of her lungs.

Coolly, the masked gunman unloaded half a clip into Power's body, before walking around to the passenger's side of the car. As Kimba saw him take position near her and square up, she urinated on herself from pure fright. She shivered uncontrollably, attempting to hide in the small space between the floor and dashboard, as the gunman leveled his gun and pointed it towards her.

Kimba's soft eyes met the gunman's menacing pupils for seconds that seemed to last a lifetime. He placed the index finger of his right hand to his lips, motioning her to be quiet, as he gripped the handle of the nine in the southpaw stance. His brown skin was visible through the holes for his eyes that were cut out of the knitted mask.

Fear gripped her fragile soul. She closed her eyes tightly and screamed loudly, as she squirmed around in the pool of blood and glass on the floor, trying to find a safe haven. There was no place to move and no place to go. Her heart pounded in her chest.

The seconds quickly turned into minutes of eerie silence, as she awaited the inevitable. Her sobbing was interrupted by two teenagers that were walking home from a house party, sharing a forty ounce of Old English. They noticed the shattered window glass on the pavement next to the beemer, and upon further investigation, they found Kimba sitting on the floor of the car, shivering as she leaned her back against the door. Warm tears were streaming out of her blood shot eyes.

"Yo, Miss. You alright?" One of the boys asked.

She didn't acknowledge him. Through unfeeling eyes, she stared at the bloody diamond ring she held in her hand. Power's lifeless body lay beside her.

About fifteen minutes later in the Bronx, Carson received a page that he rushed to return from a payphone next to his favorite bodega. It was Dickson's code, and Dickson's voice he heard on the other end of the phone after he dialed the number.

"It's done," Dickson said calmly.

"Everything's straight?" Carson asked.

"The last ice cream man has been retired today. We don't have to worry about any more deliveries."

"Good. I'll get up with you later."

After hanging up with Dickson, Carson called *Sonny's Chicken and Rib,* and reached Gunner who promptly put his boss on the line. Carson had let Sonny know about the little side business he was conducting a few months back, and he gave him his blessing for a small percentage and also the promise that Carson's dealers weren't going to be profiting in the areas in which he operated. Their shit was cool. He just wanted to give him a heads up on the latest developments.

Sonny answered the phone in his deep baritone voice and said, "What's going on baby? Speak to me."

"We're all good, everything from BK to the Bronx has been shut down."

"Good, good. So, all your little hustlers have been retired?"

"Taken care of."

"Alright, we'll get up later."

"Cool," Carson replied. He was just about to hang up the phone when he heard Sonny say, "Yo, Cee. You still there?"

"Yeah, what's up?"

"What happened to the cats you had intercepting the supply channels?" He asked, trying to be as vague as possible.

"We laid off our little helper from the Bronx a few weeks back."

"Oh, that's unfortunate. I hope that his family will be able to get by without the extra income."

"Yeah, they should be fine."

"What about the two delivery boys you sent by here to see me before?"

Carson paused for a second, realizing that he was referring to Nan and Joe. He thought out his words before speaking, finally saying, "One is out on disability and the other never really worked for us. There's no need to be concerned about them."

"I want them to be officially laid off as well. We can't take any chances," Sonny responded in a serious tone.

"Like I said, they're of no concern," Carson responded firmly.

"If it was me, I would separate both them niggas from payroll. But that's on you, I'll let you make that call. If it comes back to haunt us, that's on you as well."

With that the line went dead. Sonny had hung up. His message was understood.

Lost and found

$\mathcal{J}$oe woke up out of his sleep in a cold sweat. His *Fruit of the Looms* t-shirt was uncomfortably pasted to the skin on his wet back. He glanced over at Shay who was sound asleep by his side, hugging a pillow as she snored lightly. He envied her. She had the uncanny ability to knock out as soon as her head hit the pillow. On the other hand, he had tossed and turned all night uncomfortably as he dozed in and out of a light sleep.

He had so much on his plate between school and tutoring, but surprisingly none of that was on his mind. His thoughts were elsewhere. No matter how often he tried to ease his mind, he kept thinking about Nan. His stomach churned uneasily as he stood up from the bed and walked into the bathroom.

Splashing water on his face, he thought about when they last spoke about a week ago. He couldn't believe that he was still with Leslie. Never in his wildest dreams did he think that Nan would actually find someone to replace Latoya. But he did, and Joe was extremely happy for him. He also had found a job, which made Joe proud as well.

Nan had never told him about the events that led up to him being shot. In the hospital he brushed it off, and never answered Joe's questions or addressed his concerns. And as he recovered from his wounds during the weeks that followed, he always found a way to avoid the topic. It was typical of Nan.

Joe had personally been overwhelmed with his own day-to-day activities, but he decided that he needed to have a heart to heart with him when they got up with each other tomorrow. If Nan was going through some drama, he had to be there for him. No matter what it entailed, that was his brother. He'd give his life for him.

After finishing up in the bathroom, Joe headed into the living room and sat down in a swivel chair in front of his wooden desk. Moonlight eased through the slats in the blinds, creating a calming atmosphere. After a minute or two, Joe turned on his desk lamp before he grabbed a small stack of fifty or so white papers that he had piled up neatly next to his typewriter. He thumbed through them slowly. It was a self-biographical piece titled, "Lost and Found," that he had started writing before he encountered a mild case of writer's block.

Looking through the pages closely, he encountered some minor grammatical errors, which he highlighted before scribbling notes in the margins. This was his first attempt at writing a novel, and it was based on his childhood. He wanted it to be just right. He started reading it from the beginning again. As he scanned the double spaced lines, his eyes started getting heavy and before long he started to doze off.

His head was resting on the wooden desktop when the intercom buzzer in his apartment sounded off. He popped his head up and wiped the saliva off of the corner of his mouth, before he walked over and pressed the button on the intercom.

"Who is it?"

Through the distortion, he could hear a female with a Spanish accent on the other end say, "I left my key in my apartment. Can you let me in please?"

Joe wiped the sleep out of his eyes and said, "I'll be right there."

This was inconvenient, but it wasn't out of the ordinary. The intercom mechanism that allowed keyless entry into the building broke recently, and unfortunately for him, he lived on the first floor. Over the past two days, he had to let in at least five people.

He placed his manuscript on a wooden table next to the door and started undoing the lock. He made a mental note to speak to his landlord in the morning about this. An ominous feeling came over him as he opened his door and stepped out into the hallway. It was indescribable, but awkward nonetheless.

Turning as he headed towards the apartment building's front door, he could feel the presence of someone else in the hallway. He planted his feet just as a stocky figure lunged out of the shadows swinging a switchblade wildly. The swift action caught Joe by surprise, but he avoided the brunt of the attack, adeptly stepping backwards just as the blade sliced through his t-shirt and tore a layer of flesh that lined his chest.

A stinging pain shot through him, but he regrouped quickly and parried the next attack before turning and retreating back to his apartment. His attacker gave chase as he scurried. He could hear the deep heavy breaths behind him. The footsteps clanging against the tiled floor grew louder as the distance between them lessened.

Joe crashed into the metal doorframe, as he frantically stumbled into his apartment, and hurriedly attempted to slam the door behind him. His bloodied hand gripped the brass handle, almost closing the door completely before the figure on the other side pushed it in forcefully, sending him reeling backwards. He knocked over the small table next to the door, sending the loose paper from his manuscript flying through the air like confetti.

Joe's heart skipped a beat. He planted his feet and raised his arms defensively, preparing to face his stocky attacker. Fear gripped his heart in an unbreakable grasp. It was written all over his face.

The next attack came swiftly and unprovoked. In the apartment's narrow hallway, Joe was unable to dodge his attacker's vicious lunge. He thought about Thaddeus briefly, as the jagged blade ripped into his stomach muscles. He wondered what he would do in a similar situation. He wished that he had given in on the countless occasions that Nan tried to coax him into practicing the arts again.

Bloody drool ran out of his mouth, as he struggled with his attacker, valiantly attempting to pull the knife out of his stomach, to no avail. His enemy was too powerful. He pinned Joe's back against the wall, leaning his shoulder into his chest as he ripped the knife upward, tearing through his flesh violently. Joe grunted in pain, as blood lined the spaces between his teeth.

His thoughts drifted, as he thought about a recurring nightmare he had as a teenager. As his assailant plunged the knife deeper into his flesh, a revelation came upon him. After all of these years, he finally realized that the faceless man with the innocent eyes being stabbed to death in his dreams, was actually him.

The struggle ended quickly. Joe slid down the wall slowly, leaving a bloody streak behind him, before collapsing to the floor with a thud. A pool of blood poured out of his stomach, drenching the pages of his manuscript that were littered across the floor. He mustered as much strength as he could, forcing himself to look into the bedroom that was directly to his right. Through the darkness his eyes met Shay's.

The disturbance had awakened her only seconds earlier. Without talking, she was able to read his facial expression. Something was terribly wrong. His eyes warned her. He was already gone, and he desperately wanted her to save herself. Hesitantly, she inched off of the mattress, and slid underneath the Queen sized bed. Sneakers and shoes lined the side of the bed facing the door, but the end that she was on near the window was clear.

As she inched further beneath the bed, her body tensed up out of fear, and a cold sweat slicked her skin. She thought about Joe, wondering who had done this to him. Her nose ran as the tears came down her face. She didn't breathe, didn't move and didn't utter a sound when the killer walked into the bedroom startling her.

A flashlight scanned the room and footsteps echoed as they touched the polished wooden floor. Dickson bent down on his knees and shined the flashlight underneath the bed. Shay thought she felt her heart stop as the light radiated her face. Dickson looked from side to side, missing her in the sea of shoes and sneakers. Standing back on his feet, he opened the bedroom closet and looked inside quickly.

"All clear in here Digangi," Dickson yelled out as he walked back into the hallway.

Shay let out a sigh of relief as he walked out. In the hallway, she heard muffled voices speaking. She listened on hearing what she could.

"Let's spread the shit out and get the fuck outta here. I'll put the coke in the kitchen," Digangi said.

"I'll put the gun and the money in the bedroom," Rodriguez said in a whisper.

A sudden calmness came over Shay. The shivering stopped. The pounding in her chest slowed to a delayed beat, in preparation for whatever her fate would be. The sound of footsteps echoed across the floor again. She felt the presence of someone nearby. They were hovering over the side of the bed where she hid.

A ripping noise could be heard as a knife sliced through the side of the box spring. The bed creaked and slumped in the middle as the figure she saw enter the room climbed on the bed and placed a gun under the pillow. Footsteps clanged against the floor again, echoing as they left the room.

Shay exhaled a deep breath, listening intently as she heard voices whispering in the hallway.

"We're good. One down one to go."

Then there was complete silence. She lay in the fetal position, arms hugging her knees. Her emotions coming to a head, as she sobbed uncontrollably. She was frozen in fear.

Outside, Digangi, Rodriguez and Dickson discretely filtered back into the rear of the van. The streets were fairly empty, and those still out were completely oblivious to what had just taken place.

Carson was seated behind the steering wheel. He turned around with a devious look in his eyes and asked, "Is it done?"

"Yeah, easy as pie Sarge," Dickson responded confidently.

Carson's facial expression was unmoved. It didn't express elation or dissatisfaction. With coldness in his eyes, and a latent menace in his voice he said, "Let's go finish this shit."

Confidently, Dickson smiled and said, "Shiiit...the way this is going, I may be home in time to catch the reruns of *Sanford and Son*," laughing under his breath sarcastically.

Carson didn't find him the least bit funny. In anger he contorted his face and hissed, "Fuck *Sanford and Son*. Focus on the shit at hand. This motherfucker Nan is a whole different breed, than the nigga you just killed."

With that, he started the van and pulled away from the curb slowly. They were headed to the Manhattan Bridge, en route to Albany Avenue in Brooklyn.

BETRAYAL: 5

NAN RELUCTANTLY TOOK OFF his leather bomber, before bending down and picking up the sword. He stared into Thaddeus's eyes. His facial expression was one of deep concentration. The anger and bitterness his body emitted, shot through Nan like a cold winter wind. Fear gripped his heart, as he wrapped his hand around the sword's handle and prepared to fight his Master.

"I came here for your help. I need you to help me, and you want to kill me. What's this all about?" Nan asked in a hollow voice, almost pleadingly.

In the same bitter tone but a slightly more pronounced accent, Thaddeus responded, "I told you to leave, but you didn't listen."

"So, because I didn't listen, you wanna kill me?" Nan asked dumbfounded.

Thaddeus begin to move around him slowly in a circular manner, lessening the distance between them with each step. As they moved deeper into the dojo, darkness enveloped them. The translucent candlelight from the back room only provided a soft glow. Thaddeus's eye focused in on Nan's silhouette.

"I warned you. I told you that a true Samurai is bound to any man who has put his own life on the line to preserve the life force that exists within the Samurai. *Seen? But, ya not listen.*"

Recognizing his strategy, and capturing his movements, Nan began to walk foot over foot to his right, emulating Thaddeus.

"So, what does that have to do with me? I need your help!" Nan yelled out, his words full of angry emotion.

Unfazed and still in deep concentration, Thaddeus responded, "Many years ago, I was on a classified mission, in the jungles of South America. The thing go wrong, and we soon come across an enemy that was better equipped than we...and much better trained," he paused mid-sentence to study Nan's movements, noticing that he was attempting to greaten the distance between them. He changed directions mid-step, throwing Nan off as he said, "I lay face down in the middle of the jungle, blood oozing from me chest. I was ready to meet Jah, just as a young soldier come upon me. He threw me over his shoulder and dodged enemy fire, risking his life for the sake of mine. From that day on, I made a life long blood oath, to forever be indebted to the marine that sacrificed his own well being, to save me life. That Marine's name was—"

"Mark Carson," Nan said, finishing his sentence for him. There was a look of revelation on his face. It was all beginning to make sense now. The night when he flipped out in the dojo, he remembered that

Thaddeus said he was bound to two men for eternity. His Sifu, that was dead, and a man that was alive. He vowed that he would give his life for either man. Nan completely understood. Thaddeus had not only taught him the arts, he had taught him about the culture, intently focusing on instilling values that reflected honor, courage and commitment.

Thaddeus nodded, acknowledging that Nan was correct.

"You always were quick witted."

"So, all of this time *you knew* what was up? *You knew* what I was going through and you just let it happen to me."

Inside, Thaddeus was paining. The words hurt him, because he truly did care about Nan. He was more than a student, he was like a son to him. But, the value he placed on his blood oath came first, and nothing could change that. He had accepted that. And, even though he struggled to deal with the inevitable, so did Nan.

"I had no commitment to you but to teach you the art of war...the skill of self defense. Teachers teach, and good students listen and learn. If you had only listened a *likkle* bit more, you would not be in the situation you're in."

"You're defending someone that didn't deserve to live in the first place. That's why I pumped shotgun shells into him when he tried to kill me. He lied to me. He—"

Thaddeus interrupted Nan's sentence by launching a swift attack with his sword. As he leaped inwards, Nan parried the attack. He evasively moved to his right, before performing a high jump and an outward fan kick *(Tengkong Waibailian)* in midair that connected flush against Thaddeus's jaw.

Thaddeus paused to wipe his hand across his face, and lick the blood off of his lip. His yellow teeth were visible in the darkness, as a sinister grin came across his face.

"I see you've been practicing. I underestimated you once, but I won't do it again brethren."

His next attack came without warning, with the quickness and precision that Nan remembered from the days when they sparred in the gym. Back then Thaddeus would perform a slew of moves that he never bothered to teach the boys. His sword cut through the air, slicing through the sleeve of the camouflaged shirt that Nan wore, catching his shoulder in the process. He didn't let up, continuing forward as he fended off Nan's feeble attacks and attempts to defend himself.

"More chi," he yelled out, as he forcefully delivered a pushing palm strike *(Tuizhang)* with his left hand to Nan's stomach, followed by a sword attack that Nan tried to block in vain. It sliced into his right forearm, causing blood to spray in the air. His sword sailed across the room as it flew from his hand.

The wind was knocked out of him, and excruciating pain shot through his body. The attack was too quick for Nan to defend himself. Even when he managed to block the blows they hurt intensely. He struggled to catch his breath as he retreated backwards. Thaddeus's dreadlocks swung wildly in the air, as he followed in quick pursuit, yelling as he delivered a punishing tornado kick *(Xuanfengjiao)* to Nan's chest.

The force of the blow knocked him off of his feet and on his back.

Nan rolled over and slowly hopped back on his feet, searching through the darkness as he tried to locate Thaddeus. He turned to his left just as a vicious backhanded smack was delivered to his face, causing blood to flow into his left eye as Thaddeus's knuckles ripped a gash into his eyelid. It felt like his eye socket was busted. Nan saw stars, as he balled up his fists weakly and limped backwards.

Thaddeus changed styles, moving towards Nan in the stumbling fashion of a drunken monk. The powerful front flex kick *(Zhengtitui)* that he delivered to Nan's chest seemed to come out of nowhere. The impact sent him flying backwards, crashing through the metal blinds before breaking the glass panes in the window. Glass shards flew in the air, landing on the shoddy fire escape that was right outside the window, while other pieces fell to the floor with the blinds. Rays of light shot into the room revealing Thaddeus who was now standing in front of Nan clutching his sword with both hands.

Nan was seated in the windowsill. He fidgeted slightly as he sat looking at Thaddeus's menacing figure approach him. The fight in him was gone. His limbs felt weak. He mentally prepared himself for death as all true Samurai should.

His mind drifted to thoughts of his mother...seeing visions of his father...Joe...Leslie.

As Thaddeus slowly approached in attack mode, he menacingly mumbled, "Prepare to return to the essence."

Nan thought about Latoya...little Nathan.

The attack came swiftly, as Thaddeus swung his sword, sending it through the air cutting through the wind. Nan closed his eyes as he listened for the sounds that to most are often not heard. With his eyes closed, he was able to see what to most would go unseen. With the sword less than a foot from his head, he ducked and dropped into a bow stance *(Gongbu)*, before quickly grabbing a glass shard with his right hand and delivering an upward strike.

The sharp pointy end of the jagged glass tore through the muscles that lined the front of Thaddeus's throat, ripping a gaping hole to the back of his neck as it severed his esophagus. The attack caught him by complete surprise. He was ill prepared to defend himself. His sword dropped to the floor making a clanging noise, before he fell to his knees clutching his neck with both hands. His mouth was wide open, emitting thick bloody foam as he gasped for air. He had trained his student well...perhaps to well. He stared at Nan in a state of shock, smiling slightly before his eyes rolled back in his head and he fell forward on his face with a thud.

"More chi, Master...more chi, train harder." Nan mumbled to himself, as he turned towards the window, and used the light from the street lamps to study himself. The breeze coming in felt good as it blew against his battered face. The sleeves of his shirt were ripped to shreds. He tugged at a piece that was hanging off of his shirt and used it to dress a wound on his arm that he had suffered from the sword attack. Snow flurries had started to fall, coating the ground with a light cushion. He wiped the sweat off of his forehead with one of his tattered sleeves, adrenaline still rushing through his body.

"Bravo. Bravo. Very well done. I was just about to leave, when you arrived. Man, I would have been pissed off if I missed that *Enter the Dragon* shit that just went down," the voice bellowed from behind him. Nan knew the voice all to well. But, how could it be, he wondered? He killed him. He blasted him off of his feet with his shotgun.

He turned around and looked at Carson standing in front of him. One arm was in a sling, and the other he used to steady his hand that gripped a 9mm semiautomatic pistol. A sinister smile was on his face as he said, "You look like you seen a ghost."

"I fuckin' killed you nigga," Nan spewed out. Hatred filled his words.

Carson chuckled before saying, "Body armor baby. Same shit I had Rodriguez give you. If you had worn it a few months back, those fuckin' curry goat eatin' Jamaicans wouldn't have almost killed your ass. But, that's you, never changed. Still the same old stubborn assed *Lemonhead*."

"Don't call me that motherfucker. I did all this shit for you. To protect your ass, and this is how you repay me?" His words were full of emotion.

Carson cracked a sarcastic grin. "Damn, don't take this shit personal baby. It wasn't all for me. You had a good run…took your little money off of the top and shit. You never complained about that, right? But, everything comes to an end. This shit is just business."

"Business? Just business? You were like a father to me. I would of died for you."

"And you will," Carson sneered. He stared at Nan through unfeeling eyes, before finishing his thought.

"Remember that day at my crib when you asked me if I would kill someone over money. *Remember that shit?* Well, damn skippy nigga. In a New York minute if it's what's necessary to protect my interests. And you would too. Me and you are one and the same."

"Fuck you...I'm nothing like you," Nan responded scornfully.

Carson laughed cynically, "Nah, we're cut from the same cloth, that's why I knew you'd pop up over here sooner or later. We think just alike...just different interests. Like you said, you would of died for me. And shiitt, you managed to kill a few drug dealers because you thought you were protecting Joe. *Same shit, just different interests.* I'm a businessman and you're a heartless killer and a ruthless assassin."

"I didn't just go out and kill nobody. I was forced to do what I did. I defended myself. "

"Hmm...the dreds, Roach and his niggas. Need I say more? Oh yeah? I almost forgot Jerome Reddy?"

"What about him? That's the only body that you can put on me. And that nigga got what he deserved."

Carson laughed aloud cynically.

"You're right, he did...*about three years ago.* That pipe head overdosed shortly after he killed your parents. Heroin or sumthin. I never got around to telling you that shit. It slipped my mind I guess," Carson said with a smile.

Furiously Nan said, "You're a liar…a fuckin' liar. So, who was that nigga I killed?"

"Different Jerome. That motherfucker was an informant. A little favor for a friend," Carson said, pausing as he cracked a sinister smile.

"Plus, I wanted to see how far you would go, and I was right. You're a killer. I knew that you were the right nigga to help me out of my financial bind."

Taken aback, Nan looked at him in disbelief before asking, "What about one on one? That was all bullshit too?"

"Fuck one on one. This shit is about doe-ree-mi. Like I said, it's business Nan. It's the American way," he responded belligerently.

His words were intentionally cold, as he raised the gun and pointed it at Nan's chest. Nan shook his head in disgust, fearlessly looking down the barrel of the gun.

"What about Joe? What are you gonna tell him? How are you gonna explain this shit to him?"

Carson laughed aloud unfazed. "I ain't gonna tell him shit. Matter fact, you can tell that nigga the whole story when you join him."

Nan's jaw dropped, and his heart felt like it skipped a beat. "What…what the fuck do you mean?" He asked in a weak tone, already knowing the answer.

"I sent that nigga to join his parents just before we visited your house," he paused to laugh coldly before adding, "Maybe after I shoot your ass, all of you can get together and have a big family reunion or some shit."

Anger burned through Nan's veins as he rushed towards Carson with all his energy. He made it two steps before the bullets started hitting him.

"*Pop! Pop! Pop, pop, pop!*"

Five shots to the chest blasted him backwards, his body landing in a sea of shattered glass and blood next to Thaddeus.

Carson blew the tip of his gun like a cowboy in an old western, before coolly placing it in his holster. Then he reached into his pocket and grabbed a clunky gray cell phone that he had bought a few days earlier, and dialed a seven-digit number. After a few seconds, a male on the other end picked up and said, "Speak."

"It's done, Sonny." Carson said.

"Good," he responded, before hanging up.

A cool breeze blew through the window behind him, as Carson put away his phone and pulled a whiskey flask out of his back pocket. He turned around towards the window smiling widely.

"I'm a just pour a little liquor out for my homeboys who ain't here no more."

Carson glanced down at the floor, and saw Thaddeus still lying in a pool of blood, but Nan was gone. Frantically, he ran over to the window, and looked outside at the fire escape. There were footprints and little drops of blood visible in the cottony snow. Carson climbed out onto the fire escape and descended the ladder.

When he reached the sidewalk, he glanced down towards his feet. Laying in the concrete was a bulletproof vest, with hot rounds still stuck in it. It was the same kind he wore. The same kind that he told

Rodriguez to give to Nan. He cursed under his breath as he followed the path of the footprints. There was no trace of them once they made it to the street.

Nan sped as fast as he could down the snow-slicked streets of Brooklyn, parking his car up the block from Latoya's crib. It was eleven fifty-five. The streets were bare. He took shallow breaths, wincing as sharp pains shot through his chest. He figured that a couple of his ribs had probably been bruised when he took the barrage of bullets from Carson's gun. His arm was still bleeding, and he undoubtedly required some form of medical attention.

He waited in between two brownstones directly across the street from Latoya's house, taking advantage of the dark cover they provided. At twelve o'clock, Latoya walked out slowly, carrying little Nathan. He was wide awake, squirming in her arms as she opened the car door and strapped him into the car seat. She started the car in order to warm up the engine, while she got out and scraped ice off of the windows, constantly looking down at her watch.

At ten after, she still sat in her car, tears streaming down her face as she sobbed uncontrollably. Nan looked on, wanting to join her, wanting to hold her in his arms. But, as much as he yearned to, he knew that he couldn't. He had some loose ends to take care of if they were ever going to have a future together. Plus, he had to avenge the deaths of Joe, Leslie, Ms. Cooper and her grandson D.J.

At twelve fifteen, Latoya slowly pulled away from the curb teary-eyed. She looked right in Nan's direction, unable to see him concealed in the darkness.

He stared at her face, as a warm tear fell from his own eye. His stomach churned as his emotions got the best of him. He vowed to join them one day. He swore that they would be a family.

Back at the dojo, Carson was sitting outside in his car getting loaded off of whiskey, when his cell phone rang. He just got the phone and had only given the number to a select group of people, so he knew it had to be important.

"This is Carson," he said as he answered his phone.

"Hey, what's up my main man. It's Dave."

"Oh, what's up, Dave?" Carson responded dryly. Dave Williams was a cop that started on the force with him years ago. Now he worked dispatch out of a precinct in Manhattan. They were still close friends, but Dave's timing wasn't always the best.

"Damn, sorry to disturb you my man, I know that you must be pulling your hair out and shit."

"Yeah, things is a little hectic. But, what's up?"

Now whispering in a low tone Dave said, "You looked out for me a couple of weeks ago with that money to put the down payment on my crib, so I wanted to return the favor."

"Don't worry about that shit. You know how we do Dave. I'll hit you up if I need it back."

"Nah, this ain't about the money," Dave responded.

"What's up then?"

"I just got a call from a chick named Shedanka. She was blowing her nose in the phone sobbing and shit, saying that her apartment got broken into last night. I was about to send one of my guys over there to check it out, but when she said that her boyfriend was murdered as well, I thought I should call you. I thought you'd be interested." Dave said calmly.

"Why's that? What else did she say?" Carson asked, in a tone that reflected his newfound interest.

"She said that the killers planted drugs, money and guns in her apartment before they left. She didn't see faces, but she heard a couple of names. "

Carson gulped before asking, "She was there?"

"Yeah, hiding under the bed the whole time the killers were there."

"Where's she at now?" Carson asked in a concerned tone.

"She's still at the apartment....delirious. I don't think she ever got out from under the bed until she called me. Anyway, I told her to stay put. We'd send an officer right over. I could send someone over to question her, if you're not interested."

"Nah, Nah...good looking out. I'll go pay her a visit," Carson responded coolly. He didn't know how he got his cell number, and he didn't care. Before Dave could say, "No doubt," he was speeding off down the snow covered street en route to Manhattan. On his mind were evil thoughts...in his lap was a fully loaded 9mm.

Nan: The Trifling Times of Nathan Jones

TO BE CONTINUED...

The Nanhunt Continues in Part Two ...

NAN:
THE GAME OF TRIFE

IN STORES FALL 2007

For exclusive updates visit:

MindCandyMedia.com
TriflingTimes.org/NAN
and
myspace.com/TriflingTimes

MOSES MILLER
MIND CANDY, LLC
"Intelligent Urban Fiction"

About The Author:

Moses Miller is an author, journalist and co-founder of Mind Candy, LLC, a company focused on book publishing and creative screenplay development. A native New Yorker, Moses exhibits the uncanny ability to capture the pulse of the streets with intelligence, strong character development and well thought out storylines. Moses has contributed articles and written for various websites and publications including The Voice, Newsday, 88HIPHOP.com and F.E.D.S. Magazine. He holds a Bachelors degree in Business Management and a Masters of Science degree in Technology Management. His first novel, Nan: The Trifling Times of Nathan Jones has received critical acclaim from critics, readers and book clubs around the world.

For book club meetings, speaking engagements or to provide feedback directly to the author please email:

Moses@MindCandyMedia.com

CHAPTER 1

It was approximately 8 o'clock on a Saturday night, and 138th street was uncharacteristically silent and dark. This was the area of Harlem known as "Striver's Row", because of the fancy brownstones that had been built in the 1920's, which became occupied by the black upper class. Even after forty years had passed, the buildings still looked physically appealing, even though the tenants had changed.

The sun had set, and the only illumination came from the streetlights that lit up the hard pavement. Long gone were the people and the hustle and bustle that existed only hours before. Those that remained scattering about, were just hanging out jive talking or making plans for the evening. The ladies were home digging through their closets, trying to scrap together their best digs to wear over to Mr. B's, Woody's, Shalimar or Big Wilt's club. They knew that the hustlers and gamblers would be out in force tonight, and only the finest freaks would have a shot at catching their eye and spending their cash.

John Williams sat slouched down behind the steering wheel of his rusty old blue 57' Chevy Impala. He was draped in a raggedy pair of blue overalls, and a dingy white t-shirt that had oil and dirt smeared on it from a hard day's work. Although he looked older, John was only twenty-three years old. Years of working as a mechanic and a handyman, had left him with a face sculpted with hardened features and a chiseled frame. He took the painstaking trip up from the south with his 17 year-old brother Sam earlier in the year, in search of opportunities in the big city. At that time, he confidently told his girlfriend Michelle that he would send for her as soon as he got things situated. He was always good with his hands, and was certain that he wouldn't have any problems finding work and decent pay.

The opportunity well had run dry in South Carolina, and John and Sam found themselves doing petty robberies and muggings in order to provide money to put food on the table. In the big apple, he wouldn't have to sit incognito outside of a juke joint, waiting for an unsuspecting patron to leave drunk at the end of the night, so he could pounce on them. Those days were over…so he thought. Six months passed like the blink of an eye, and John was still broke and struggling to find work to help ends meet. He began to realize that the racism that was prevalent in the South, existed in a more subversive fashion in the North. At least the bigots he encountered in South Carolina called him "nigger" to his face. Up here they plotted against you behind your back, while they smiled in your face.

When he lived down south, the good ole' southern cooking helped keep his 5-11' frame thick at a healthy 215 pounds. Lately, the lack of money and infrequency of meals, had visibly taken its toll, causing his physique to slowly decay. As his sweaty palms gripped the steering wheel, John stared at himself in the rear view mirror. He looked beyond the hairy stubble forming on his face, shocked to see how thin and drawn in his once round face had become. After studying himself for a couple of minutes, he gazed back at the streets, regaining his composure and concentration. He didn't have time to think about anything else but what he came here for tonight. He tried to do the right thing and live by the straight and narrow, but he felt himself being forced back into a life of crime.

A light drizzle began to fall from the sky, glazing the ground with a light coat of rain, and increasing the humidity significantly. Those that were still on the street scattered in sight of the summer rain, as if they thought a little water would make them melt.

"I'm hungry as hell," Sam said. He was always at John's side as far back as he could remember. Racist Klan's men gruesomely murdered their father when they were still in grade school, and their mother had succumbed to the pains of cancer just last year. Since then, John had been doing his best to provide for himself and his little brother.

Sam looked like a younger version of John, except he was slightly thinner and his complexion was a shade lighter. Even though he was only seventeen, his young eyes had seen a lot in his short life, and he was wise beyond his years. The two of them were so close that they sometimes finished each other's sentences for one another. And they always seemed to know what the other one was thinking. Sam sat in the passenger's seat keeled over holding his stomach, with his head resting on the dashboard.

"Just be patient, we'll get some food in a little while," John said assuredly.

Exasperated, Sam glared at John in disgust. "You said that an hour ago. Man, I'm fuckin' starving," he said while moaning loudly to add more emphasis. John glanced over at him. He did look like he was in a great degree of agony. John was just about to reach into his pocket and give him a half eaten *Mary Jane* bar, when he noticed a break in the darkness in his peripheral vision.

It was Hayward Jones, the local numbers runner who was making a little money for himself, judging by his tailor made silk and suede wears. Hayward was a flamboyant character who liked being noticed, and was always looking for attention. Even though no one was out on the block, he bopped slowly across the street, as if he was walking down a red carpet to a movie premiere.

BOOK EXCERPT

John had been following his routine closely for the past week, studying his every move carefully. He was right on time as usual.

"Here," John said throwing the candy bar over to Sam. "I'll be right back."

As soon as the candy bar hit the seat, Sam snatched it up like a starving hostage and took a healthy bite out of it.

"Where you going?"

"I got some business to take care off."

"I'm coming too," Sam said adamantly. He was used to going everywhere with John.

"No, stay here," John responded sternly. "Sit behind the wheel n' start the car when you see me come out the door." That was all he needed to hear to be content. He didn't have a driver's license, so he cherished every opportunity his brother gave him to drive.

"O.K." Sam said, cracking a wide grin.

"Remember. Pump it twice before you turn the key, and don't over pump—" John started to remind him, before being interrupted.

"I know, I know."

The darkness of the night enveloped John, as he walked briskly but quietly across the wet pavement. He was trying to blend in discreetly, but his raggedy clothes made him stick out like a sore thumb. Hayward had just entered the building. John waited patiently, before pushing the door open behind him slowly and entering the vestibule.

After completing a handyman job earlier that day for the tenant downstairs, he had rigged the door jam by placing a wad of gum in it, so the lock didn't fully engage when you closed the door. John knew that Hayward's apartment was on the second floor, because he had followed him here before. He quickly removed his dirty work shoes and left them at the bottom of the stairwell, before creeping up the rickety old staircase that led to the second floor.

The stairs made a slight creaking noise under the pressure of his body weight, but not enough to alarm anyone. Hayward had just unlocked his door and was about to enter his apartment when John reached the top of the steps.

"Yo, Hey," he yelled out. His tone was just loud enough to get him to turn around, but not so loud that it would garner the attention of his neighbors.

"Who dat," Hayward asked, as he put his right hand on his brow and peered down the poorly lit hallway.

"It's me," John said as he continued to walk towards his direction. Once he got closer, Hayward cracked a sinister smile as he recognized who it was.

"Country? What the hell is your old simple ass doing in my building boy?" He asked sarcastically.

"I'm still looking for work. Do you have any thing for me yet?"

"Look at you nigga. Yo, dumb ass so po that you ain't even got no shoes on your feet. Shiittt...Simple ass nigga. Last time I seen you, didn't I tell you not to ask me for work no more, nigga?" Hayward said agitatedly as he glared at John. His muscular frame began to tighten up as he became more upset.

"Actually, you said next time I ask you for some work, you was gon' kill me," John said, as his voice cracked out of nervousness. His southern drawl was more pronounced now, as it always was when he was upset or agitated.

"So, what the fuck is you doing here, you dumb motherfucker?"

"Well, I asked for work...and I ain't dead yet," John said sarcastically, as he glanced directly into Hayward's eyes with a slight smirk on his face. His blood felt like it was beginning to boil due to the adrenaline rushing throughout his body. He gathered his thoughts, and continued talking. "So, not only is your word worth shit, but you ain't got a lick of balls on ya' either."

Hayward shot a menacing glare at John, as he angrily yelled out "Motherfuc—"

Before he could finish his sentence, John swiftly pulled a sharp sharecropper's knife out of the back pocket of his overalls. Hayward's eyes widened, but he was completely caught off guard as John sliced his throat in one motion, violently ripping through the muscles that lined his neck. Blood shot out splattering the white hallway wall, and spraying John in the face.

Instinctively, Hayward lunged forward forcefully grabbing John around the throat with both of his pudgy hands. John tried to maintain his stance, but his socked feet couldn't gain any traction on the slippery polyurethane floor. Hayward easily used his upper body strength to plow him backwards, slamming him into the wall. As he banged into the hard plaster, the knife jarred loose from John's hand, and slid across the floor.

A steady flow of thick blood ran out of Hayward's neck, drenching the front of his white silk shirt in a deep red color. John struggled valiantly, trying to pry his hands from his neck, but to no avail. His mouth fell open as he gasped for air, while the grip continued to grow increasingly tighter around his neck. It was as if the loss of blood was making Hayward stronger instead of weakening him.

"Ughhh…Ha….mug…Uh," Hayward spewed out inaudibly, struggling to put together a sentence. Blood seemed to stain every one of his exposed teeth, as he cracked a smile and continued to flex his muscles, effectively putting more pressure on John's neck. The sarcastic grin on his face made it obvious that he was trying to taunt him, but the wound to his neck was causing the words to come out as incomprehensible gibberish. John tried to muster as much strength as he could to knee him in the groin, but Hayward's massive body was pressed too tightly against his frame for him to gain any type of leverage. As he started to feel lightheaded, he made a mental note. No matter what happened, he would never underestimate a foe again…if only he survived this ordeal.

Hayward's smile widened, realizing that John's body was growing limp, and his defenses were weakening. Bloody drool ran down his chin in a steady stream, as he continued to crack his menacing smile. His eyes were locked in a dead stare with John, as the precious seconds that passed seemed like an eternity. Veins were visible in Hayward's forehead as he strained. He continued to flex his muscles, putting all of the strength he could muster into his wrists.

"Uhhhhhh!" Hayward yelled out in extreme agony, as he spit a mouth full of thick blood and saliva into John's face. His grip loosened, as his body went limp and crumpled to the floor with a loud thud. John put his hands to his neck and coughed a few times as he struggled to get oxygen and breathe normally. After gaining his composure, he wiped his face and looked downward at Hayward's limp body, noticing that his sharecropper's knife was protruding out of his back. When he looked back up, he saw his little brother Sam standing there.

Sam was stone faced, and there was a slight glint of madness in his cold eyes. John walked over to him and gave him a tight hug. He couldn't remember ever being so happy to see his little brother's face. He had intentionally told Sam to stay in the car because he didn't want things to escalate. He knew that Sam had a bad temper, and tried his best to keep him away from testy situations. Ironically, Sam had just saved his life.

BOOK EXCERPT